"Richly authentic detail. Nobody writes Indian romance quite like Holly Harte."
—Elaine Barbieri, winner of the *Romantic Times* Lifetime Achievement Award

KISSING LESSONS

"Will you give me my first lesson now?" he asked.

"Yes." She smiled up at him. "Now, the first thing you need to know is, there are all kinds of kisses." As she spoke, she brought her face closer to his. "There's the soft little hello peck, like—" she demonstrated—"that. Then there's the teasing kiss, for when you're in a playful mood." Starting at one corner of his mouth, she nibbled on his lips, working her way to the opposite corner with slow, deliberate precision.

When she broke contact, she reveled in the fact that his breathing was as uneven as hers. Looping her arms around his neck, she slid her hands into his long hair and clutched the thick, silky strands with her fingers. "And then there's the passion kiss," she said in a throaty voice. "The one that takes your breath away and makes your knees weak. The one that sets your heart to pounding so hard you're afraid it will leap from your chest."

She looked up at him, noticing his flared nostrils and hooded eyes before focusing on his mouth. "Ready?"

Other *Leisure* books by Holly Harte:
APACHE LOVER

APACHE DESTINY

HOLLY HARTE

LEISURE BOOKS NEW YORK CITY

For Vern, my destiny and the love of my life.

A LEISURE BOOK®

October 2001

Published by

Dorchester Publishing Co., Inc.
276 Fifth Avenue
New York, NY 10001

ISBN 0-8439-4930-9

The name "Leisure Books" and the stylized "L" with design are trademarks of Dorchester Publishing Co., Inc.

Printed in the United States of America.

Visit us on the web at www.dorchesterpub.com.

APACHE DESTINY

Chapter One

Chiricahua Mountains, Arizona Territory, 1864

Chino's heart pounded with fear. He had to escape the fury of the Thunder People. They shot another of their fiery lightning-arrows across the sky, filling the air with an eerie bluish glow. Their deafening shout of thunder instantly followed. The earth shook violently, tossing Chino to the ground. He landed with a grunt, dazed, his head ringing and his breathing labored. When another bright streak of a lightning-arrow flashed, he knew he should move. But he couldn't make his body obey.

Then everything went black.

A heavy mist swirled around him, a thick layer of gray clouds or dense smoke, he couldn't tell which.

7

Chino squinted, trying without success to make out his surroundings. Abruptly, the mist vanished to reveal a cloudless sky with sunshine so intense, it hurt his eyes. He blinked several times, then glanced around. Neither the hill where he stood nor the valley below, where a small herd of horses grazed, looked familiar. His gaze drawn to the horses, he studied each one carefully. Recognizing that they came from an excellent bloodline, he smiled, hoping one day he would own such horses.

The sharp report of a rifle filled the air. One of the horses screamed and reared, a splotch of blood appearing on its yellow flank. Chino's smile changed to a frown. Anger churned in his belly. His hands curled into fists. Who would shoot one of these horses? Who could do such a vile and unforgivable thing? He could not imagine hurting one of the animals he loved.

He started down the hill at a run, determined to stop whoever fired the rifle. After he'd taken only a few strides, the valley began to disappear. He slid to a halt in the tall grass, nearly losing his balance.

"No," he yelled, "I must help the horses."

His pleas were for naught. The valley grew fainter and fainter, finally fading completely behind another heavy curtain of swirling mist. Once again Chino could see nothing, but a voice drifted to him from out of the darkness.

"When the time is right, you will help."

*   *   *

Chino awoke with a start, the raindrops cold on his face. Blinking the water from his eyes, he sat up and looked around. He was not on a hill. There was no valley below. No herd of horses. He was in the mountains of his people, the Chokonen Apache, where he'd been caught in a sudden thunderstorm with two of his friends, Tu Sika and Nacori. The close strike of one of the Thunder People's lightning-arrows had tossed him to the ground.

Chino got to his feet, remembering the valley, the horses and the blood appearing on the one with a shiny yellow coat. Had he been dreaming? He frowned. It was not like any other dream he'd ever had. Maybe what he'd seen and heard was a vision from the Spirits. He would seek out the shaman of his band. Spotted Wolf would know the answers to his questions.

Near Arivaca in Arizona Territory, 1877

Abigail Madison straightened from the strenuous task of cleaning out horse stalls, then rubbed the small of her back with a gloved hand. She'd done the chore hundreds of times since the death of her husband two years earlier, and although the work remained one of the hardest tasks she'd been forced to take over, at least now her muscles had grown accustomed to the physical labor.

She sighed, brushed a wisp of hair off her forehead, then moved to the final stall. To relieve the monotony of her work, she passed the time by thinking of the herd of horses grazing in one of the valleys on the ranch.

Other than her son and daughter, and Marita and Cesar Zepeda who had worked for her husband even before he'd bought the land that became the Flying M Ranch, she loved those horses more than anything in the world. The herd was small but growing steadily, their number increased by a dozen foals the previous spring. By the time those foals were two-year-olds, Abby hoped to be able to start selling a few head for the income the ranch desperately needed. Provided she withstood the growing pressure to sell out.

While holding her dying husband in her arms, she'd promised him she would fulfill their dream to turn the Flying M into a successful, well-respected horse ranch and create a worthy legacy for their children. Remembering her promise, and the circumstances that had forced her to say the words, she held her breath, waiting for the agony to strike her. But there was no crushing pain in her chest, no enormous lump in her throat, no blinding tears filling her eyes. The devastating grief she'd first experienced had eased since his death, but not until that moment had she realized how much. Now the only reminder she had of her painful loss was a warm, sweet ache in her heart. She drew a shuddering breath, wondering how that could be. Alan had been her rock, the man to whom she'd given her heart, the man who'd fathered her children. How could she have allowed the heartrending pain of losing him to fade so quickly?

She squeezed her eyes shut for a moment. *Dear God, I can't forget Alan! Please don't let—*

"Momma, Momma."

Her son's shout jerked Abby from her painful introspection. She turned toward the door and watched Teddy enter the barn at a run, then slide to a halt.

"Momma, where are you?"

Abby took a step forward. "I'm here. What's wrong?"

"There's a damned redskin sittin' on the hill in the north pasture."

Abby set aside the pitchfork and approached her son. "Theodore Alan Madison, you know better than to use language like that."

"But that's what you call the men who killed Pa."

Abby cringed at the truth of her son's words. She *had* called the raiding band of Apaches that killed her husband damned redskins, which actually was one of the kinder terms she'd used. But hearing her own hatred coming from the mouth of her six-year-old son hit her like a physical blow. For the first time, she realized her mistake in spewing her grief and anger within earshot of Teddy and his sister. Drawing a shaky breath, she wondered what else she might have done to spoil the innocence of her children.

"I know I did, Teddy," she said, cupping his chin with one hand and tilting his face so his gaze met hers. "But those are horrible words. Words I shouldn't have used, and I don't ever want to hear you say them again. Is that clear?"

Abby could see the mutinous gleam in his hazel eyes, the flattening of his lips. He'd grown up so quickly after his father's death, taking on responsibilities around the ranch when he should have spent his time enjoying a carefree child's life. She longed to pull him into her arms and hug him tight, but knew he'd object to being hugged by his mother—that was for babies.

When he remained silent, she said, "Teddy, I asked if that's clear."

He pulled his chin from her grasp, then nodded. "Yes, ma'am."

Abby managed a gentle smile and risked his reaction by ruffling his thick, dark brown hair. "How do you know there's an Indian in the north pasture?"

"I saw him."

"When?"

"A couple of minutes ago, when I went there to fetch the cows. That's when I saw him."

"What was he doing?"

"Nothin'." Teddy scrunched up his face in concentration. "He was just sittin' there, lookin' toward Cerro Colorado."

"Did he see you?"

Teddy shook his head. "Don't think so. Leastways he never turned around."

"And he was by himself?"

"Yup," he said with a nod. "Just him and his horse."

Abby frowned. What was a lone Apache doing on her land? If he planned to raid the Flying M, he wouldn't be sitting in the open. And he wouldn't be alone. If there was one thing she'd learned about Apaches, it was that they never took unnecessary risks. They never planned a raid if they weren't confident their efforts would be successful. Determined to make sure the Apache who'd made the mistake of crossing onto her land wouldn't be there much longer, she stripped the gloves from her hands.

"Go find Cesar," she said to Teddy, tossing the gloves aside. "Tell him to meet me in the north pasture, then go to the house and stay there with Marita and your sister."

"But I saw the Indian first. Why can't I go with you?"

"Because I want you to stay with Marita and Susanna."

"Aw, geez, I never get to do nothin'," he replied,

scuffing the toe of his boot in the dirt floor of the barn.

She grasped his shoulders, bending so her eyes were level with his. "Your time's coming, Teddy, I promise you. But for now, I need you in the house. If Marita or your sister gets frightened, someone needs to be there to keep them calm. That's a big job, one I'm counting on you to do for me."

Teddy held her gaze for several seconds, then finally drew a deep breath and exhaled heavily. "Yes, ma'am. I'll do it."

Abby smiled, her heart squeezing with love for her son, who looked so much like his father and possessed the same stubborn streak. Before Teddy could object, she leaned forward and kissed his nose. "Thanks, son," she said in a husky voice. "Now go find Cesar."

As soon as Teddy left to follow her instructions, she grabbed the rifle propped beside the barn door, then racked a shell into the chamber. Squaring her shoulders, she marched from the barn and turned north. Sooner or later her horses would move to the north pasture to graze, and she wasn't about to let a damned redskin anywhere near them.

Chino Whitehorse scanned the valley below. Once again he saw no horses, nothing to indicate impending danger, nothing to tell him if this was where his first dream-vision would finally come to pass after all these years. A few days earlier, when the Spirits sent him a vision telling him to come to this place, he'd been relieved. At last, the vision plaguing him since his youth would become reality. He would save the horses from an attack, then he could get on with his life.

Yet so far nothing had happened, nor had he felt a shaking of the flesh in his outer thigh—a sign something bad would occur, and a warning he always heeded. He sighed, wondering if he'd somehow misinterpreted his most recent vision. His personal Spirit, a great white horse with blue eyes, had appeared and told him to find Cerro Colorado—the red hill—then go beyond to a small valley between the sister hills where he was to stay until the horses were no longer in danger. He looked around at his surroundings and nodded. Yes, he'd found Cerro Colorado and the valley, but—A noise behind him pulled him from his thoughts.

Someone was coming up the hill, making no effort at silence. Since he was probably on private land, he'd expected someone would confront him sooner or later. Obviously, the boy he'd glimpsed a few minutes earlier had also seen him and wasted no time reporting his presence.

Chino got to his feet, then slowly turned around, hoping he could explain why he—His breath whooshing from his lungs, he stared at the sight before him. A woman strode up the hill with determined strides, the sun's angle casting her in a golden glow and reflecting streaks of fire off her hair.

When she stopped across the hilltop from him, his gaze dropped to the rifle she held. Raising his hands, he started toward her. After he'd taken a couple of steps, she shifted the rifle so the barrel pointed directly at him. The metallic click of the gun's hammer being pulled back brought him to a halt.

"Do you speak English?" she said.

Chino nodded. "I thought the boy's father would be the one to come here. You are very brave to come alone."

"My son's father is dead, thanks to raiding savages like you."

Chino had been the target of such biased hatred countless times. But for some unknown reason, the venom in her words stung much more than he would have thought possible. Shaking off his unexpected reaction, he turned his attention to defusing what could escalate into a deadly situation. He kept his voice soft when he said, "I did not kill your husband."

"Ha! You'd never admit it even if you had killed him, especially since I'm the one with a gun. You probably won't even admit that renegade Apache bands are still raiding and killing, let alone that you're one of them."

"I am proud to be Apache," he said, trying to remain calm. "I am from the Chokonen band, one the

White Eyes call Chiricahua. I know there are some Apache who continue to raid. But I have never joined them."

The woman glared at him for a long moment, her lips pressed into a thin line. The sun slipped behind a rare cloud in the Arizona sky, giving Chino his first good look at her face. Her skin was a golden color with a sprinkle of freckles across the bridge of her slightly turned-up nose. Eyebrows several shades darker than her light reddish-brown hair arched above wide-set brown eyes, flecked with bits of green. Tilted at a defiant angle, her squarish chin bore a small indentation in the center.

Chino had the sudden urge to run a fingertip over her freckles, skim his fingers down one cheek, explore the fascinating cleft in—Her voice interrupted his fanciful musings.

"Why should I believe anything you tell me?"

"You do not know me, so you have no reason to believe me. But I speak the truth. Lying is a great offense to the Apache."

When her only reaction was the narrowing of her eyes, he said, "When was your husband killed?"

"Two years ago last month."

A fresh wave of pain clutched at Chino's heart, a reminder of his own loss at nearly the same time this woman had lost her husband. He drew a deep breath to ease the tightness in his chest. "I was far from here two years ago, recovering from an injury. I could not travel for many months."

She stared at him for a few moments, then said, "I'm not saying I believe you, but if you are telling the truth, what are you doing on my ranch now?"

Chino looked over his shoulder at the valley below, then again met her gaze. "It is a long story."

Her hands tightened on the rifle. "So give me the short version. I don't have all day."

He had to bite the inside of his cheek to halt a smile. This White Eyes woman was more than brave; she had spirit, a fearlessness he admired. Not sure where to begin, he finally cleared his throat, then said, "Do you have horses on your ranch?"

She made a snorting sound. "Do I look stupid enough to tell you what's on this ranch so you, and the other Apaches that are probably hiding around here somewhere, can come back on a raid?"

"I came alone, and I told you," he said, his voice rising in volume, "I do not raid."

At her withering glance, he tamped down his growing agitation, then folded his arms across his chest and spread his legs in a wider stance. "I will start again." He took a deep breath, blew it out slowly. "I know there are horses here. Horses like none I have ever seen, and they need my help."

"And just how is it you know all that?"

"As a boy, I had a vision about horses. I was standing on a hill, looking down into a valley where the horses grazed. Then I heard a gunshot. One of the horses, one with a yellow coat and a black mane and tail, was struck on the flank."

The color drained from the woman's face, and her throat worked with a swallow. "Are you . . . are you saying someone is going to shoot one of my horses?"

"Yes, that is what I am saying."

Her chin tilting up again, she lifted the rifle barrel a little higher. "Maybe that's just a story you made up in case you were discovered before you could do the shooting."

Chino unfolded his arms, took a step closer. "I would never do such a thing," he said in a fierce voice. "Someone who would hurt a horse is the one who should be shot."

She stared at him for several tense seconds, then uncocked the rifle and lowered the barrel. "Okay, for now I believe you would not shoot one of my horses."

Chino waited until the last of his momentary anger receded before speaking. "I thought the horses would be in this valley, but I have not seen them."

"They graze in a number of valleys on my ranch."

"Does one of your horses have a yellow coat and a black mane and tail?"

"Yes, I have a mare with that coloring. She foaled this year. All the more reason why I wouldn't want to see her hurt."

Chino nodded. "The Spirits did not show me the

foal in my visions, but they sent me here to protect the mare and the rest of your herd."

"Wait a minute," she said, irritation again creeping into her voice. "You keep mentioning visions and spirits. I think you'd better explain what you're talking about."

"Visions are sent by the Spirits. The Apache Gods. Some of my people hear only voices in their visions. Others see pictures in their heads. Some visions come during the day. Some while we sleep, but they are not the same as dreams. All visions are messages from the Spirits, but learning to understand their meaning takes time. After the Spirits sent me my first vision, I went to a shaman in my band and asked him to explain what it meant. He said one day I would save the horses I saw being attacked in my vision. That when the time was right, the Spirits would tell me where to find the horses."

"So you're saying these spirits told you to come here, to the Flying M?"

He nodded. "I have had the same vision several times since the first one. But until the Spirits sent me another vision a few days ago, I did not know where to find the horses. In the most recent vision, I was told to find Cerro Colorado, then go beyond it to a small valley between sister hills and stay until the horses are safe."

She shifted her gaze to look over his shoulder at Cerro Colorado, then glanced at the hill on the other side of the valley, the hill matching the one on which they stood. "Sister hills," she murmured.

"Yes. I am certain this is the valley I was told to find. It is between two hills that look the same."

The woman snapped out of her momentary trance, her piercing glare once again focused on his face. "And you came here because you think my horses are in danger. Did I get that right?"

"Yes, your horses are in danger, and I plan to stay until they are safe."

"Oh, you're staying all right." She nodded toward his dark bay horse, which stood dozing nearby. "Grab the reins, but don't mount up. And don't even think about trying anything funny."

"Funny?" He frowned. "Why would I want to make you laugh?"

"That's not what I meant. Trying something funny means—" She exhaled with a huff. "Never mind. Get your horse, you're coming with me."

"Where are we going?"

"Down to the ranch house. Since you seem to know a whole lot more than I do about the safety of my horses, I want you where I can keep an eye on you."

When he made no move to follow her order, she said, "You heard me. Now do it, and don't take a sudden notion to jump on your horse's back and take off. This rifle isn't just for show. Believe me, I know how to use it. If you don't do as I say, I'll have absolutely no qualms about blowing a hole in your chest."

"I will not try to take off," Chino said, moving slowly toward his horse. "I give you my word."

"I don't place much stock in the word of an Apache."

Chino snatched his horse's reins off the ground, his jaw clenched against the urge to shout his outrage at this infuriating woman. Instead, he took a calming breath, then said, "I told you, I speak only the truth."

"Oh, that's right," she replied in a sugary drawl. "How could I have forgotten?" Using the barrel of the rifle, she motioned for him to move. "And I don't make idle threats," she said, her previous sweetness replaced by a layer of ice. "Do as I say, or I swear, I'll shoot you dead."

Chapter Two

Abby took a deep breath, eased it out slowly, then started down the hill behind her prisoner. Though she tried to look elsewhere, she couldn't make her eyes obey. Her gaze remained on the man in front of her. He was of average height, she decided, and on the lean side, with broad shoulders and the easy stride of a man who was comfortable inside his skin. A perfect example of what a man should—She frowned at the direction of her thoughts and forced herself to look away. But that did little good, because her mind immediately filled with more images of him, this time of his face. His features were so sharp they could have been carved from stone, an intriguing combination of planes and angles. Prominent cheekbones. Wide, sensual mouth. Narrow, slightly hooked nose. High forehead bisected by a headband made from a strip of white cloth. Arched eyebrows over deep-set, dark brown eyes.

His eyes. There was something about his eyes, but she couldn't quite put her finger on what it was. His horse nickered, pulling her from her mental wanderings.

Her gaze returned to him, drawn by a power she couldn't overcome. She noticed how the wind ruffled his blue-black hair across the shoulders of his calico shirt, how his buckskin trousers hugged his buttocks and thighs like a custom-made glove. She inhaled sharply, her cheeks burning with a blush. What in the world was wrong with her? Thinking about the fit of a man's trousers!

From the moment she'd seen the Apache, she'd taken leave of her senses. Though she'd managed to maintain her composure during their confrontation, her insides had been anything but calm. A wild tingle had sizzled through her veins, a sensation she had no business feeling for a man she should hate. Yet even now, in spite of her efforts to keep her mind on the matter at hand, unwanted thoughts continued to pop into her head. Wondering what running her fingers through his long hair would be like. Longing to test the strength of his muscular arms and chest. Wanting to place her lips in the shallow indentation at the base of his neck and touch her tongue to his bronze-colored skin.

She clamped her mouth shut, stifling the urge to

scream her frustration. What possessed her to think such things? He was an Apache, one of the savages who'd killed her husband! How could she even think about touching him with her hands, much less her mouth and tongue?

The reprimand she gave herself was meant to bring her wayward thoughts to a standstill, but in reality the silent lecture had the opposite effect. Another curl of heat ignited low in her belly, the beginnings of something she knew was much more dangerous. Desire. She bit her lip to hold in a moan.

Unlike some women she'd heard complaining about their wifely duties, the intimate side of marriage had always been a source of great pleasure for her. Alan, fifteen years her senior, had been a kind and considerate lover, and he'd taught her well. She missed him for a hundred reasons, but never more than at night when she lay in their bed alone, aching with need.

She drew a shuddering breath, realizing her two-year abstinence had to be the reason for this unwanted stirring of desire for the man ahead of her. Because wanting a man she'd only just met, a man she should despise, was ludicrous. Why, she didn't even know his name.

She told herself she couldn't care less about his identity and had no intention of asking for information she didn't want. But what if the story he'd told her wasn't true? What if she found out he'd been hired to drive her off her ranch? In that case, she would need his name so she could send word to the county sheriff.

"By the way," she called to him, "what's your name?"

He stopped, then turned to face her, his eyebrows drawn together in a frown. Finally, he said, "The White Eyes call me Chino Whitehorse."

"That isn't your real name?"

"It is hard to explain. The White Eyes in charge of the White Mountain Reservation could not say most Apache names. He gave names to some of the others, but I did not want a name he chose, so I told him to call me Chino, my boyhood name, or Whitehorse. He decided to call me both names.

"Why Whitehorse?"

"It is part of my Apache name."

She thought about his response for a few moments, then nodded. "I guess that makes sense."

Before she could tell him to get moving, he said, "What should I call you?"

Abby wanted to say, "Not a damn thing," but managed to quell the urge. Instead she said, "I'm Abigail Madison. Most folks call me Abby. Now let's get going."

"Abby," he said in a husky whisper. His intense stare roamed over her face with slow deliberation, rooting her to the spot.

After he turned around and continued down the

hill, she released her breath and tried to will her racing heart to slow. She had to stop reacting to this man so strongly or she'd end up in deep trouble. Really deep trouble!

She'd taken only a few more strides when he stopped again. She came to a halt several paces behind him. "What is it?"

"Someone is coming."

Abby moved so she had an unobstructed view down the hill. Cesar was hurrying toward them, moving as fast as his arthritic knees would allow.

"Señora Abby," he called in a wheezing voice, "I came as quickly as I could." When he reached her, he gave her a quick appraising glance. "You are not hurt, sí?"

"I'm fine, Cesar."

He released a long sigh. "*¡Gracias a Dios!* When Teddy told me where you went—" he nodded toward the other man—"I was afraid you would be hurt by this *bastardo rojo.*"

Abby glanced at Chino. His back was rigid, his lips pressed into a thin line, and a muscle ticked in his jaw. Keeping her gaze on him, she said to Cesar, "I told you, I'm fine. But you'd better watch what you say. Chino Whitehorse apparently understands Spanish."

Cesar tightened his grip on his rifle and glared at the younger man. "I do not care if he understands me."

"Maybe so," Abby replied, turning to look at Cesar, "but you'd better not use words like that around Marita. I don't think she'd approve of you calling an Indian a red bastard."

Cesar's gaze snapped back to meet hers, a deep frown adding more creases to his sun-wrinkled brown face. "Marita knows I would never say such a thing about her ancestors. I am proud she carries the blood of the Aztecs."

"To some folks, one Indian is the same as another."

"Sí, but to not me," he replied. "There are good and bad in all people."

When Abby's only response was a frown, Cesar took a step closer. "What are you planning to do with him?"

Before she could open her mouth to answer, unwanted images again flashed in her mind. Smooth bronze skin. Naked, above her. Muscular legs entwined with her much paler—She gave her head a shake to chase away the erotic pictures. After clearing her throat, she said, "I . . . uh . . . haven't decided yet. He says the horses are in danger. That someone is going to shoot a yellow horse with a black mane and tail. Claims he saw it in a vision."

When Cesar opened his mouth to respond, she held up a hand. "Yes, I know Marita believes in such things, but I'm not so sure he's telling the truth. To be on the safe side, I figured I'd better keep him around for a while."

Cesar dropped his voice to a whisper. "You think he is working for Señor Warner?"

She shrugged. "I don't know," she replied in an equally low voice. "But I aim to find out."

When Chino got his first glimpse of the ranch house, a sense of peacefulness settled over him, a calm he hadn't experienced in years. Though he'd never been to this valley or this ranch, he felt as if he had returned home.

He scowled. That was not possible. How could he belong on the ranch of a White Eyes woman? Especially one who hated all Apache for killing her husband. He belonged nowhere and refused to think about settling in one place until he'd completed his mission to avenge the deaths of—The woman's voice pulled him from his thoughts.

"You can put your horse in the corral next to the barn for now."

He nodded, then turned to follow Abby's instructions. Once he'd released the bay in the corral, he returned to stand in front of her. When she didn't speak, he folded his arms over his chest and arched an eyebrow in anticipation.

For a few tense moments, she stared up at him, the green flecks in her eyes becoming darker, more distinct. Her breasts rose and fell with a deep breath, then her tongue flicked out to wet her lips, sending a rush of blood to his groin. Surprised and shocked by the intensity of his reaction, he clenched his teeth in frustration.

She must have noticed the change in his expression, because her eyes suddenly went wide. Taking a step back, she motioned for him to go first. "We'll talk on the ramada," she said in a slightly uneven voice. "Behind the house. It'll be much cooler there."

Chino followed her directions and soon found himself beneath the heavily shaded ramada. The beams supporting the roof were attached to the back of the main house on one side and to a smaller house on the other. The ends of the ramada were open, allowing a refreshing breeze to pass through the structure. Plants hung in pots from some of the beams, and a large clay olla filled with water sat near the door to the main house.

Abby indicated he should have a seat; then she turned to Cesar. "Please ask Marita to keep the children inside for a while longer."

After the man went into the house, Abby moved to the olla. Using a dipper made from a gourd, she filled a cup with water and lifted it to take a drink.

Chino watched her from beneath hooded eyes, his attention drawn from the movement of her throat to a drop of water that escaped the cup. He followed the drop's journey over her chin and down her neck. When the droplet disappeared inside her blouse, he wished he could take the water's place. Angry at himself for having so little control over his thoughts, he jerked his gaze away from her to stare blindly at the adobe wall of the house.

He heard her dipping more water, but refused to look in her direction. Then she stood in front of him, offering him a cup of water. He allowed himself a quick glance at her face, then wished he hadn't. In spite of the deep shade of the ramada, he thought he detected something in her expression, something beneath her obvious hatred, something she seemed to find as confusing as he found his attraction to a White Eyes. Pushing those thoughts aside, he murmured his thanks, then took the tin cup from her.

She took a seat across from him, but did not speak. After Cesar returned and sat in a chair next to hers, she turned to look at Chino.

"Now, tell me again about the visions you had and why you came to the Flying M."

Chino took a drink of water, then said, "It was during my fifteenth year. I went hunting in the mountains with two friends from my band. We were caught in a fierce thunderstorm. Before we could find shelter, we were thrown to the ground by the force of a powerful lightning strike. I was dazed and could not move. That is when the Spirits spoke to me in my first vision."

After telling them about the vision—the valley with horses like none he'd ever seen, hearing a shot and seeing blood on the flank of a yellow horse—he said, "When I found my friends, they said they had also received visions during the storm, but none of us understood what the Spirits showed us. When we returned to camp, we went to Spotted Wolf, a shaman in our band, and asked him to interpret our visions. He told me when the time was right, I would be the one to save the horses because I would receive horse power from the Spirits. I was pleased by his words. Even as a boy, I had much skill with horses."

Cesar leaned forward in his chair. "You received this horse power?"

"Yes. Several years later, the Spirit of the horse, a great white horse with blue eyes, came to me in another vision. That is when I was given a new name. *Yiiltsen liligai*—the one who sees the white horse."

Chino saw Cesar and Abby exchange a quick glance, but when neither spoke, he continued. "The white horse spoke to me, telling me what I must do to receive its power. Since then the Spirits have sent me only a few visions. None were the same as the first one, until a few days ago. In that vision, the white horse told me where to find the horses that were in danger."

"That's when you were told to find the red hill—Cerro Colorado," Abby said, "then go beyond it to the valley between Twin Peaks—what you called sister hills?"

When Chino nodded, she said, "How did you

know where to look for Cerro Colorado?"

"I knew where it was. It was customary for my band to spend the time of Ghost Face, winter, far to the south in Mexico. When we returned in early spring, during the time of Little Eagles, sometimes we followed the river that flows through the valley east of here. Cerro Colorado can be seen from the river. After I moved farther to the north, I no longer made that trip. But when the white horse told me to look for the red hill, I remembered seeing it as a boy."

Abby let Cesar mull over Chino's words for a few minutes before turning to him and saying, "What do you think?"

Cesar sat back in his chair, one hand rubbing the graying stubble on his jaw. "Everything he said could be true. Marita strongly believes in visions. And I have heard others speak of what he calls receiving power."

"Then you believe he came here alone?"

"I think it is very possible." When Abby didn't reply, he turned to look at her. "You do not agree? You think he is working for someone else?"

"Maybe." She looked at Chino. "Nothing would surprise me." She saw him lift a hand to one of the earrings she hadn't noticed dangling from his ears. Entranced, she watched his long fingers play with the single white bead that had been strung on a thick piece of string.

Finally, she said, "I wouldn't put anything past Neville Warner. He'll do anything." Her eyes widened at the abrupt change in Chino's expression. There was no mistaking the look on his face.

Cesar must have noticed, too, because he said, "How do you know Señor Warner?"

Chino's fingers went still on his earring. He dropped his hand to his thigh, trying to cool the fury bubbling up inside him. "I know the name," he said, curling his hand into a fist.

"I'd say you know more than that," Abby said, watching his face to gauge his reaction, "which means you could be working for him. Maybe that's the real reason you came here. Maybe he hired you to spy on me. To figure out a way to change my mind about selling my ranch."

"I do not work for him." His dark eyes bored into hers, unmistakable anger swirling in their depths. "I would never work for such a man. I spoke the truth about my reason for coming here. The Apache lifeway teaches truth speaking. To my people, being accused of telling a lie is a great offense." He looked away from her for a moment, his chest rising with a deep breath. He relaxed his fist, then looked back at her, his eyes no longer hot with anger. "It is Warner who wants to buy your ranch?"

Abby nodded. "One way or another, I think he intends to have this land. He first approached me about selling out six months or so after Alan was killed. Then every couple of months, he'd come back to repeat his offer. Last time he was here I lost my temper and told him I would never sell out. When I ordered him off the Flying M, the look he gave me made my skin crawl." A shiver wracked her shoulders. "I can still see the change in his eyes. They burned with what I can only describe as pure evil. Then just as quickly, his usual cool glare slid back into place. He gave me that smug little smile of his and said he admired my grit even if it was misplaced. I'll never forget what he said before he turned to leave. He told me I should be more careful about saying never, because things have a way of changing."

Cesar made a sound of disgust. "If only I had been here that day. If I had heard him make such a threat, I would have done more than talk to him."

"Calm down, Cesar," Abby said, reaching over to squeeze one of his work-gnarled hands. "Getting yourself all riled up won't help matters."

"Sí, you are right," he replied with a sigh.

Abby smiled at him, then withdrew her hand and turned her attention back to Chino. She stared thoughtfully at him for a moment, mulling over what he'd said about Warner. "You claim you would never work for a man like Neville Warner. So, how do you know what he's like?"

"I saw him once. Saw what he is capable of doing."

The harshness of his last words surprised Abby. "What did he do?"

He lifted the cup to his mouth and drank the last of the water, then met her gaze. "You are right to think he is evil. He is filled with poison, a wicked need to control everyone and everything in his life. He will do anything to get what he wants, even killing the innocent, the defenseless." He squeezed his eyes closed for a second. The muscles in his jaw tightened.

When he opened his eyes, Abby saw shadows in them, remnants of pain, perhaps the lingering result of a devastating loss in his past. Whatever the cause, the pain she recognized in his eyes had something to do with Neville Warner. She was sure of it.

He released a deep breath, then said, "I will never forget what happened that day." His voice dropped to a fierce whisper. "A day I have sworn to avenge."

She sucked in a quick breath, a prickle of uneasiness teasing her skin. "What . . . what happened?"

Chino turned his head to stare at the distant mountains, his mind traveling back in time, back to that day two years earlier when his life had changed forever.

After a moment, he began speaking in a low voice. "Four of us had permits to leave the White Mountain Reservation and travel south to visit the Chiricahua Reservation. We had just stopped for the night when three White Eyes rode into our camp. Two of the

36

men moved closer. One said we were on private property and their boss had no stomach for trespassers, especially filthy savages. I tried to tell them we would move, but the third man, the one who stayed farther away, told the others to kill us. Before I could do anything to stop them, they drew their guns and started shooting. They shot me first, then—" his shoulders rippled with a shudder—"the other two."

"Oh my God," Abby whispered, her heart constricting at the anguish reflected on his face.

Chino swallowed hard, his surroundings fading from his mind, replaced by a scene he would never forget. He remembered the moment the bullet struck him, hitting him in the chest with so much force it knocked him to the ground. He tried to get up but couldn't make his body respond. As he watched in horror, more bullets struck their intended targets, jerking one then the other off their feet. They lay crumpled nearby, their lifeblood gushing from their wounds. His mind screaming in protest, he fought the encroaching blackness long enough to reach out to the body closest to him. Wrapping his fingers around the small wrist, he slid into unconsciousness.

His hand tightening on the cup he held, he wondered again why the Spirits had spared his life that day. Why they had kept him alive only to make him suffer a pain many times greater than being shot. Eventually, his grief had lessened to a dull ache, but the need for revenge still—Abby's voice jarred him back to the present.

"You said four of you had permits to leave the reservation, but only three of you were shot. What happened to the other person?"

"He went to look for game as soon as we stopped that day and had not returned," he replied, turning to look at her. "He heard the shots, but by the time he reached our camp, the White Eyes were gone. I was seriously wounded, but the others—" he drew a quavering breath—"had passed to the Spirit World."

Abby swallowed the sudden lump in her throat. "That's the injury you were recovering from when my husband was killed?"

"Yes. For several weeks, I was near death. I did not want to live, but the Great Spirit would not let me pass to the Spirit World. When I started to recover, I had only one thought: revenge."

For a few moments, Abby considered everything he'd told her, then said, "You're sure Neville Warner was one of those men?"

"Yes. The one who gave the order to kill us. He did not fire the shots, but he is just as guilty."

"How do you know Señor Warner was the man who gave the order?" Cesar asked.

"As soon as I was strong enough to ride, I started looking for the three White Eyes who rode into our camp that night. Three months ago, I found two of them hiding far down in Mexico."

Abby nearly asked what had happened, but the fierceness of his expression halted the question. Instead, she said, "They told you the identity of the third man?"

Chino stared at her for several seconds, then shrugged. "Not at first. They would not tell me his name until after I . . . persuaded them to speak the truth."

Abby couldn't suppress a shudder. She didn't want to know how he'd persuaded the men or what he'd done to them afterward. She'd met Chino Whitehorse barely an hour earlier, yet instinctively she knew he possessed skills she didn't want to contemplate. Though he had to be the most dangerous man she'd ever met, she found herself drawn to him by a force stronger than anything she'd ever experienced.

Why had this man been brought into her life? And more importantly, what should she do about him? She closed her eyes and offered a quick prayer to ask for divine guidance. After a moment, she blew out a deep breath, then opened her eyes.

Right or wrong, she'd reached a decision.

Chapter Three

Abby rose from her chair and turned to Cesar. "I need to speak to you privately." Looking over at Chino, she said, "Excuse us, Mr. Whitehorse, we'll be right back."

Abby led Cesar away from the ramada, far enough to prevent their voices from reaching Chino. "You still believe his story?"

"Sí, I think he is telling the truth." Cesar stared at her through narrowed eyes. "Do you think he is?"

She tucked a loose strand of hair behind her ear. "I'm not sure. I want to believe him, but all that talk of visions and spirits sounds so far-fetched." When he opened his mouth to reply, she held up a hand. "I know. You don't have to say it. Marita believes. I guess I just have to have more proof."

"Marita should talk to him. She will know if he speaks the truth."

"Maybe I will ask Marita. One thing I do believe is his hatred of Neville Warner. That seems genuine."

Cesar nodded. "I do not think he could pretend to hate someone that much."

"I agree," she replied, glancing toward the man sitting under the ramada. She sighed, then once again met Cesar's gaze. "I'm going to ask him to stay. If you have any objections, you'd better voice them now."

Cesar's thick gray eyebrows lifted. "You want an Apache to stay on the ranch?"

"I know," Abby replied with a smile. "Sounds like I've taken leave of my senses. But, yes, I do." Her smile disappeared. "For a long time, I kept thinking that sooner or later Neville Warner would accept the fact that I have no intention of selling this ranch. But I've come to realize that notion was plain foolish. He won't give up. And if he can't buy me out, I wouldn't put it past him to try to run me off." She drew a deep breath, then exhaled with another sigh. "We can't stop him by ourselves, Cesar. We need help."

"Sí, and there is no one else around here with the *cojones* to stand up to Señor Warner."

"Exactly," Abby said with a smile, then immediately sobered. "I know Chino Whitehorse is only one

41

man, but he's the only option we've got."

The old man lifted a hand to rub the back of his neck. "You are right. But can you trust him?"

Abby drew a deep breath, then exhaled slowly. "No, but I plan to stick close enough to keep an eye on him." The idea of sticking close to Chino White-horse sent a flush of heat over her body.

When Cesar didn't respond, she said, "Is there anything else you want to say?"

He cleared his throat. "You know Marita and I think of you and your *niños* as family. We worry about you working so hard. And now that Señor Warner has—" He cleared his throat again, then swiped a hand under his nose. "You must promise to be more careful."

She smiled. "You and Marita are family to us, too. I promise to be careful." Looping her arm through his, she said, "Come on, let's get this over with."

When Abby entered the ramada, she found Chino in the same spot. He sat staring at the cup he held, his eyebrows knitted in concentration, lips pressed into a thin line. At her approach, he lifted his head.

She noticed the shadows once again lurking in his eyes, and had the sudden urge to chase them away, to see those dark brown eyes alight with laughter, or burning with desire. Irritated by her inability to stop such inappropriate thoughts, she took the seat she'd occupied earlier.

"Cesar and I have discussed the situation, Mr.

Whitehorse," she said, "and we would like you to stay on the ranch until this business with Neville Warner ends."

She paused, waiting for Chino to say something, but when he didn't, she continued. "I can't afford to pay you wages, but if you agree to help us, I'll give you a horse from my herd."

Chino shifted his gaze from Abby to Cesar, then back to her. "I did not come here to be paid," he said at last. "I came because the Spirits sent me, and because I care for horses and do not want to see any of them hurt. I planned to stay until the danger to the horses has passed, so yes, I will help you. But I do not want you to give me anything."

"That's admirable of you. But you haven't seen the horse I have in mind. When you do, you may want to reconsider my offer."

Once again, she got to her feet. Turning toward Cesar, she said, "Tell Marita what we've decided, then you can go back to whatever you were doing when Teddy came to fetch you."

As Abby and Chino made their way across the yard a few minutes later, she said, "Earlier, you said you have great skill with horses. What did you mean?"

"The Spirits gave me many skills with horses. How to gentle and ride the wildest ones. How to heal them of sickness and injury."

"So, you've broken a wild horse?"

"Yes, many times."

"That's good," she said, walking toward a corral a short distance from the barn. "Because you're going to need that skill if you want to break—" she stopped at the corral fence and nodded toward the lone occupant—"this fella."

Chino moved to stand beside Abby, his breath catching in his throat. Fearing his imagination had played a trick on him, he rubbed a hand over his eyes. No, he wasn't seeing things. On the opposite side of the corral, in the shade of a thick stand of mesquite, stood a magnificent white stallion. The horse turned toward them, ears pricked forward, nostrils flared to catch their scent, staring at them through clear blue eyes.

Abby watched Chino's reaction, then smiled. "You still want to turn down my offer of a horse?"

He turned his head, his gaze locking with hers. "You would give him to me?"

She nodded. "After you told me about your visions and how you got your name, I knew this horse was meant to belong to you. I've never been a strong believer in fate, but I think your coming to my ranch and my owning a white horse with blue eyes is more than coincidental. It's almost like this was supposed to happen. Like our meeting was—" a shiver raced up her spine—"destiny."

He stared into her eyes for a several seconds. "What you said is true," he said in a low voice. "This was supposed to happen. The visions from the Spirits told me to come here."

"But your Spirits didn't tell you I had a white horse with blue eyes, did they?"

"No, they did not reveal that to me."

"I wonder why."

He shrugged. "I do not know why the Spirits reveal some things and not others. But that is their way." He nodded toward the stallion. "Why are you willing to give up such a magnificent horse? He would give you many strong foals."

"I know. He's already sired some of the best foals in my herd. But I have several other stallions, so losing him is a small price to pay if it means saving the rest of my horses and my home. If you'll help me keep Neville Warner from getting his hands on this ranch, this fella is yours."

He turned to look at the stallion. A full minute passed before he moved. Then swinging around to face her, he said, "I accept your offer."

Abby gawked at him. She couldn't help it. His lips were curved in a broad smile, revealing a dimple in his left cheek and a series of crinkles at the corners of his eyes—eyes no longer filled with shadows but sparkling with merriment. She'd thought his looks striking before, but when he smiled, he was beyond description. The transformation staggered her, sending her pulse into a wild cadence and her imagination winging toward lustful thoughts best left unexplored.

Somehow she managed to return his smile; then she drew a steadying breath. "I . . . uh . . . probably shouldn't tell you this, since you've already agreed to help me. But it's only fair you know the truth. This white devil is the most intelligent horse I've ever been around, but he's also the most stubborn. My husband tried to work with him but finally gave up, and my efforts weren't any more successful. And lately, I haven't had the time to try again. You'll need every bit of your—what did you call it?—horse power, and maybe then some, to get him to do what you want."

"A little stubbornness is good," Chino replied. "But I will not have a problem with him."

Abby stared at him for a moment. There was no hint of bragging in his words, no arrogance in his expression. He'd merely stated what he believed to be fact. She knew some folks might be put off by such self-confidence, but she found no fault with him for speaking honestly.

"Well," she finally said, "I hope you're right. Now that we've reached an agreement, let me show you around."

Chino glanced one last time at the horse in the corral, then turned to follow her.

Abby took him through the horse barn, explained the reasons for the various corrals, then showed him

46

a smaller building, actually little more than a lean-to, built for their two milk cows. On the way back to the house, she said, "After Cesar milks the cows each morning, he turns them out into one of the pastures for the day. Then Teddy brings them back late in the afternoon."

"The boy does that by himself?"

"Yes," she replied with a smile. "He's only six, but he wants to help, so I thought fetching the milk cows was something he could do."

Chino frowned, but didn't speak.

"What's wrong?"

"Nothing is wrong."

"Then why are you frowning?" When he didn't respond, she said, "Don't Apache children have to help their parents? Is that it?"

"From the time Apache girls are old enough to walk, their mothers begin teaching them what they will need to know when they become wives and mothers. How to gather and prepare food. How to make baskets and clothes for their family."

"What about the boys?"

"They are taught how to make and use weapons. How to hunt so they can provide food for their families. How to fight the enemy. Much of their time is spent competing against the other boys to practice those skills."

Abby thought about what he'd said for a minute. "What about gathering wood and hauling water?

47

Don't the boys have to do chores like that?"

He shook his head. "Those are women's tasks. Apache men would be laughed at if they did those things."

"Life on this ranch is entirely different," she said, trying to keep her temper from boiling over. "We all pitch in and do whatever needs to be done. So I'm warning you. You'd better get used to the notion, because sooner or later you may have to do work you think is beneath you."

Chino glanced at her, resisting the urge to chuckle. "There is no need to become angry. What I told you about teaching our children was the Apache life-way of our grandfathers, and their grandfathers before them. Now everything has changed. The old ways are dying. We lost our homeland and much of our life-way when the White Eyes forced us onto a reservation."

Abby stared straight ahead, surprised by her reaction to his statement. Shaking off her unwanted compassion for an Apache, she summoned the hatred she'd nurtured for the past two years. "Yes, well, you brought it on yourselves. Raiding and killing at will. What else was the American government supposed to do with you?"

He stopped and turned toward her. His bronze cheeks darkened with a flush; unmistakable anger radiated from him. "You ask me to work for you," he said in a harsh voice, "to help stop your ranch from being taken from you. Yet you think your government was justified in forcing the Apache off their homeland, that there is nothing wrong in treating us like cattle." A muscle worked his jaw. "When will you White Eyes understand? Apache are human beings like you. We are not animals. We have a lifeway we do not want to see die. We have children we love and—" His voice broke. "And we want to see them live to be adults."

He paused, glaring at her, then said, "You talk from both sides of your mouth. You say you must keep the land you call home, but you see nothing wrong with the Apache losing their home."

Abby opened her mouth to respond, then changed her mind and clamped her lips shut. She might hate the Apache for killing her husband and for leaving her children fatherless, but one thing Chino had said struck a nerve. The Apache were human beings. She'd let her grief and anger color her views, continuing to paint all Apache as bloodthirsty savages, who took whatever they wanted and killed anyone who stood in their way. But Chino made her realize she might have been wrong in her assumptions.

She squinted up at the late afternoon sun, then brought her gaze back to his face. "I . . . uh . . . shouldn't have taken my anger out on you, Mr. Whitehorse. And I'm sorry for what I said. I had no call to speak to you the way I did."

The tightness of his features eased a little. "If we

are going to be working together, you should call me Chino or Whitehorse."

"All right," she replied, "Chino. And please call me Abby."

He gave her a curt nod, then turned and resumed walking toward the house.

Abby fell in step beside him. After walking a short distance, she said, "Down there—" she pointed to their right—"along the creek bank is our garden. If not for Cesar being such a talented gardener, putting enough food on the table could become a serious problem for us."

Chino took a deep breath, struggling to push away the last of his anger, then glanced in the direction she indicated. He noted the well-worn path, heading down a slight slope, toward a stand of trees growing along the creek.

A few more seconds passed before he trusted himself enough to speak. "How many live on your ranch?"

"There are six of us. My son and daughter, Marita and Cesar, Nestor and myself."

"Who is Nestor?"

"Nestor Zepeda. Cesar's nephew. He does chores Cesar can no longer do, chores that would be too difficult for me. Having Nestor here has been a great help. He's not only taken over most of the heavy work, but he offered to accept only room and board as payment until I can get the ranch back on its feet.

50

I can't imagine what I'd do without his help. If I had to pay him wages, well—" she drew a deep breath— "I'd rather not think about what would happen."

They walked the rest of the way across the yard in silence. Abby led Chino back under the ramada, then to the back door of the house. Holding the door for him, she said, "Come inside so I can introduce you to Marita and my children."

Chino nodded, then stepped through the doorway. Inside it was considerably cooler, the thick adobe walls keeping out the worst of the summer heat.

"Marita," Abby called, "come here, *por favor.*" A female voice answered, drifting to them from somewhere deeper in the house.

While Chino waited for Marita to appear, he took the time to look around. This room was the kitchen, with a hard-packed dirt floor, a stove in one corner and a long table in the center. A large window took up most of one wall, the deep sill was crowded with containers holding a variety of plants.

He moved closer to the window to study the plants growing there. He recognized several; others he had never seen before.

"Marita uses some of those in her cooking," Abby said, after noticing his interest in the window garden. "The rest she grows to treat sickness and injuries. She is very knowledgeable about healing with herbs and plants. Since there are no doctors nearby, her abilities are a great comfort to me."

"Where did she learn such knowledge?" he asked, touching the leaf of one plant.

"Her healing skills have been handed down for generations in her family."

"Sí," Marita said, entering the kitchen, "From both my Aztec ancestors and my grandfather, who was a skilled *curandero Mejicano* —Mexican healer."

Chino had turned at the sound of Marita's voice. She was shorter and plumper than Abby, her silver-streaked black hair pulled back from her round face and secured in a knot at her nape.

She swept her gaze over him in silent assessment, then said, "You are the one who had the visions about Señora Abby's horses, sí?"

"Sí," Chino replied. "The Spirits have sent me several visions, showing me horses from this ranch."

The older woman studied him in silence for several seconds, then gave a quick nod and said, "*Bueno.* He speaks the truth."

"Just like that?" Abby said. "You're satisfied he's telling the truth?"

"Sí."

"You're sure? You don't need to ask him anything else?"

Marita shook her head. "His eyes. They do not lie."

Abby eased out a long breath. She had already decided Chino Whitehorse had spoken the truth about his visions and his reason for coming to her ranch, but having Marita confirm her conclusion came as a relief. Perhaps the woman's uncanny ability to read people came from her Indian blood, but whatever the source, she was seldom wrong.

After Abby made the introductions, she said, "Where are the children?"

"In the *sala*," Marita replied. "I should get them?"

"No, I'll go. Why don't you pour us some lemonade?"

Several minutes passed before Abby returned to the kitchen, her children at her sides, their small hands clutched tightly in hers.

"Chino," she said, "I'd like you to meet my children. Theodore and Susanna." She looked down at her son, then her daughter. "Teddy. Susanna. This is the man I told you about. Mr. Whitehorse will be staying on our ranch for a while."

Though Chino wondered at the reason for the flush on Abby's face, he turned his attention to her children. The boy—the one he'd seen earlier from atop the hill—met his gaze with a mutinous glare. His eyes nearly matched the brown-and-green mix of his mother's. The girl, younger than her brother, stared up at him with the open curiosity of a child. Her eyes were the bright green of the Time of Many Leaves—late spring—and her hair, several shades lighter than her mother's, hung in a thick braid past her shoulders. The tightness in Chino's chest—the two-year-old ache that never went away—intensified, making it difficult to breathe. If only he hadn't decided to visit the Chiricahua Reservation, then perhaps he would—Abby's voice jerked his thoughts back to the present.

"Children, what do you say to Mr. Whitehorse?"

The boy shifted his glare to his mother. "Do I hafta?" he asked in a low voice.

Abby frowned. "We've already discussed this, Teddy," she replied in an equally soft but firm tone. "And I'm not going to go over it again." She tipped her head to one side, giving him a stern look, one that brooked no argument. "Now, mind your manners and do what I asked."

The boy's chest rose then fell with a deep breath. Turning to look at Chino, he said, "Pleased to meet you, sir."

"Me, too," Susanna piped up. "Peesed to meet you."

"I am pleased to meet you, Theodore," Chino replied.

"Teddy," the boy said. "Momma's the only one who calls me Theodore, and that's only when I done somethin' wrong."

Chino nodded, trying to hold back a smile. But when he turned to the little girl, who stared up at him with such open curiosity, he gave in to the urge. "I am pleased to meet you as well, Susanna."

Abby blinked, taken aback by the expression on Chino's face. The completely genuine smile, the gentleness in his voice, the kindness in his eyes, all were a surprise to her. An odd warmth swirled around her heart, a sensation she quickly squelched.

She didn't want to like this man. She wanted to continue hating him, wanted to call him every vile name she'd ever heard. But when he shifted his gaze, his dark eyes locking with hers, she instinctively knew accomplishing what she wanted would not be easy.

Chapter Four

After enjoying a glass of lemonade, Abby said to Chino, "Supper won't be ready for a while, so how about I show you where you'll be staying?"

"I need to take care of my horse," he replied.

"Of course. Feel free to put him in one of the empty stalls in the barn."

"He is not used to being inside."

"One of the stalls has a rear door that opens into a small corral. You can put him in there, if you like. There's a barrel of water and a bucket just inside the barn door, and you'll find plenty of hay in the loft. While you're seeing to your horse, I'll hunt up some bed linens and sweep out the bunkhouse. Meet me there after you finish."

"Are you sure you want to do that for me?"

"Of course. Offering a roof over your head is the

least I can do." When his only response was a frown, she said, "What is it?"

"Other White Eyes I have worked for told me to sleep outside, or in the barn, with the other animals."

His words startled Abby, causing empathy to well up inside her—a reaction that came as yet another surprise. For the past two years, she'd shared the view that Apaches were nothing more than animals and deserved to be treated as such. So why did she now find the idea so repellent? Realizing the reason for her change in attitude was the man standing in front of her, she finally said, "Well, not me. I insist you stay in the bunkhouse."

Chino stared at her for several seconds. Satisfied she spoke the truth, he saw no reason to argue further. He nodded, then left the house.

While he worked, stripping the saddle and bridle off his horse, then giving him a quick rubdown with a handful of straw, he was struck again by a feeling of peacefulness, a sense of belonging.

In the two years since he'd left the White Mountain Reservation on that ill-fated trip, he'd done a lot of traveling, picking up work wherever he could while looking for the men who'd forever changed his life. But never during that time had he found a place where he wanted to stay for more than a few weeks. Never had he found a place where he felt he belonged. Not until he'd arrived on the Flying M.

He drew a deep breath, then released it slowly. He

glanced around at the surrounding hills and the mountains in the distance, wondering what was different about this ranch. Maybe the land, part of the Apache ancestral home, spoke to a place deep inside him. Or maybe his appreciation for the herd of horses was responsible for his unusual reaction. Or perhaps the answer was Abigail Madison. His mind tried to recoil from that thought, but he forced himself to consider the possibility.

He couldn't deny his attraction to the White Eyes—something he still found disturbing. But if Abby was the reason for his sense of peace and belonging, there had to be more than the desire she stirred in him. He shook his head. No, Abby couldn't be the answer. She'd made her hatred of his people clear, so to consider that there might be something between the two of them would be foolish. That argument made sense, except for one thing. The Spirits had sent him to the Flying M. The Spirits were all-knowing. And yet, in spite of knowing about the death of Abby's husband and her resulting hatred of all Apache, the Spirits had sent him a vision to come here, to her ranch.

The more Chino thought about it, the more confused he became, so he finally gave up trying to find answers. He knew if the Spirits had more to tell him, they would do so when the time was right.

A few minutes later, Chino headed toward the small adobe structure sitting away from the other ranch buildings. The door stood ajar; the single window at the front of the building had been opened.

When Abby noticed him standing in the doorway, she finished smoothing a blanket over one of the room's bunks, then straightened. "I'm sorry for the way this looks. My husband had so many plans for this ranch, like building this bunkhouse. He said we'd need it for the hands he planned to hire. He had more he wanted to do on the inside, but he was killed before he could—" She took a deep breath. "Anyway, at least the roof looks sound."

Chino stepped inside and looked around the room. Besides two bunks, built against opposite walls, the only other furnishings were a crudely built table and two chairs. "You are sure you want me to stay here?"

"I thought we'd already decided that." When he didn't reply, she said, "Is there a problem?"

"No, this will be fine." He took a step into the room, then placed a buckskin bag and his rifle on the table. His back to her, he added, "Thank you."

The huskiness of his last words, spoken as an afterthought, told Abby this man rarely had reason to offer thanks to anyone. She had to clear her throat before she could speak. "You're welcome."

When he said no more, she said, "Well, unless there's something else I can get for you, I'll leave you to get settled."

He turned to face her. "I do not need anything."

Abby swallowed hard, suddenly aware of the

smallness of the room. She could sense the heat of his body, his wonderful male scent. Light-headed and in desperate need of fresh air, she started toward the door. "If you change your mind, let me know," she said, trying to slip past him.

He shifted at that exact moment, causing her shoulder to brush against his chest. She took a step to the side, bumped her leg against a bunk and lost her balance.

Chino grabbed her arms, preventing her from tumbling onto the bunk. Several seconds passed while he stared into her eyes. Finally, he said, "You are all right?"

She managed a nod. His gentle but firm grip and the concern on his face and in his voice made getting a word through the tightness in her throat impossible. Where his hands touched her, twin bursts of heat danced up her arms, swirled through her chest, then dipped lower and combined to create a burning throb low in her belly. Summoning all the strength she could, she said, "You can . . . um . . . let go of me now."

He stared at her for a moment longer, then slowly uncurled his fingers and took a step back.

Abby straightened the bodice of her dress and smoothed her skirt, using the time to get her overwrought senses back in control. When her nerves calmed, she said, "Marita will have supper ready in about an hour."

He acknowledged her words with a nod. She crossed the room, then stopped in the doorway. She told herself looking at him was dangerous, yet she couldn't heed her own warning. When she turned her head, he lifted his gaze and met hers. Something flickered in his dark eyes, a powerful and alluring force that tugged at the very center of her being. Her mouth went dry, and her pulse kicked into a wild rhythm. She licked her lips, then said, "We need to discuss the situation with Neville Warner, but not around my children. I don't want to frighten them."

"I understand."

"Good. Teddy and Susanna go to bed early, so we can talk after they're asleep."

At his nod, she left the bunkhouse and hurried across the yard. She could still feel the heat emanating from him, the fire caused by his touch. Biting back a groan, she lifted the hem of her skirt and practically ran to the house.

When she reached the ramada, she stopped to collect her thoughts. Her attraction to Chino Whitehorse still came as a shock, hitting her without warning and with an intensity she never could have foreseen. Never in her twenty-five years had she experienced anything even approaching what she felt whenever Chino was near, not even with Alan.

Oh, God, Alan! She sucked in a sharp breath, feeling as if she'd been doused with a bucket of cold water. Squeezing her eyes closed for a moment, she released a heavy sigh. She had to figure out how to stop her unwelcome reaction to Chino every time he leveled those mesmerizing dark eyes on her. Moving beneath the ramada to the back door, she frowned. The easiest solution would be to stay away from him. But since he would be on the Flying M for as long as it took to make sure she kept the ranch, steering clear of him wasn't an option. In spite of everything he'd said and the fact that Marita believed him, she didn't trust Chino Whitehorse. And the only way to find out if he'd told her the truth—that he hadn't been sent to the ranch to spy on her—was to watch his every move. She considered having Cesar or Nestor stick close to him, but immediately vetoed the idea. She couldn't take over the chores of either one of the men, so the job of sticking close to Chino would have to be hers.

Her only hope was that the novelty of having an attractive man as her constant companion would be short-lived. Once the newness of his presence wore off, her reaction to him would diminish. At least, she prayed that was what would happen. Heaving another sigh, she entered the house.

By the time Abby took her place at the supper table, she'd managed to wrestle her libido back into control, as well as collect her thoughts. Hoping her children's presence would keep her mind occupied for as long as the meal lasted, she was determined to concentrate on the two of them and their usual happy chatter.

After everyone's plate was filled, she picked up her fork, content with the notion that the meal would go as she'd planned.

Then Teddy turned to look at Chino and said, "How many scalps have ya taken?"

Marita gasped and crossed herself. Cesar made a choking sound, then reached for his glass of water.

Abby's fork slipped from her grasp, and clattered onto her plate. "Teddy! You know better than to ask a question like that."

"Why?" he replied, meeting her gaze, his eyebrows pulled together in a frown. "He's Apache, ain't he?"

"*Isn't* he," she said automatically, certain her face had turned bright red. "Yes, Mr. Whitehorse is Apache, and he's also our guest. Neither gives you the right to be rude."

The boy's frown deepened into a scowl. "I didn't mean nothing. I was just curious."

"I know, son. But you do owe him an apology."

Several seconds passed; then Teddy's chest rose and fell with a deep breath. "I'm sorry I was rude," he said in a low voice.

Chino accepted the apology with a nod, then said, "I will answer the question."

Abby's gaze flew to his face. Rather than the anger she expected, his expression reflected what appeared

63

to be indulgence mixed with mild amusement. "Are you sure?"

"Yes," he replied, then turned to look at her son. "Many believe we take the hair of our enemies. But my band, the Chokonen, does not do this. It is not part of our life-way. I have heard that warriors from some Apache bands have taken the scalps of their enemies, but I do not think they have always done this. I think Apache did not take scalps until after it was done to our people."

There was more Chino could say, but he didn't want to discuss the sordid details about the bounty offered by the Mexican government. About the Apache camps that were attacked by scalpers for the sole purpose of killing every man, woman and child for the money their scalps would bring. Pushing aside the painful memory of another of the horrible atrocities done to his people, he said, "Does that satisfy your curiosity?"

Teddy nodded, then said, "It's kinda like what the Bible says, an eye for an eye. But Momma says we shouldn't do something to somebody just 'cause they did it to us. Two wrongs don't make a right." He turned to look at his mother. "Ain't—I mean, isn't that what you say when Susanna kicks me and I wanna kick her back?"

"Yes, Teddy, that's what I say."

Teddy smiled, then turned his attention to the food on his plate.

Abby gave Chino an apologetic smile, and although she tried to put the incident from her mind, her thoughts returned to what he'd said about taking scalps. After she'd arrived in Arizona Territory as a new bride, she'd heard Alan speak of scalpers—unscrupulous men who received a bounty for every Apache scalp they turned in to the Mexican government. At the time, she hadn't given the practice a second thought, accepting the bounty system established by several Mexican states as a necessity of life in that part of the country. But now the idea of paying men to hunt down and scalp every Apache they could find turned her stomach. Swallowing the bile rising in her throat, she wondered how many other things she'd heard about Apaches were also incorrect.

Several times, during a lull in conversation, her gaze strayed to the fascinating man sitting across from her. Appalled by her own rude behavior and her apparent inability to keep herself from staring at him, she forced herself to look elsewhere. Not quickly enough though, since she was certain he'd caught her staring at him at least once. But when she allowed herself another quick peek to see if she could read his expression, his stoic face revealed nothing.

Abby had no idea what she ate that evening, not tasting a single bite of the food she put into her mouth. She simply chewed and swallowed by rote. She barely heard anything said by the others at the table; her mind was overflowing with a jumble of thoughts—her growing concern about keeping the Flying M and whether she'd be able to fend off Neville Warner's attempts to force her to sell out, her confusing attraction to Chino Whitehorse and whether everything he had told her really was the truth.

By the time she put her children to bed and returned to the kitchen, Marita had just finished cleaning up.

The woman dried her hands, then turned. "If there is nothing else, Señora Abby, I will say *buenas noches*."

"No, there's nothing else, Marita. Good night."

Marita nodded, then said, "Cesar tell me to say he waits on the ramada with Señor Whitehorse."

"Okay, thanks."

After Marita left, Abby took a deep breath, blew it out slowly, then stepped through the back door. She paused to let her eyes become accustomed to the heavy shadows. Taking another deep breath, she moved toward the two men waiting for her.

Chino stood with his back to her, staring out at the mountains to the south, their peaks still visible against the fast-darkening sky. He turned at her approach.

"I want to apologize for Teddy," she said, sitting in the chair she'd occupied during their earlier conversation. "He is a very curious child. When he hears something, well, he just naturally wants to find out more. I hope you understand."

"You do not have to apologize for the boy. Asking questions is one way to learn."

"Yes, that's true. I'm glad you feel that way, but—" she toyed with the fabric of her skirt—"I hope you weren't offended when he quoted my lessons to him. About two wrongs not making a right."

"No, I was not offended, but the beliefs of my people do not agree with what you teach your son. We do believe in revenge. If an Apache is killed, his family must seek revenge by killing the one who is responsible."

"That's pretty bloodthirsty, don't you think?"

"And the killing of my people, even women and children, for their scalps was not bloodthirsty?"

"Of course it was," Abby said, a knot forming in her stomach at the horrible picture his words painted in her mind. "Look, I didn't come out here to debate what constitutes a bloodthirsty act. I just wanted to tell you I'm sorry for the things Teddy said, so can we leave it at that and move on to what we need to discuss?"

Chino huffed out a deep breath, then said, "Yes, but I have a question first. Where is this Nestor you told me about? Does he not take his meals with you?"

Cesar shifted in his chair. "Sí, normally my

nephew eats with us. But today he went to check on the cattle."

"We keep about twenty-five head," Abby said, "so we can have fresh meat. The herd drifts from one area to another, going where the grazing is best. If Nestor has trouble finding them, he could be gone until tomorrow."

"What about your horses? Where are they?"

"Like the cattle, they move around. Last we knew, they were south of here, near the ranch border."

Chino thought about her statement for a moment, then said, "You know Neville Warner wants your ranch, but you let your horses roam wherever they want. Why do you not keep them closer?"

"If you're asking that because you think they're in danger, let me remind you of something: Until you showed up with your talk of one of my horses getting shot, I didn't know they were in danger. Therefore, I had no reason to consider moving my horses closer. And for another, they need grass and, in case it's escaped your notice, ranches here aren't fenced. Letting the herd graze on its own is the only option. Besides, keeping them nearby would require not only putting up fence, but also cutting and hauling grass. That much work would be impossible without a lot more help than I've got."

Chino moved to one end of the ramada, where he leaned one shoulder against the adobe wall of the house. Several minutes passed before he spoke. "Is there a place closer to the house where the horses could find enough grass for a few weeks?"

"The valley north of here, where I found you," Abby replied. "And there's another not far to the west." She looked at Cesar. "The horses haven't been to either of those for what, three or four weeks?"

The older man bobbed his head in agreement. "As you say, the herd has been close to the south boundary of the ranch for perhaps three weeks."

Abby shifted her gaze back to Chino. "What are you thinking?"

"The horses will be easier for me to protect if they are closer. We should move them as soon as possible."

"We can do that, but then what?"

"I worked for a man in Mexico. He raised mules for a freight company. There was a horse with the mules, one with a bell tied around its neck. He called the horse a bell mare, and wherever she went, the mules followed. Is there such a horse in your herd? One the others will follow?"

"Yes, a sorrel mare. There's no bell around her neck, but whenever the herd moves, she leads the way."

"She can be hobbled or tied?"

"I don't think either would be a problem. Right after my husband bought the herd, he realized she was the leader and started working with her. He wanted to get her accustomed to being around humans, and said earning her trust was important. I remember wondering if all his time and effort were really necessary, but now—" she took a deep breath, exhaled slowly—"looks like it's a good thing he did."

Cesar patted her hand. "All things happen for a reason, Señora Abby."

"Yes," she replied with a smile. "That's what you're always telling me. So," she said, turning to Chino, "I take it you plan to hobble or tether the sorrel mare to keep her from wandering off with the herd. What then?"

"I will stay near the horses during the day."

"What about at night? Seems to me that would be the best time for an attack, when darkness hides a person's identity and what he's up to."

Chino shook his head. "That is not what the Spirits showed me."

"And your spirits couldn't be wrong about this?"

He crossed his arms over his chest. "The Spirits have always told me the truth."

"Maybe so, but shooting at horses in broad daylight is foolish. Who would run the risk of getting caught by—" She gave an indelicate snort. "On second thought, I know exactly who would do that. Neville Warner. I knew he wanted my ranch. I just didn't realize how much until now." She clenched her teeth, trying to rein in her anger. "The conniving snake in the grass."

Cesar grunted. "That is too kind. He deserves to be called much worse."

"You won't get any argument from me," she replied, flashing a quick smile. "Okay, so the first thing we need to do is get the horses. Let me know as soon as Nestor returns. Maybe he saw the horses while checking on the cattle. After I talk to him, Chino and I will leave to bring the herd back here."

"But, Señora Abby, I should be the one to go with you."

"No, *tío abuelo,* we might have to ride a long ways. That much time in the saddle would be bad for your arthritis. You will stay here with Marita and the children, *por favor.*"

"Sí, I will stay," he replied. Casting a quick glance toward Chino, he dropped his voice to add, "You must be careful with this one. He has eyes for you."

"What?" Abby's heart thumped hard against her ribs.

"It is true," he said. Pushing himself out of his chair, he raised his voice to say, "I will leave you now." Crossing the ramada, he said, *"Buenas noches,* señor, Señora Abby." Then he disappeared through the door to the smaller house.

The soft click of the door closing sounded overly loud in the silence of the Arizona night. Abby drew a deep breath, eased it out slowly. She had always loved this time of day, when the heat gave way to the cooler nighttime breezes, when all creatures on the ranch settled down for the night. Chino's voice startled her, pulling her from her thoughts.

She turned to look at him. "I'm sorry. What did you say?"

"There is nothing more you wanted to talk about?"

"No. If you want to turn in, go ahead. I'm going to sit here for a few minutes."

He murmured a good night, then turned on his heel and silently melded into the deepening darkness.

She released a long sigh, then closed her eyes and let her head drop against the back of her chair. She hoped she had the strength she needed to get through the days ahead—not just to save the Flying M, but to control her reaction to Chino Whitehorse. The latter, as she'd discovered just a few hours earlier, might prove to be the more difficult of the two tasks.

The sky was glowing with a bright golden-pink as the sun crested the mountains behind Neville Warner's house.

He stood at his office window, hands clasped behind his back, staring toward the west in his normal morning routine. He enjoyed watching the day's first rays of sunlight splash over his ranch. The Warner Land and Cattle Company. From his location, he had an unobstructed view of the Santa Cruz River and the broad valley that stretched far beyond—the exact reason he'd had his house built on higher ground. He wanted to look outside and see nothing but Warner land. Land he owned. His personal kingdom.

He found the notion of owning a kingdom, of being a king, strongly appealing. Smiling, he allowed himself a moment to bask in that heady thought. Then reality intruded into his vision of the future.

He didn't own all the land he could see.

His morning ritual ruined, he muttered a curse, then turned away from the window. Taking a seat at his desk, he drummed his fingers on the desktop.

There had to be a way to put an end to Abigail Madison's stubbornness. Sitting back in his chair, he thought again of his most recent conversation with one of the men on his payroll. The man had already proven he'd do anything for money, but for the time being, his job was giving the widow plenty of reason to change her mind about selling the Flying M.

Neville hoped the plan they'd devised a few days earlier would produce the desired results. But if not, he had no qualms about asking the man to do something more drastic.

He wanted the Flying M, and by damn, no matter what, he would have it.

Chapter Five

Abby stood at the edge of the ramada looking out over the ranch yard. She'd spent a restless night; the thoughts and images churning in her mind allowed little sleep. As soon as the sky had begun to change from inky black to a dull gray, she'd given up trying and rose from her bed. After a quick sponge bath, she'd dressed, then headed to the kitchen to put a pot of coffee on to boil.

She yawned, stretching her arms over her head. The days were already long enough—most requiring her to work from dawn until well past dusk—but her lack of sleep would make today even longer. Well, there was no help for that now. She'd just have to make the best—Movement to her right halted her musings. Squinting in the morning's pale light, she scoured the area toward the creek until she found the source of movement. Chino.

Her pulse quickened at the sight of him. Wondering what he was up to, she decided to find out. She slipped from beneath the cover of the ramada and followed him, taking care to stay in the shadows. When he stopped in an open area not far from the bunkhouse, she crouched behind a clump of mesquite.

From her hiding place, she watched him drop a small bundle onto the ground, then turn to face the east and lift his arms to the rising sun. Noticing how his hair stuck to his neck and shoulders, she realized he'd gone to the creek to bathe. Her gaze traveled from the thick strands of wet hair to the well-defined muscles of his bare back, then down to the sinfully tight buckskin trousers and knee-high moccasins.

She bit her lip, her pulse speeding up even more. Not wanting to give away her presence and intrude on his privacy during what appeared to be some sort of spiritual rite, she straightened and carefully made her way back to the house.

After Chino ended his morning prayers to the Great Spirit—Ussen, the Creator of Life—he went into the bunkhouse to finish dressing, then headed to the main house. When he entered the back door, he found Abby sitting at the dining table with a man he didn't recognize—a man he assumed was Nestor Zepeda.

She glanced up at him. "Chino, I'm glad you're here. I want you to meet Nestor." She nodded toward a chair opposite hers. "Have a seat."

As Chino took the chair she indicated, Marita brought the coffeepot to the table. "You would like coffee, señor?"

Chino nodded, pushing an empty cup toward her.

While Marita poured his coffee, Abby made the introductions, then said, "I was just about to ask Nestor if he saw the horses yesterday."

Nestor waited for Marita to refill his cup, then said, "Sí, I saw them. They were south of Black Mesa."

"Good," Abby replied, looking at Chino. "Then we should be able to get back with the herd before nightfall."

Nestor's heavy eyebrows pulled together in a frown. "You are planning to bring the horses here?"

"Yes. Chino and I will be leaving as soon as we finish eating."

"I do not understand. Why do you want to move the horses? There is plenty of grass where they are."

As Abby explained Chino's fears for her horses' safety and her decision to move the herd closer, Chino studied Nestor. The man looked a little older than his own twenty-eight years, with a narrow face dominated by a wide nose; a thick, drooping moustache; and pale brown eyes—eyes as cold as any Chino had seen. Taking a drink of coffee, he wondered at the reason for the coldness in this man's eyes. Anger perhaps, or frustration. Or maybe the cause was hatred—a reaction he'd encountered countless times. Yes, one of those might be the reason.

The door swinging open ended Chino's contemplation of the man. He looked up to see Cesar enter the room.

Abby rose to help Marita serve breakfast. After everyone's plate had been filled, she took her seat. "You got in late last night," she said to Nestor. "Did you have a problem finding the cattle?"

"I found them early yesterday afternoon," he replied, keeping his eyes focused on his plate.

"They look good, sí?" Cesar asked.

Nestor hesitated, then finally said, "Sí, Tío Cesar, the ones I saw looked good."

"What does that mean, the ones you saw?"

"Part of the herd is missing."

"Missing?" Cesar's eyebrows shot up. "How many?"

Nestor shrugged. "Perhaps half."

The older man dropped his fork onto his plate with a muttered, *"¡Díos mio!"*

Marita's gaze skipped from her husband's shocked expression to Nestor's face. "You look for the missing cattle?"

"Sí, Tía Marita, for the rest of the day. I did not find them."

"But they have to be somewhere," Abby said.

"I look, Señora Abby, but they are gone."

"Gone," Abby whispered in a hollow voice. "How can that be?"

"I cannot explain it," Nestor replied, "but it is true."

Silence followed Nestor's last words, broken only by the occasional clink of silverware as everyone resumed eating.

Finally, Chino said, "Did you see tracks around the herd?"

Nestor reached for his coffee cup. "What do you mean?"

"Tracks left by horses. A trail that could be followed."

"If you're talking about my horses," Abby said, "they aren't shod. Their feet are hard as rock. Every time Alan tried to shoe one of them, the nails bent. Besides they have never grazed with the cattle."

"I did not mean your horses." When the furrowing of her brow was her only response, he said, "You do not think it strange that half your cattle would leave the herd at the same time?"

Abby's frown deepened. "Yes, that is odd. We've had to look for one or two strays before, but not— Oh my God, are you suggesting the missing cattle didn't wander off on their own?"

"It is something you should consider."

Nestor set down his cup with enough force to rattle the other dishes on the table. "You accuse me of stealing the cattle?" The ice in his voice matched the cold stare he directed at Chino.

"No. I am saying it is possible someone stole them. That is why I asked if you saw tracks made by horses."

"Stolen," Abby said with a shake of her head. "Who in the world would want to—" Her gaze met Chino's. "Warner."

His lips pressed into a grim line, he nodded.

Nestor gave a snort of laughter. "Why would Señor Warner want your cattle? There are at least a thousand head on his ranch."

"He wouldn't steal half my cattle because he wants to add to his herd," Abby replied. "He would do it because he doesn't want me to have them. Undoubtedly another tactic he thinks will help his efforts to buy this ranch. Reduce our food supply, and I'll become eager to sell."

"If what you say is true," Marita said, "he would steal all the cattle, sí?"

"My guess is he's playing games," Abby replied. "Stealing half my herd is a warning. If I ignore it, he'll do something to apply more pressure."

Cesar looked from Abby to Chino, then to his nephew. "You did not answer Señor Whitehorse's question. Did you find hoofprints?"

Nestor dropped his gaze to his plate. "No, tío, I saw nothing."

"Well," Abby said with a sigh, "if Warner is behind this, and I'd be willing to stake my life that he is, we could never prove it. He's too clever to let the blame fall on him."

When no one offered a response, another heavy silence fell over the table.

Though Chino turned his attention to the plate of food in front of him, his mind remained on Abby's last statement. Yes, Neville Warner was clever, and proving he was behind the disappearance of her cattle would be difficult. The man was not stupid; he would hide his involvement. But he was also arrogant. His arrogance had caused him to make a mistake two years ago by paying off the two men he'd ordered to shoot Chino and the others, then telling them to disappear. He never suspected Chino had survived, never suspected how persistent Chino would be in tracking down the men who'd fired those shots.

Yes, if Warner operated true to form, sooner or later he would become overconfident and let down his guard. When that happened, Chino planned to be there. In fact, he relished the idea of making sure Neville Warner received just punishment for what he'd done.

A child calling for Abby broke the silence. Both

she and Marita set down their forks and started to push away from the table.

"I'll go," Abby said, getting to her feet.

She returned several minutes later, a sleep-tousled Susanna in her arms. Teddy followed his mother and sister into the room, rubbing the sleep from his eyes with a fist.

"Good morning, *niños*," Marita said with a smile. "You are ready for breakfast, sí?"

Teddy nodded, then climbed onto a chair. Abby took her seat at the table, settling Susanna on her lap. The little girl yawned, pushed a wisp of hair off her face, then flashed Chino a bright smile.

Chino swallowed hard, captivated by the open sweetness of that smile. "You slept well, *sha?*"

Her brow furrowed. "My name's Susanna."

"Yes, I know," Chino replied, resisting the urge to grin. "I called you *sha,* Apache for sunshine, because your smile is bright, like the sun."

An even bigger smile curved her rosy mouth as she looked up at her mother. "Momma, he called me *sha* 'cuz my smile is like the sun."

"Yes, sweetheart, I heard. That was a very nice thing to say, wasn't it?"

The girl gave a vigorous nod, then looked back at Chino. "Can I sit with you?"

"Susanna," Abby said, "it's impolite to ask questions like that. Besides, Mr. Whitehorse is eating and—"

"I do not mind," Chino said, pushing his chair away from the table to make room for the girl.

Abby's gaze snapped up. After her momentary shock passed, she arched her eyebrows at him, silently asking if he was sure.

When he nodded, she loosened her hold on Susanna and let the girl slide to the floor.

Susanna ran around the table, her thin, cotton nightgown flapping around her legs, then scrambled up onto Chino's lap. She tipped back her head and smiled at him, then reached up to pat his cheek.

Her eyes widened. "No scratchies."

"Scratchies?"

"Whiskers," Abby said. "She calls them scratchies because they're rough against her skin."

"Ah, now I understand," Chino said, smiling at Susanna.

"How come you ain't got no scratchies?"

Chino's smile broadened. "I pull them out."

"Why?"

"All Apache men pull out the hair on their face."

"Why?"

"Apache men have always done this. It is part of our life-way."

"Why?"

"Susanna," Abby said, "stop pestering Mr. Whitehorse with questions."

The girl looked at her mother. "I wasn't peserin' him."

"Was, too," Teddy said. "Yer always pestering everybody, asking why all the time."

"Teddy, that's enough. Your sister's only three—"

"Me almos' four," Susanna said.

"Yes, sweetheart, you'll be four in a couple of months." Turning back to her son, Abby said, "Susanna is full of curiosity, the same as you were at her age. And you asked just as many questions."

The boy frowned at that, but finally said, "Yes, ma'am."

Susanna looked up at Chino again. "Was I peserin' you?"

"No, *sha,* you are curious," Chino replied with a laugh, surprised to hear the sound coming from his mouth. He couldn't remember the last time he'd laughed.

Marita set a bowl in front of Susanna. "Eat, *niña.*"

The girl wiggled to get more comfortable on Chino's lap. " 'Kay," she said, reaching for her spoon.

Abby watched the interaction between her daughter and Chino with amazement. Though Susanna wasn't a shy child, she always had been reserved around strangers, never taking to anyone as quickly as she had to Chino Whitehorse. Picking up her coffee cup and taking a sip, Abby studied the man over the rim.

She had to remember he was Apache. A fierce and

dangerous man. One of the red devils who struck fear in the hearts of every Anglo living in Arizona Territory. Yet, sitting at her table, with her daughter on his lap, he had shown only impeccable manners, kindness and gentleness—traits she wouldn't have thought any Apache possessed. Even though she'd witnessed such a display, she still found the shattering of her preconceived notions hard to accept.

She narrowed her eyes, looking at him more closely. Maybe his behavior was an act. Maybe he was deliberately trying to lull her into thinking he posed no threat to her or her family.

Yes, that was a definite possibility, one she should consider. And she would, she decided, swallowing the last of her coffee. Deep inside, intuition told her he wasn't acting, but she refused to listen.

Abby set down her cup, then pushed away from the table. "I'll be ready to leave as soon as I change. Meet me in the barn, in ten minutes."

Chino looked up. The harshness of her expression took him by surprise, banishing the joy he'd experienced with Susanna. Wondering at the reason for the sudden chill in her eyes, he nodded.

A few minutes later, he was tightening the cinch on his saddle when Abby entered the barn. He didn't turn around, trying to concentrate on his task. But he heard the clomp of her boots on the hard-packed dirt floor, the creak of the stall door swinging open, the soft murmur of her voice as she spoke to her horse, and then the animal's answering nicker.

For a moment he allowed himself to imagine what living on a ranch such as the Flying M would be like. His days would be spent working with the horses, but he would leave time for his children, to teach them what they needed to know as adults. Then once the children were asleep, he would enjoy the evening by sitting on the ramada with his wife. They would talk quietly about their day or their plans for the future. Or maybe they would go for a walk in the moonlight, to a secluded spot where they would—

"Chino. Are you all right?"

He blew out a deep breath, grabbed the reins, then turned. "Yes, I—" He blinked, momentarily stunned. "What are you wearing?"

Abby frowned. "What do—" She looked down at her clothes. "Oh. I'm so used to dressing this way, I forget how people react." She met his gaze, her chin lifted at a defiant angle. "After Alan died, I had to take on a lot of additional work, much of it on horseback. Wearing layers of skirts and petticoats while spending hours in the saddle was impractical, so I took Alan's trousers and cut them down to fit me. They're more comfortable, and I intend to continue wearing them." She tilted her chin a little higher. "I don't care if you, or anyone else, is shocked. And I sure don't need your approval."

Chino pursed his lips to halt a smile. A smile he knew she would misinterpret. She wouldn't understand that his amusement over her prickly defense of her clothes came from admiration, not criticism. She stared up at him with a mutinous glare, feet spread, hands on hips. So courageous. So full of pride. Just looking at her caused a strange warmth to fill his chest. When her eyes narrowed, he realized his silence had given her the wrong impression.

"You are right," he said. "You do not need my approval for what you wear, but I do approve."

Her eyes narrowed even more, but she didn't respond.

"You are a strong and wise woman. When you became the leader of your family, you had to make decisions. Decisions you do not have to defend. What others think does not matter. They have not lived your life and should not judge you."

She continued staring at him for a moment. Finally, her chin lowered and the stiffness in her back eased. Wetting her lips, she said, "Um, well, thanks."

He nodded, then started toward the barn door.

A few minutes later, they mounted up and headed south. As soon as they crossed the creek, Abby settled her hat more firmly on her head, then kicked her chestnut gelding into a canter. She looked around at the rolling hills with their blanket of grass and sprinkling of mesquite trees. Riding the ranch always gave her such a wonderful sense of peace and serenity, a joyful oneness with the land that never failed to soothe her aching heart, or replenish her flagging spirits.

Her worries momentarily forgotten, a laugh bubbled up from her chest. Urging her horse into a run, she bent over his neck, loving the feel of the wind on her face.

At the top of a hill, she pulled her horse to a halt, then turned to watch Chino rein his horse in beside hers. Knowing a silly smile was probably on her face, she said, "Isn't it a wonderful day?"

He nodded, his dark eyes studying her quietly.

She glanced around them. Mountains could be seen in all directions, some far in the distance, others much closer. She inhaled a deep breath, then sighed. "When Alan brought me here, the oddest thing happened. I felt as if I'd been waiting my entire life to come to this place. On this wild land, I found a peacefulness and a sense of belonging I'd never experienced. And just that quick—" she snapped her fingers—"I knew this was where I was meant to spend the rest of my days."

She dragged her gaze from a distant mountain peak and met his. "I suppose that sounds ridiculous," she said with a sheepish smile.

Chino's lips curved upward. "No. I understand."

"Really?"

"The Apache have a deep closeness to the land that has been our home for countless generations. The land gave us food and shelter, but that is not the same as what you feel for this place. You feel more than gratitude for what the land gives you. You feel you are part it. Your breath is its breath. Your heart beating is its heart beating. You feel a connection—a bond you cannot break."

For a moment Abby couldn't speak. Her heart was thundering against her eardrums; a huge lump wedged itself in her throat. In just a few simple words, he'd expressed her feelings perfectly. It was as if he somehow had reached inside her and touched her soul. Swallowing hard, she willed her heart to slow, forced herself to breathe normally.

Finally, she said, "You *do* understand. You've felt that bond, haven't you?"

He nodded.

"Did it hit you as quickly as it did me?"

"Yes, it happened quickly."

"Where is this place?"

He turned to stare off into the distance. "That is not important."

"But don't you long to go back there?"

A muscle in his jaw jumped. "We cannot always have what we long for."

Not waiting for her to respond, he moved his horse away from hers. With a touch of his heels, the dark bay lunged forward, then settled into an easy lope.

Abby held her gelding in check, her thoughts centered on the complex man riding away from her. There was so much she didn't know about him—

things, she was startled to realize, she wanted to know. After several seconds, she blew out a deep breath, then gave her horse his head.

As her gelding lengthened his strides to catch Chino's bay, a battle raged in her mind over whether she should allow her surprising revelation to become reality and learn all there was to know about Chino Whitehorse. She feared if she did, she would become even more attracted to him, which could end up involving her heart.

Common sense told her she should stay away from him. His people were responsible for Alan's death, and she didn't need to add more heartache to the list of obstacles she already had to overcome. Yes, staying away from him would be the safest choice, but there was one major problem with that line of thinking.

She wasn't sure she could.

Chapter Six

After Abby caught up with Chino, she didn't try to strike up a conversation. Though her discovery that she wanted to know everything about the man remained fresh in her mind, she held her tongue, not sure how he would take to being barraged with a string of questions. Patience is a virtue. Wasn't that the old adage she'd preached to Teddy countless times? Only this time, she needed to follow her own motherly advice. Being patient could prove difficult, especially given her curiosity about Chino—not to mention the strength of her attraction to him. But she'd do her best to exert all the patience she could muster; she'd force herself to be content with gathering snippets about Chino whenever the opportunity arose.

They had traveled several miles in silence, their

horses walking side by side, when Chino said, "You called Cesar great-uncle. He is family?"

"Not by blood, but I think of him that way. From the minute I arrived here with Alan, both Marita and Cesar have treated me with only kindness and love. They're the closest I have to real kin."

"You have no family?"

"A brother somewhere. Joe. He left home when I was ten. Our parents died of a fever three years later. I had no idea where Joe was, so I couldn't send word to him."

"You have not seen him since he left?"

"No. He didn't come back to East Texas before I married Alan and moved here. So, unless he went back after I left, he'd have no way of knowing where to find me." She sighed. "If he even wanted to."

"You were young to be on your own."

"I was thirteen and could've taken care of myself. But Papa owed money on our place, and as soon as the bank found out about my parents, they told me I had to pay off the loan or get out. One of our neighbors offered to take me in. Alan's brother and his wife."

"That is how you met your husband?"

"Yes. Alan came to visit, and we hit it off right away. He was so kind to me, and we could talk about anything. He told me about his plans to head west. How he wanted to buy some land and start a ranch. A year later, he said he was leaving. But before he left, he told me he wanted to marry me when I was old enough and asked me to wait for him. I said I would, and then he was gone.

"He wrote me a couple of times, telling me about the land he'd bought, how it wouldn't be much longer before he'd come for me. He rattled on and on about Arizona Territory and all the plans he had for the ranch he named the Flying M."

Abby vividly remembered those letters, recalling how his words had conveyed his excitement. "Anyway, four years after he left, he kept his promise and came back to East Texas. We were married a week later, and three days after that, we left to come here."

She laughed. "I'll never forget that trip. Those miserable weeks of riding in constantly rocking, bouncing stagecoaches, through every kind of weather. It's a wonder I wasn't covered in bruises from that bone-jarring ride. But then we arrived here, and I saw the Flying M for the first time—Well, suddenly my exhaustion vanished. All the discomforts I'd endured were a small price to pay for how I felt when I first laid eyes on this ranch."

Chino thought about what she'd told him, then said, "You have been back to where you were born?"

"No. I've got no reason to go." When Abby noticed his odd expression, she said, "You look like you don't agree. My life is here now, with my children. What reason would I have for going back to where I was born?"

"For you and other White Eyes, maybe none. But to my people, our place of birth is important. All Apache children are told where they were born. Whenever their band is near the place, parents take their children there and roll them on the ground."

"Why in the world would they do that?"

"To seek the holy good of the directions for the child. They are first rolled to the east, the most sacred direction, then to the west, north and south."

Abby gaped at him for several seconds. "You're not serious?" When he gave her a glowering glance, she added, "You are!"

"I told you I speak only the truth."

"Yes, but rolling a child around on the ground?" She shook her head. "That's really strange behavior."

"Not to me. It is part of the Apache life-way." The corners of his mouth curving upward, he added, "Do you White Eyes not do things that are strange?"

"I guess I've never thought about it. You think we do?"

He nodded, then said, "I once worked for a White Eyes near Mesilla. Behind the door of the barn he kept a knife in a jar filled with water. I asked him why he did this. He said it was to protect his horses."

She turned to look at him, narrowing her eyes to study his face. Unable to tell if he was pulling her leg, she said, "Okay, I'll bite. Protect his horses from what?"

"Evil spirits."

She shook her head again, then chuckled. "I had to ask."

He smiled. "You agree? What the White Eyes did was strange?"

"Yes, and I get your point," she replied, returning his smile. "Anglos have some pretty strange customs, too."

He held her gaze for several seconds. Then his smile faded, and he turned to look straight ahead.

Again they rode in silence, Abby's thoughts dwelling on their conversation. Her curiosity had once more been piqued by Chino's comments about what he called the Apache life-way. She definitely wanted to know more, but she'd already admonished herself about the need to be patient. After contemplating the situation for a few minutes, one answer dawned on her. The man and his culture were inseparable, therefore whatever she learned about one would teach her something about the other.

When the sun was nearly straight overhead, Abby pointed out a thick grove of mesquite as a place to stop and rest the horses.

After dismounting, she took her canteen and a cloth-wrapped bundle she'd removed from her saddlebags to where Chino had already taken a seat beneath one of the trees. She sat down next to him, set her canteen on the ground beside her, then opened the bundle. Handing him a tortilla rolled around strips of dried beef, she said, "Black Mesa isn't far from here, so I'm hoping the horses are still where Nestor saw them."

He accepted the food with a nod of thanks. "If they are not, we will find them."

"Yes, of course we will. I just don't want to be gone from the house any longer than necessary."

Chino swallowed a bite of the beef-filled tortilla, then said, "Tell me more about Neville Warner."

"Actually, I don't know a great deal. The first I heard of him was about three years ago, when he moved onto his ranch. But Alan thought he'd probably been buying land up and down the Santa Cruz River Valley for years before that. Anyway, the headquarters of the ranch is near Tubac, but his land stretches well to the north, and as far south as the Mexican border. In the last couple of years, he's added more land by buying out smaller ranches in the area."

"Why did the owners sell to him?"

"We heard one man sold out after his wife took sick and died. Another one sold his ranch after the biggest share of his cattle turned up missing. Word around these parts was that the cattle had been run off by a band of raiding Apaches, but now I wonder if . . ." Abby frowned, then turned to look at Chino. "Do you think the missing cattle could've been Warner's doing?"

Chino shrugged. "If he is hungry for more land, I think it is possible."

"Yes, he definitely wants more land. About six months before Alan was killed, Warner got a contract with the Army to supply beef to the posts in this part of the territory. That's when he started the Warner Land and Cattle Company. He was already running a pretty large herd on his ranch, but after getting the military contract, he increased the number. And the more cattle he had to feed, the more grazing land he needed."

Abby uncapped her canteen, then lifted it to her mouth and took a long drink of water. Closing the canteen, she continued. "That's when he approached Alan about buying our ranch. Alan turned him down, of course, and I forgot about it until—" she squeezed her eyes closed for a moment—"Warner paid me a visit. He said a widow with two young children didn't belong on a ranch in the middle of Apache country. He tried to make it sound like he was doing me a favor. Offering a fair price to take the land off my hands."

She clenched her jaw, her fingers tightening on the canteen. "I wish now that I'd shot the sorry excuse for a man."

Chino resisted the urge to smile at Abby's fierce expression. "You know what it is like to shoot a man?"

"No, but if Neville Warner is as determined to buy

my ranch as I think he is, then I'm willing to find out."

"Do not worry about him. I will see that he pays for what he has done."

"You think I'm not capable of shooting him?" she asked, her chin tilted upward.

"I did not say you are not capable. But I would not want you to have to spend the rest of your life knowing you killed a man. For some, that is a burden the mind cannot accept."

Abby stared at him for a moment. Then releasing a deep sigh, she lowered her chin and relaxed her rigid posture. "I'm sure there are people who never recover from the experience. But, I swear, if Neville Warner hurts, or even threatens, someone I love, I won't hesitate to take that chance."

Chino understood her desire to protect her family, so he made no effort to try to convince her to change her mind. But he understood something else, as well. He knew firsthand, that in spite of a person's best efforts, providing protection for loved ones wasn't always possible. Not wanting to upset her, he kept his thoughts to himself.

They ate in silence for a few minutes, then Chino said, "Does Warner have a wife, children?"

Abby shook her head. "Not that I know of. When he first came to this part of the territory, we heard rumors that he had a wife back East somewhere. But Alan spoke with a man who'd been to the Warner ranch, and he said Warner claimed he wasn't married. I hope not, because he had a young Mexican woman living with him, and she wasn't there just to keep his house, if you get my meaning."

Chino smiled. "She shares his bed. Is that your meaning?"

"Exactly," Abby replied, hoping the shade cast by the mesquite trees hid the blush burning her cheeks.

"You do not approve because the woman sharing his bed is Mexican or because he is not married to her?"

"I didn't say I don't approve. I couldn't care less who shares Neville Warner's bed. I mean, everybody has . . . well, needs. And if he chooses not to marry her, that's none of my concern. But I *would* disapprove of him carrying on with any woman if it turned out he has a wife somewhere."

"You have reason to think he does?"

"No. Like I said, he claims he's not married."

"You do not think he would lie?" Chino replied, then popped the last of his tortilla into his mouth.

She mulled that over for a moment. "Based on what I know about him, I'm inclined to believe he's capable of most anything—especially lying—if it gets him what he wants."

Chino nodded. "You are right to believe that, because it is true. My people would call him *naaldluushi*—coyote. He is sly. A trickster. Hard to see and find."

"Coyote, huh?" Abby said with a smile. "I'd say that description fits him pretty well."

He returned her smile, then uncapped his canteen and lifted it to his mouth. She watched the muscles of his throat work as he swallowed. Her pulse increased, her breath caught in her chest, heat pooled between her thighs. She felt as if there was more to the moment than her viewing the simple act of his taking a drink. Her body reacted as if they were sharing a much more intimate encounter. Forcing herself to look away, she searched for something, anything to divert her attention from the magnetic power Chino unknowingly had over her.

A few minutes later, much to Abby's relief, they swung back into their saddles and resumed their trek to find her horses. When they reached the south side of Black Mesa, Abby pulled her gelding to a halt. Looking in all directions, she frowned. There wasn't a horse in sight.

She released a heavy sigh. "Thinking they'd still be here was too good to be true."

"You are sure this is where Nestor saw the horses?"

"Yes, of course this is the place." When Chino didn't respond, she turned to look at him. "What? You think Nestor didn't tell me the truth?"

Chino's lips flattened, but again he didn't speak.

Her eyes widened. "My God, you do! I'll have you know, Nestor is as devoted to the Flying M as his aunt and uncle. If he said the horses were here two days ago, then I believe him."

Chino appeared to debate her words for a moment, then finally shrugged. "What do you want to do now?"

Abby drew a deep breath, then exhaled slowly. "Keep looking. Maybe they haven't wandered too far."

At his nod, she said, "We'll start by checking the closest water." Swinging her horse around, she touched her heels to the gelding's sides.

Chino stared after her for a moment, then urged his bay forward.

The ride to the spring was short, and when they arrived, Chino dismounted to check the ground surrounding the pool of water.

"Well," Abby said after Chino made his inspection, "what did you find?"

"They were here this morning."

"You're sure?"

Chino looked up at where she still sat astride her horse. "You doubt the word of an Apache? Do you not know we are the best trackers?"

The sarcasm in his voice took Abby by surprise. "I—well, yes, I heard that's why the Army used Apaches as scouts."

"The White Eyes Army could not track down those who fled the reservation, so they hired the only ones who could. To admit Apaches are superior at something must be bitter medicine for the White Eyes government."

Abby had no idea how to respond to that, so she didn't try. Instead she said, "Can you tell which way the horses went?"

"There," he replied, pointing to the east.

By mid-afternoon, Abby's anxiety was growing stronger with each passing minute. Chino had followed the trail as far as he could, losing it in a rocky area—even Apaches couldn't track over solid rock—and had yet to pick it up again.

As Chino studied another area of ground, a chuckle bubbled up from Abby's chest. "I remember the first time I saw the horses scale a jagged slope," she said. "Watching them was amazing. From then on, I considered hard feet a desirable trait in a horse. But right now, I wish they weren't so surefooted on rock. That would certainly make following their trail easier for you."

He straightened and turned toward her. "We will find them."

She looked up at the sun's position in the sky. "Well, it had better be soon, otherwise, we won't get back until well after dark."

"The horses are not far away."

She gave him a weak smile. "Thanks for trying to reassure me. But I know they could be miles from here by now."

"I was not trying to reassure you. They are close by."

"Really, and just how is it you know that?"

Chino mounted his horse before replying. "I received a sign that something good will happen soon."

"A sign. You received a sign that something good would happen?"

At his nod, she said, "And the something good is finding my horses?"

Again he nodded.

"Would you mind telling me what this sign was?"

He appeared uncertain about responding, but finally he said, "I had a shaking in my leg. Here." He touched the inner muscle of his right thigh. "That is a good sign. And I know it means we will find your horses."

"I take it a shaking is like a muscle twitch?" When he nodded, she said, "When did you have this shaking in your leg?"

"Just now, while I was looking for tracks."

She rolled her eyes. "I'm willing to keep an open mind about your having visions because Marita believes in such things. But now this . . . this shaking—" she bit her lip to halt the threatening laughter—"as you call it. Do you expect me to believe a muscle twitch can predict what's going to happen?"

"I do not *expect* you to believe anything. But I speak the truth."

She studied him in silence for a moment. His jaw

clenched, his lips pressed into a thin line and his dark eyes returned her stare without a blink. Such a proud man, she mused, and from all she could tell, also an honorable one.

"I want to believe," she said. "So, why don't you tell me more about these twitches you have?"

He held her gaze for a few moments longer, then looked away. Nudging his horse into a walk, he waited for Abby to bring her horse abreast of his before he began speaking. "To my people, shakings of the flesh are another way for the Spirits to speak to us, messages sent to inform us of something. From the time I was a boy, I have paid attention to each one I had, and I would remember what happened afterward. When I was older, I knew a shaking of the flesh on the inside of my leg was a sign something good would happen. A shaking on the outside of my leg was a sign of something bad."

"You're not the only one to have muscle twitches. So why are yours any different than someone else's?"

"I do not know if mine are different. I think it is just that I have spent much time studying the shaking of my flesh, and others have not. My people say the Spirits have given me a great power, just as they gave me horse power. And I must honor both powers."

Abby mulled over his explanation, then said, "I don't understand how you know what good or bad thing will happen when you have one of these muscle twitches. For instance, how did you know the one you had a few minutes ago means we will find my horses?"

"I have learned a shaking in my flesh is about what I am doing when the Spirits send me the sign. Today, we are looking for your horses, so I know the good sign from the Spirits means we will find them."

Abby turned to look at him, then frowned. "No offense, but interpreting your muscle twitches still seems a little too far-fetched to me. I'm more a believer in cold, hard facts. I believe we'll find my horses when I actually see them with my own eyes."

"You should not question the shakings of my flesh," he replied, pulling his horse to a halt. "They have never been wrong."

"Is that right?" She stopped her gelding beside his horse. "Well, I hate to trample all over your confidence about these muscle twitches of yours, but there's a first time for everything."

He turned in his saddle, scanned the surrounding area before his gaze settled on her face. "It is true. There is always a first time." He shrugged. "Maybe I am wrong. Maybe the shaking of my flesh did not mean we will find your horses."

"No, don't say that," Abby said. "Look, if I've offended you, I'm sorry. But all your talk about muscle twitches is a lot for anyone to accept. Please tell me I'm forgiven, that you'll still help me find my horses."

He stared at some point over her shoulder for several long moments, then said, "You are forgiven."

Abby eased out a relieved breath. "And you'll help me find my horses?"

He nodded, bringing his gaze back to meet hers.

"Thank good—" She scowled. Was that amusement in the depths of his dark eyes? And a smile tugging at the corners of his mouth?

"Well," she said, lifting her chin, "you obviously find this amusing, so go ahead and laugh. Then when you get it out of your system, we can—"

"Get off your horse."

"What?"

"Get off your horse."

Chapter Seven

Chino held Abby's stare for several seconds, the angle of her chin telling him her exasperation hadn't completely faded. He watched her struggle to overcome the last of her irritation, then she did as he'd instructed and dismounted.

"Okay, now what?" she said.

He swung his right leg over his horse's neck and slid to the ground. Moving a few feet away from the horses, he beckoned to her. When she stood in front of him, he said, "Turn around."

She tipped her head to one side, brow furrowed, eyes narrowed. "What's this about?"

"You will see. Now, turn around."

He watched the emotions play across her face. Annoyance, impatience, curiosity. When the latter finally won the battle, she huffed out a breath and slowly turned.

"All right," she said, a hint of irritation lingering in her voice, "what am I—" Her words ended with a gasp, followed by a moment of stunned silence, then delighted laughter.

He smiled at her reaction to seeing the herd of horses working their way down the rocky slope of a nearby hill.

"You did it," she said, spinning around to face him again. "You found them."

He returned her smile, then looked past her to watch the horses. "I told you they—" The grip of her hand on his arm took him by surprise. And when she moved closer and pressed her mouth to his, surprise turned to shock. He sucked in a sharp breath, filling his head with her scent—a tantalizing mixture of wildflowers and the musk of her sun-heated flesh.

Then just as quickly, she pulled away, leaving his lips tingling and his blood roaring in his ears.

She stared up at him, the green flecks in her eyes more prominent than usual. He managed to collect his scattered thoughts enough to realize the startled expression on her face undoubtedly matched the one he wore. Before he could find his voice, she spoke.

"I . . . um . . ." She cleared her throat, and took a step back. "I don't know what—It's just that I was so excited about finding the horses, and before I knew it, I was kiss—" Her eyes closed for a second, and her chest rose with a deep breath. "Anyway, I'm sorry. I don't usually get carried away like that."

Chino lifted a hand and stroked one of her flushed cheeks with the backs of his knuckles. "There is no reason to be sorry."

She blinked. "Are you sure? I mean, I don't know anything about Apache etiquette, but I hope my behavior wasn't too forward. I didn't mean to offend you."

He stared at her for a moment before responding. "Apache girls are taught to stay away from boys in their band, to remain untouched for their husband. Even talking to a boy would be considered forward. When they become women, most are very shy around men and would never consider kissing a man. It is considered much too personal. Even after women marry, some never kiss their husbands."

He saw the hope in her eyes change to disappointment before she lowered her head. Struck with the need to touch her again, he resisted doing so by crossing his arms over his chest. "I did not tell you about Apache girls to make you feel bad. I told you to make you understand why your kiss surprised me."

When she didn't respond, he said, "You did not offend me."

Her head came up. "Honest?"

He arched his eyebrows in response.

Her brow furrowed, then just as quickly cleared. "How could I forget?" The corners of her mouth lifted in a weak smile. "You speak only the truth."

"Yes," he replied. "I was surprised, not offended. I know the ways of our people are different. I have seen this many times in the two years I have lived among the White Eyes. You are not the first White Eyes woman to surprise me."

Her eyes widened. "Other women have impulsively kissed you?"

He chuckled. "That is not what I meant. Last year, I went to see a friend in Tucson. There I saw one White Eyes woman start a fight with another. She did this to defend the honor of the man who had captured her heart." Giving in to temptation, he touched a finger to the small dent in her chin. "What I saw that day also surprised me. But you are the first to kiss me."

Her throat worked with a swallow. "I'm glad." The words were softly spoken, yet ripe with a hidden meaning he couldn't grasp. She held his gaze for a moment more. Then turning away, she said, "Let's go get my horses."

Chino watched her grab her horse's reins, then step into a stirrup and settle onto her saddle. As he turned to mount his own horse, he tried to forget the image of Abby swinging her leg over the gelding's rump and how the movement pulled the seat of her form-fitting trousers even tighter. He had little success, fearing the memory had been etched permanently in his mind. Right beside the one of her mouth pressed to his.

Because Abby knew the lead mare was familiar with her scent, she suggested Chino wait a short distance away until she could get a rope on the mare.

Chino nodded, then pulled his horse to a halt while she slowly moved closer to the herd.

The sorrel mare's head came up at Abby's approach, ears pricked forward and nostrils flaring.

"Easy, girl," Abby said. "Nobody's going to hurt you." She continued moving closer, talking in a constant soft croon. When she untied one of the leather thongs attached to her saddle, releasing a coil of rope, the mare tossed her head, then pawed the ground, but luckily didn't bolt.

Abby held the gelding at a painfully slow walk, finally stopping beside the mare. "Thatta girl, you're doing fine. Just hold it right there." Using slow, deliberate movements, she leaned closer and dropped a loop of rope over the mare's head.

"See there," Abby said, still using a gentle tone, "I told you nobody would hurt you." She tightened the rope until it was snug around the mare's neck. "Now be a lady, and don't cause trouble."

The mare nickered, bobbing her head as if in agreement. Abby smiled. "Think you're pretty smart, don't you?" Again the mare bobbed her head.

"Guess you are," she said, turning the gelding.

"Now, let's see if we can get your friends to follow us." She started toward the spot where Chino waited, giving the rope tied around the mare's neck a gentle tug. The horse seemed hesitant at first, but then moved forward without further resistance. After going a few yards, Abby glanced back at the rest of the herd. Happy to see the other horses following behind them, she released a relieved breath.

When she reached Chino, she said, "Since I've got the herd moving, I think we should keep going."

He nodded. "Where do you want me to ride?"

"Beside me is fine."

Again Chino nodded, then nudged his horse into position next to Abby's gelding.

They rode side by side, the creaking of saddle leather and the occasional nicker of a horse the only sounds other than the soft murmur of the wind.

Chino looked back at the loose-knit herd, then said, "Tell me more about the horses."

"What would you like to know?"

"Anything. Everything."

"Well, let's see," she said with a chuckle. "The man who sold them to my husband said they have pure Spanish blood. According to him, the ancestors of this herd were brought to Mexico from Spain many years ago."

"They are fine-looking horses."

Abby nodded. "The finest ones I've ever seen. They aren't as big as a lot of breeds, which some folks would say makes them undesirable as saddle horses. But anyone who can't see beyond their size is a fool. These horses have amazing strength. They can carry a two-hundred-pound man and a heavy saddle for long distances with no difficulty. Besides their stamina, they have speed, intelligence and tremendous courage. Their feet are on the small side, but their hard hooves more than make up for that, a definite advantage in rocky terrain. I've seen them climb mountainsides other horses would never attempt. In my estimation, they're the perfect horses for this part of the country, because—" she glanced over her shoulder at the herd—"they're so much like this land: incredibly beautiful yet extremely rugged."

"It is true," Chino said, his gaze lingering on her face. Thinking about her last words, he decided they could be applied to her as well. Like the mountains and valleys around them, she, too, possessed a wild, natural beauty. And as for being rugged, she'd shown him her fearless spirit when they first met. And now he knew her ability to survive, without a husband and in such a remote area, proved she had toughness and determination in abundance. Yes, Abby Madison and this land were a perfect fit.

He turned to look straight ahead, annoyed with himself for not being able to keep thoughts of Abby from filling his head. The Spirits had directed him to find her ranch so he could protect her horses. But they had not given him an indication of how he was supposed to deal with the woman herself. It was a situation that became more complicated with each passing hour.

As the afternoon wore on, their progress remained painfully slow. After another long silence, Abby turned to Chino.

"Would you check the herd, make sure all of the horses are keeping up? I'd like to increase our pace, but I'm concerned about this year's foals. They should be strong enough by now, but if any of them are already struggling to stay with the herd, I won't risk it."

Chino nodded, then wheeled his horse around.

A few minutes later, he returned and pulled up next to her. "I saw ten foals. They are keeping up with the others."

"Good," Abby replied. "Then let's try moving them a little faster and see how they do." Checking to make sure the rope leading the mare was securely wrapped around her saddle horn, she touched her heels to her gelding's sides.

Once the pace was set at an easy trot, Chino periodically checked the herd for stragglers, as much to ease Abby's mind as to give himself something to keep his thoughts occupied. When the foals began to show signs of tiring, they slowed their pace to a walk, then a while later resumed a trot.

Though he tried to concentrate only on the horses—getting them settled in a valley closer to the ranch house before dark, and what he'd do to protect the herd once they were there—Abby continued to intrude into his thoughts.

There was no point in trying to deny the truth; his attraction to her was too strong to pretend it didn't exist, too strong to believe it would quickly fade as soon as her ranch was safe and he left. All he could do was pray to Ussen, asking for the Great Spirit's guidance and the strength he would need to ride away from her when the time came.

They continued alternating their pace for several hours, then Abby said, "I think we should stop for a while. Let the horses have a longer rest." She glanced up to check the angle of the sun. "I'd say we've still got a solid four hours of daylight, so getting back to the ranch by nightfall shouldn't be a problem."

Chino also checked the sun's position, then scanned the mountain range just ahead of them. "You know of a place?"

"There's a dry wash not far from the other side of the pass we'll take through the mountains. We'll stop there."

When he nodded, she said, "I think it would be best if you rode in the rear until we're through the pass. It's wide in some parts but really narrow in others. That's where the trail has some twists and turns, with several canyons branching off the main one. Too many places where the herd could easily get split up."

"I will keep the horses together."

"I know you will."

As Chino started to turn his horse, she reached over and grabbed his arm. Startled by her sudden move, he frowned. Controlling his horse with his knees, he looked up to find her staring at him, an odd expression on her face.

"Chino, be careful."

He studied her for a moment, then said, "What is it?"

She shivered slightly. "I don't know. All of a sudden, I had the strangest feeling." She frowned, releasing her grip on his forearm. "I can't explain it. I just had the urge to tell you to be careful." She drew a deep breath and exhaled slowly. "It's probably nothing. Just my overactive imagination. I'm tired and hungry, and anxious to get the horses moved closer to the house. That must be what it was, right?"

He continued staring at her, then said, "Being tired and hungry can make you imagine things." He flashed her a smile. "Or maybe you received a message from the Great Spirit of the White Eyes."

She made a snorting sound. "Like one of your visions?"

He shrugged. "It is not possible?"

"Sure, it's possible. When horses sprout wings and fly."

Chino furrowed his brow. "I thought you believed me."

"If you're talking about whether I believe *you* have visions, yes, I do. But all I've ever experienced is woman's intuition. And I'm not so sure that even exists."

"Some would say this intuition is like messages from the Spirits."

"And I'd say those same people are crazy."

"You will never have visions if you do not open your mind to the idea."

She scowled. "I'm not looking to have them, all right, so I don't need to open my mind to anything."

"I was—"

"Can we just drop the subject?"

He gave her a long, considering look, then finally nodded. Wheeling his horse around, he headed to the rear of the herd.

A short time later, just as they reached a narrow, twisting section of the pass, the flesh on the outside of Chino's right thigh started shaking. Immediately on the alert, he followed the herd around a large boulder, his gaze moving constantly, checking their surroundings for any sign of trouble.

Off to his left, he caught a flash of gray. Squinting into the sun, he finally made out what had captured his attention. One of the horses, a dark gray, had broken from the herd while Chino's sight had been hindered by the winding trail. The horse was perhaps fifty yards away, heading toward the mouth of a narrow canyon.

Chino leaned over his horse's neck, urged the bay into a gallop, then whispered his thanks to the Spirits. If not for their warning, he might not have seen the fleeing gray.

Even from a distance, he could tell the horse was full of energy, relishing the chance to run. His black mane and tail fluttering, his legs stretching in long, easy strides, he raced over the ground. When Chino finally caught up with the young stallion, getting close enough to get a rope on him took some careful maneuvering. After several failed attempts, he succeeded. Snugging the rope a little tighter around the gray's neck, Chino slowed his own horse, forcing the stallion to slow as well. Winded, his excess energy spent, the gray didn't fight the rope but followed behind Chino's horse without resistance.

They had almost reached the herd, when a shot rang out, echoing through the pass. Chino's head snapped up, his heart thundering with both surprise and anticipation. Finally, the scene from his dream-vision had begun. Tightening his grip on the reins, the thought occurred to him that the Spirits hadn't sent him another warning. He'd had only one shaking in his leg.

Before he could consider the idea more fully, another shot rang out, followed by the scream of a horse. He couldn't see which horse had been hit, but he didn't have to. He knew it was the yellow mare. She and her foal had been near the rear of the herd when he'd left them to chase after the gray.

A third shot pinged off a boulder, sending up a spray of rock shards. The gray whinnied, tossing his head and sidling away from Chino's horse. Easily controlling his mount with his knees, he tried to get closer to the gray. He had to get the rope off the horse before releasing it. If he didn't, the dangling end could get caught on something and cause injury to the young horse.

As he worked to get into position, the yellow mare, her foal and several other horses raced past him. Noting which direction they took, he continued with his task, finally getting close enough to the gray to slip the rope off his neck. The stallion half-reared, then turned and raced after the other terrified horses.

Chino quickly gathered the rope into a coil, then jabbed his heels into his horse's sides, urging the bay toward the protective cover of a pile of boulders. Grabbing his rifle and sliding off his horse in one motion, he crouched behind a large boulder. Taking aim at the ridge above him, he fired off several quick rounds.

After a few minutes passed with no additional shots, he felt certain whoever had shot at the horses probably had fled as soon as he'd returned fire. His rifle still raised to his shoulder, he straightened. Sighting down the barrel, he scanned the ridge again, watching for the slightest of movements. His finger curling a little tighter on the trigger, he hoped for a target so he could vent the fury boiling inside him. Anyone shooting at such magnificent horses deserved to be shot himself.

When his scrutiny revealed nothing, he blew out a long breath. Easing his finger away from the trigger, he released the rifle's hammer and lowered the weapon.

"Chino!" Abby's shout penetrated the red haze of his anger. "Chino!"

He turned, saw her horse racing toward him. A rifle clutched in one hand, she pulled back on the reins with the other, bringing her gelding to a skidding halt a few feet in front of him.

"Are you hurt?" Her face was pinched with fear as she raked her gaze over him.

He shook his head. "Are you?"

She exhaled a compressed breath, then gave him a weak smile. "Scared spitless, but otherwise I'm fine." She glanced up at the ridge. "You're sure they're gone?"

He nodded. "They had no reason to stay. They did what they wanted to do."

"Did you see anyone?"

"No, did you?"

She shook her head. "I had my hands full trying to get the lead mare settled down. By then, the shooting had stopped."

"I need to find the yellow mare," he said, whistling for his horse.

"She was really shot?"

"Yes."

"How bad?"

When the bay trotted over to him, he shoved his rifle into the scabbard on his saddle. "I will not know until I find her."

"Did you see which way she went?"

He grabbed the reins, then mounted his horse. "That way," he said, indicating the west.

"What about her foal?"

"The foal and four or five of the other horses were with her."

"Okay, I'll go with you," she replied, returning her rifle to its scabbard, then moving her gelding closer to his horse. "If they've scattered, you can tend the mare while I see about rounding up the others."

"What about the lead mare?"

"I left her picketed up the trail. By the time we get there, I'm hoping we'll find the rest of the herd has settled down enough to make their way back to her."

He nodded, then touched his heels to the dark bay's sides. The horse took off at a trot, Abby's gelding not far behind.

They hadn't ridden far when Chino spotted something just inside one of the small side canyons. As they got closer, he recognized the yellow coat of the mare. Pulling his horse to a halt, he motioned for Abby to do the same.

"Are they all there?" she asked in a low voice.

"I cannot tell. From here, we must move slowly."

Abby nodded her understanding.

As they approached the mare at a slow walk, Chino saw the wound high on the right side of her rump. The lack of blood was a good sign that she wasn't seriously hurt, but he wouldn't know for sure until he examined her.

"Take this," he said, removing the coil of rope from his saddle horn and handing it to her. "Go to her left, but do not put the rope on her until I give you a signal."

She took the rope from his hand, then eased her horse forward at a walk.

He urged his horse closer to the mare, approaching from the right. She turned her head in his direction, nostrils flared. When she appeared ready to bolt, Chino began speaking to her in a gentle voice. As soon as she calmed, he pulled a small buckskin bag from a larger bag tied to his saddle, then dismounted and started toward her on foot. Her ears pricked, swiveling forward to catch his words, her dark eyes watching his every move. Continuing with his soft croon, he signaled Abby closer.

When her horse was in position, he glanced up and gave her a nod. As the rope dropped over the mare's head, the horse barely flinched.

Chino took a step closer, still talking to her, and reached out to stroke her sleek neck. She tossed her head once, then settled down.

"Keep the rope loose," he said to Abby, smoothing the dark mane. "I do not want to frighten her."

He resumed his litany of softly spoken words directed at the injured mare, stroking her withers, then her flank, and finally her hindquarters.

He examined the wound, relieved to see the bullet had grazed her, leaving only a shallow furrow in her flesh. He removed a container from the buckskin bag and carefully applied a thick salve to the wound. Her skin twitched at his touch, but otherwise she didn't move.

Abby watched Chino treating the mare, amazed by what she had just witnessed. She'd never seen anyone calm a wild horse the way he had. Talking to the horse, in what she assumed was Apache, he had completely mesmerized the mare. And his touch was so gentle. A shiver rippled up her back at the notion of him touching her that way. Of his competent hands skimming over her flesh. His fingers exploring and finding the sensitive places on her body.

Her breath quickened. Her pulse increased. A sudden burst of need charged through her veins, settling between her thighs in an insistent throb. She jerked her gaze from his hands, shocked by both the direction of her thoughts and the intensity of her feelings.

She squeezed her eyes closed. *Why is this happening to me? How can I want the touch of this man?*

After taking a deep breath and releasing it slowly, she opened her eyes and found him staring at her.

When he didn't speak, she said, "What is it?"

He continued to stare at her, an unreadable expression on his face. After a moment of uncomfortable silence, he shook his head, then turned away.

She swallowed hard, her heart once again pounding against her ribs. *He knows!* She bit back a groan. *Oh, God, he knows what I was thinking. Now what do I do?*

She stared across the canyon, trying to concentrate on her promise to Alan to turn the Flying M into a successful ranch, a worthy legacy for their children, but her growing need for Chino refused to be silenced. How a man she barely knew could make her quiver like a mare in season, she couldn't explain. But she knew one thing for certain. Not controlling her need would be a mistake. He was from another culture, with different dreams, different beliefs. A relationship between them would never work. And besides, as soon as they were certain her ranch was safe from Neville Warner's clutches, he would ride away.

The thought of never seeing Chino again sent a sharp stab of pain ripping through her. She'd lost one man in her life; how would she survive losing Chino as well?

Chapter Eight

Chino checked the mare for other injuries, but had difficulty keeping his mind on the task. Instead of the horse capturing his complete attention, as had always been the case, the look he'd seen on Abby's face kept interfering with his concentration. Though not as experienced as his friend Nighthawk when it came to women, he felt certain he hadn't misinterpreted that look. She desired him.

Though the discovery startled him, he had to admit great satisfaction in knowing she returned the simmering desire he felt for her. Still, he had no plans to act on what he'd learned. He hadn't been with a woman since the death of his wife, and during those two years, he'd never met a woman who made him even think about ending his celibacy—especially not a White Eyes woman. Until Abby. But becoming involved with her would not be wise. The Spirits had sent him to her ranch to save her horses. There had been nothing in his dream-visions to indicate he would share her bed.

He glanced over the mare's back at the woman filling his mind. Her unblinking stare at some distant point, her furrowed brow and pursed lips, told him she was deep in thought. Perhaps she, too, realized they should not become intimate. Or perhaps her desire for an Apache sickened her. She'd already made her feelings clear about his people, therefore such a reaction wouldn't surprise him. Even so, the possibility that Abby might find her desire for him repulsive struck him like a physical blow, as if a fist had been slammed into his belly. Clenching his jaw against the hard knot of pain, he finished examining the mare, then put the container of salve back in the small buckskin bag.

He'd never had a problem keeping his mind focused on a goal. But Abby Madison had changed that. As soon as he met her, his life had begun to shift; now he felt off balance. He needed to find a way to regain control of his life, before more of it slipped away. Based on his recent discovery, that he stirred desire in her just as she did in him, he wasn't sure he would succeed. He could only hope that saving her ranch would be accomplished quickly, so he could move on.

He scowled. Move on to where? For the past two

years, every day, every hour, every breath he'd drawn had been centered on finding those responsible for the deaths of his wife and son. And now that the attainment of his goal was within sight, he realized he'd never thought about the path he would take afterward. Instead, he'd concentrated only on his quest for vengeance.

Perhaps the time had come to begin thinking about his future. A future without Abby. Finding that idea more disturbing than not knowing what his future held, he shoved it aside, and turned his attention to helping Abby round up the rest of the horses.

After completing the remainder of their trek to the Flying M, Abby picketed the sorrel mare in a valley not far from the ranch house. Then they waited to make sure the herd settled down before leaving the horses for the night. By the time they finally headed for the house, the sky had changed to a deep purple, the setting sun creating a spectacular display of colors, casting the undersides of the wispy clouds with a glowing pinkish orange.

Abby dismounted her horse at the barn, physically exhausted and mentally drained. Leading the gelding to his stall, she rubbed the small of her back, hoping she wouldn't have to spend so many hours in a saddle again any time soon.

She heard Chino taking care of his horse deeper in the barn: the soft murmur of his voice, the clomp of a hoof, the chink of a metal bit. The sounds were a comfort, yet at the same time, unsettling. Though having Chino around eased her anxiety over the future of her ranch, his presence brought back her earlier thoughts about him. In spite of her efforts to control her reaction, need once again sizzled through her veins, creating a restlessness that was fast approaching a craving.

She rested her forehead on the gelding's neck. *Pull yourself together, Abby. You've got no business thinking about him that way.* Releasing a deep breath, she straightened, then finished seeing to her horse.

Over the next few days, Chino established a routine of checking on the herd of horses at first light, then again several more times each day. Since the attack on the horses had replicated his dream-vision, he believed the threat to them had passed. But unwilling to take a chance on another attack, he made a habit of periodically watching the herd from the hill above them. The first time he tried to move the lead mare to another spot in the valley, she balked. But using his horse power and infinite patience, he eventually accustomed her to his presence, and then she cooperated without further trouble.

When he wasn't with the herd, he began spending time with the white stallion. Getting close enough to touch the horse had taken Chino the better part of an afternoon. Even then, the stallion allowed only a stroke or two on his neck before jerking out of Chino's reach. Elegant white head held high, tail fluttering in a feathery stream, he'd trotted to the other side of the corral. The display had made Chino smile. He knew the stallion eventually would learn to trust him, and then they would become friends.

Abby hadn't underestimated the horse. Though highly intelligent, the stallion did possess a great deal of stubbornness. But Chino believed such a trait was good in a horse. He preferred stubbornness to a weak spirit. The stallion's stubbornness proved he had courage and pride, in addition to his intelligence. They were traits, he'd been annoyed to realize, that Abby also possessed. He was not annoyed because he disliked her being stubborn, courageous and proud—he admired those qualities in humans as well as horses, though he'd never expected to apply those adjectives to a White Eyes. He was annoyed that she had become so entwined in his life in such a short time. No matter what he did, what he thought about, Abby Madison was there, burrowing deeper inside him with each passing day. And even more disturbing, he was powerless to banish her from his mind.

Early one afternoon, Chino went to check on the horses. As had become his habit, for at least one of his daily trips, he went on foot, easily running to the valley and back. Loping into the ranch yard after making one such trek, he noticed Teddy watching him from atop the fence of one of the corrals. During his stay on the Flying M, he'd caught Teddy watching him several times—though he'd taken care not to let the boy know he was aware of the scrutiny.

Chino knew Teddy was wary of him and respected the distance the boy wanted to keep. At least there had been no more displays of Teddy's initial hostility, nor had the child posed more bold questions— like when he'd asked about taking scalps. No doubt his mother's instructions had stilled the boy's tongue.

But ever since that first night, Chino had seen the burning curiosity on Teddy's face whenever he caught the boy secretly watching him. But so far, Teddy had done nothing more than stare.

As Chino came to a halt, he greeted the boy with a nod. Teddy nodded in return, started to open his mouth to say something, then changed his mind. Chino moved to lean against the fence next to him, willing to wait until the boy found the courage to speak.

After a few seconds of silence, Teddy stirred, then said, "You ran all the way to where the horses are and back?"

Chino nodded.

Teddy's mouth turned down in a frown. "Then how come ya ain't breathing hard?"

"For Apache, that is not far," Chino replied, resisting the urge to smile. "Running has always been an important part of our life-way. We can run great distances. All day if we need to."

Teddy's eyes went wide, then narrowed. His frown deepened, but he clamped his lips shut.

Another few seconds of silence passed, then Chino said, "Where is your sister?"

Teddy wrinkled his nose and shrugged. "Probably playin' with those dumb old kittens."

Chino recalled seeing Susanna with the kittens. Often she put the four furry animals in a basket, then carried them down near the creek, where she'd play for hours. "You do not like the kittens?"

"They're okay," he replied, "but she treats 'em like they're babies." His face scrunched in a scowl. "She's the baby."

"Ah," Chino said, biting the inside of his cheek. "But you are no longer a baby. Among my people you would be old enough to begin your training to be a man."

Teddy turned toward him, his scowl replaced once again by open curiosity. "What kinda training?"

"Boys are taught about all the creatures around them. How to become strong. How to use weapons. How to hunt."

Teddy's brow furrowed, his mouth twisting into a thoughtful pucker. Finally he said, "Do they get taught how to run like you do?"

"Yes, that is part of their training."

Teddy stared at him for a long moment, then said, "Can you really run all day? Or were you making that up?"

"I speak the truth. To my people, telling a lie is a great offense. Apache parents teach their children always to speak the truth."

Teddy mulled over Chino's response for a few seconds, then said, "Momma tells me that, too." His cheeks darkened with a flush and his voice dropped to a whisper. "I got whupped the one time I told her a lie."

Chino nodded, but made no comment. From the look on the boy's face, he'd obviously learned his lesson about telling the truth.

Teddy glanced toward the corral holding the white stallion. "You gonna work with the stallion now?"

"Yes." Chino pushed away from the fence and started walking in that direction.

Teddy jumped down from the fence. "Can I watch?" he asked, skipping to keep up.

Chino slowed his pace to accommodate the boy's shorter strides. "You can watch, if you are quiet. Can you do that?"

"Yes, sir." Teddy fell silent for a moment, then suddenly blurted, "Could you teach me to do Apache stuff?"

Chino stopped and turned to face the boy. His brow furrowed, he asked, "What stuff?"

"You know, the stuff you told me about. What

Apache boys need to know when they become men. And how to work with horses like you do. And how to use a knife like that." He nodded toward the knife strapped around Chino's waist.

Chino curled his fingers around the handle of his knife. "You are too young for a weapon like this."

"Oh," Teddy replied, dropping his gaze and scuffing his toe in the dirt.

After a moment, Chino said, "I cannot teach you to use a knife, but I will teach you the other things."

Teddy's head came up, hope shining in his eyes. "Do ya mean it?"

Chino nodded. "If you will do exactly what I say, and your mother does not object, I will teach you."

"I will. I promise, and Momma won't care."

"You must still ask her."

Teddy bobbed his head in agreement. "If she says it's okay, can we start tomorrow?"

A chuckle rumbled in Chino's chest. "After I check the horses in the morning, we will start your lessons."

"Yippee," the boy crowed, leaping in the air. "I'm gonna go ask Momma right now."

"What about the white stallion?"

Teddy looked torn, his gaze moving back and forth between the house and the stallion's corral. Finally he said, "Can I watch ya work with him some other day?"

This time Chino's chuckle advanced to a full-fledged laugh. "Yes, some other day."

Chino watched Teddy race toward the house, his amusement fading. If only things had been different. Then he would be laughing at his own son's enthusiasm. He would be teaching the ways of the Apache to *his* son. His jaw tightened, his hands curling into fists. But Neville Warner had changed that when he uttered the words Chino would never forget. "Kill the thieving red devils. Even the kid."

His anger slow to cool, Chino finally turned and headed toward the corral where the white stallion waited. Working with horses always relaxed him; it was a time when he could concentrate on only man and horse, when everything else faded away. He hoped it would be no different this time. He wanted the escape, needed the soothing balm to forget the pain his memories had stirred.

When Chino returned from checking on the herd of horses the following morning, Teddy waited for him by the barn.

As he dismounted, Teddy said, "Can we start my lessons now?"

"Yes," Chino replied with a smile. "After I see to my horse." He started toward the corral beside the barn. "That is your first lesson," he said, looking down at the boy. "If you have a horse, it is your responsibility to see that it is taken care of before you do other things."

Teddy met Chino's gaze, then nodded, a solemn expression on his face. After the boy followed Chino and his horse into the corral, he said, "Where's yer saddle?"

"Sometimes I like to ride in the ways of my grandfathers. They did not have saddles, but used an animal skin or blanket. That is how I learned to ride."

"Oh."

As he pulled the blanket from his horse's back, he could feel Teddy watching his every move. He tossed the blanket over the top rail of the corral fence, then started to remove the horse's bridle.

Teddy took a step to the side to get a better view. "I ain't never seen a bridle like that."

"Teddy, what have I told you about using that word?"

The boy jerked around at the sound of his mother's voice.

"Momma, what are *you* doing here?"

Abby smiled at her son. "I thought I'd watch your first lesson."

"Aw, Momma," Teddy said, lower lip stuck out, "do ya hafta?"

"Just for today, son." She shifted her gaze to Chino. "If Mr. Whitehorse doesn't mind."

Just looking into Abby's eyes ignited a fire of need in Chino's belly. He prided himself on always being in control, yet when it came to this one woman, his self-control was being chipped away a little at a time. And worse, he seemed to have no way of stopping the erosion.

"Chino, are you all right?" She moved closer and touched his arm.

Chino blinked, Abby's voice and her touch pulling him back to the present. He glanced down at where her hand rested on his arm, the contrast between his skin color and hers a clear reminder of their differences. A sudden surge of anger cooled the fire in his belly. Shaking off her hand, he scowled. "Do not worry. I will not try to change your son into an Apache."

Visibly jolted by his harshly spoken words, she looked up at him with wide eyes. Pressing her lips into a firm line, she grabbed his arm and pulled him a short distance away from her son. "How dare you say such a thing?" she said in a fierce whisper.

He shrugged. "You hate the Apache."

"I . . . well, yes, I—" Her chin came up. "Never mind that. I wanted to make sure Teddy isn't too much for you. Sometimes his enthusiasm is more than I can deal with. He tires me out with all his questions."

He stared into her eyes, dismayed to feel his desire stirring again. Struck with the almost overwhelming urge to run his fingers over her flushed cheeks, somehow he forced himself to keep his hands at his sides.

Huffing out a deep breath, he moved back beside Teddy. "Your mother can stay."

The boy glanced up. The previous excitement on his face changing to sullen acceptance, he nodded.

"If you concentrate on what I tell you," Chino said, "you will forget she is watching."

Teddy flashed an annoyed look at his mother before mumbling, "I guess so."

Abby moved next to her son and ruffled his hair. "I'll stay out of the way, I promise." Looking up at Chino, she said, "Now please tell us about the bridle. I've never seen one like it, either."

"It is made in the old way of the Apache," Chino replied, turning back to the bay. "The bit is made of rope and tied under the horse's mouth." He removed the bridle and held it toward Abby for her inspection.

"Interesting," she said. "What's the rope made out of?"

"Braided horsehair. But the Apache also made rope by braiding strands from the yucca."

"Very resourceful."

"My people learned to use everything around us. It was necessary if we wanted to survive."

She slowly nodded. "Yes, I imagine so."

There was something in her voice that made Chino think her hatred of the Apache had undergone a change. Though the idea surprised him, the realization that his own attitudes toward the White Eyes also had begun to change came as a bigger surprise. Not wanting to dwell on the subject, he turned his attention to his horse.

After releasing the bay in the corral and making sure the animal had water, he turned to Teddy. "Are you ready to begin?"

Teddy took a step forward. "Yes, sir."

"Good." He opened the corral gate and stepped outside, motioning for Teddy and Abby to follow. "Apache boys must be strong to survive. They must know about everything around them. Plants, animals. All living things. They must be able to feed their families by becoming successful hunters. They must learn how to protect their families and the others in their band."

He walked to the center of the ranch yard, then stopped. "The first lesson in becoming strong is learning to run a great distance." Pointing to a hill behind the house, he said, "You will run to the top of that hill and back as fast as you can."

Teddy looked in the direction Chino had indicated, then swallowed hard. "That's an awful long way."

"Teddy's right," Abby said. "Maybe that is too—"

"Today it is a long way," Chino replied, crossing his arms over his chest. "Tomorrow it will not seem as far. And the next day it will seem even less. If he is to have a strong mind, a strong heart and a strong body, he must do this."

"I still don't know—"

"I'll do it, Momma."

She looked down at her son. "Are you sure?"

"I ain't—I mean, I'm not a baby," he said, his determination evident in the tilt of his chin. "I can do it."

She released a deep breath, then turned to Chino. "I guess it's settled then."

He nodded, then said to the boy, "Go."

Chino watched Teddy race away, then settled his gaze on Abby. "He will be fine," he said in a low voice. "Running is good for him."

She searched his face for several seconds. "I know. Teddy needs to be around men more. Cesar is getting too old to do very much with him, and Nestor is too busy. So, I want to thank you for spending time with him."

"You have a fine son."

"Thanks," she replied with a smile. "I agree."

"You should do everything you can to protect him," he said in a sharp tone.

Her smile faded. "Yes, of course, I will." She gave him a quizzical look. "Is there something you're trying to tell me?"

He turned to watch Teddy's progress. "Protecting a child should be easy. We are bigger, stronger, wiser." A piercing pain ripped through his chest, nearly buckling his knees. He clenched his jaw until the worst of the pain passed, then exhaled slowly. "But sometimes that is not enough," he said, his voice raw with regret and grief.

"What do you—" Abby gasped. "Oh my God, you lost a child!"

Though he felt her intense gaze, heard the shock and pain in her voice, he refused to look at her. He swallowed hard, then nodded. But several seconds passed before he could make himself say the words. "My son."

Abby moved closer, laid a hand on his forearm. "Chino, I'm so sorry." Her voice was thick with tears; her hand trembled on his arm.

When he didn't respond, she drew a shuddering breath then said, "Do you want to tell me about him?"

He stiffened, then shook off her hand. Swinging around to face her, he said, "I do not talk about him."

"I can see how much you're hurting." She swiped at a tear running down her cheek. "That's something I've had my share of. But I've learned that talking about it helps. I promise you."

Anger and grief welled up inside him. Glaring at her, he clenched his jaw against the urge to lash out, to tell her he would never speak of his son. But she wouldn't understand. Finally, he gave his head another shake.

"Losing someone we love has to be the hardest,

the most painful experience we have to face in life. Alan's death was difficult enough for me to deal with, so I can't begin to imagine what it—" She paused to draw another unsteady breath, to wipe away more of the tears trickling down her face. "What it must be like to lose a child. But I do know it isn't good to let the pain fester inside you. You have to let it out, so you can heal. If you don't, it could destroy you."

Even if Chino wanted to speak, he knew he'd never be able to get any words through the tightness in his throat. Unable to bear the pain and sympathy on Abby's face, he shifted his gaze back to watch Teddy.

He heard her quavering sigh before she said, "If you change your mind, I'd like to help."

When he remained silent, she sighed again. "Well, I have chores to do," she said in a tired voice. Then she turned and walked away, leaving him in the middle of the yard. Alone. Just as he was in life.

Chapter Nine

For a long time after Abby left Chino in the yard to await Teddy's return, what he'd revealed continued to haunt her. As she carried water to fill the troughs in each horse stall, she recalled the anguish she'd seen on his face. Just the thought of losing one of her children brought a fresh onslaught of tears, a tremendous pain squeezing her chest. For a moment, she thought she might faint. Swaying on her feet, she fought the dizziness. When the worst passed, she swallowed the lump in her throat, wiped her face, then drew a shuddering breath.

The pain of her imagined response had to be small compared to Chino's actual experiencing of such a tragedy. She longed to go back to him, to somehow help ease his grief, to try to soothe his suffering.

Heaving another sigh, she dipped the bucket into the barrel of water inside the barn door.

Though she knew nothing she could do would completely erase his pain, she wanted to help. If only he'd let his stoic demeanor slip just a little, maybe then he would accept her comfort. Allow her to hold him close, to touch his face, to—A sudden realization stopped her in mid-stride, causing water to slosh onto her skirt and the toe of one boot.

Chino had lost a son, which meant there was another person grieving over that loss. The boy's mother. Chino's wife.

Pain again gripped her chest, forcing the air from her lungs. She struggled to breathe, desperately trying to compose herself. She'd thought discovering how much she wanted Chino was enough of a shock for one day. But she was dead wrong. Finding out he had a wife came as an even bigger shock.

He seemed like such a solitary man, the last man she would expect to be married. Then she remembered him with her children. The sparkle in his eyes when Susanna smiled at him. His kindness and patience with Teddy's endless questions. She squeezed her eyes closed for a second. How could she have been so blind?

When she could make herself move, she continued lugging the bucket of water to another stall. By the time she'd finished filling the last trough, she decided there was one consolation to her most recent shock.

At least she hadn't suffered the humiliation of Chino rejecting her advances—a bold strategy, she admitted in a moment of complete honesty, which she'd begun to consider putting into action.

She tried to convince herself that not suffering the sting of rejection was an acceptable consolation. She tried, but rather than feeling consoled, all she felt was disappointment.

Mulling over the situation, she set down the empty water bucket, then reached for a pitchfork. While she finished her chores, she considered her options. She still needed Chino's help, so asking him to leave was out of the question. Yet having him around and not being able to touch him—She jerked her mind away from finishing that thought. Glancing out the barn door and catching a glimpse of him across the yard, she blew out a deep breath. Just looking at his wide shoulders, powerful thighs and proud bronze face made her heart quicken in anticipation, her body clench with need.

But her need would go unfulfilled, because she refused to trespass on the sanctity of another woman's marriage. And yet, simply calling a halt to her attraction to Chino would be a difficult task. But she had no other choice. Turning her attention back to her work, she tried to ignore the ache in her chest. An ache caused by grief for another loss—a relationship that could never be.

* * *

Chino watched Teddy stumble toward him, then collapse at his feet. He studied how the boy held a hand pressed to his side, his face flushed and his chest heaving. Satisfied Teddy wasn't injured, only winded, he said, "Did you run all the way?"

Teddy rolled his head from side to side on the ground. "I had to stop a couple of times," he managed to say between gasping breaths.

Chino nodded, pleased the boy had spoken the truth. "You did well for the first time. Tomorrow, you will do better."

Teddy groaned. "Do I hafta?"

"I thought you wanted to learn how Apache boys become strong."

"Yeah, I do, but . . . Does it gotta be tomorrow?"

"Yes," Chino replied with a chuckle. "It is important to run every day. You must get strong enough to run to that hill and back without stopping."

"Then what?"

"Then I will find a hill that is farther away."

Another groan rumbled in the boy's chest.

Chino crouched down beside him. "Apache fathers tell their sons they must make their legs and hearts strong because their legs and hearts are their friends. Apache boys are told this because someday they may have to run a great distance, and they must rely on their friends to do that."

"Why would they hafta run a long way?"

"When I was young, sometimes one of the men,

144

or an older boy, would run to the camp of another Apache band to deliver a message. Other times, when our warriors were fighting the enemy, some of them needed to run to escape."

"Didn't you have horses back then?"

"Yes, we had horses. But many years before, my grandfathers did not. That is when running became an important part of the Apache life-way. When I was a boy, there were many places a horse could not go. Those were the times we had to run. It is good to know the old ways."

"I guess," Teddy replied, no longer gasping for breath.

"Do not be discouraged," Chino said with a chuckle. "You did well today. Tomorrow running will be easier for you. Soon you will be ready for the final challenge."

"What kinda challenge?"

"Boys in my band were given a mouthful of water, and told they must run a great distance without swallowing."

Teddy moaned and covered his eyes with a forearm. "I ain't never gonna be able to do that."

"You will, if you do as I tell you."

"I don't know," Teddy said, moving his arm so he could look up at him. "Did you run without swallowing the water?"

Chino nodded.

"Were you as big as me?"

145

"I was older."

"How old, seven?"

"Older than that," Chino replied, trying not to smile at the boy's curiosity. "You should not worry about the challenge. You should concentrate only on making yourself strong."

Teddy thought about that for a moment, then got to his feet. "When ya gonna teach me some other stuff?"

"This afternoon, when your mother finishes your lessons."

The boy's smile quickly changed to a scowl. "I'd rather have you teachin' me. Can't you ask Momma to forget my lessons for today?"

"What your mother teaches you is important."

Teddy's scowl deepened. "Bet your mother didn't teach you stupid old readin' and cipherin'."

"Apache boys are not taught by their mothers," Chino replied, choosing his words carefully. "Fathers and grandfathers teach boys what they need to know." If Teddy found out Apaches weren't taught those skills at all, he would balk even more about continuing the lessons with his mother.

Teddy's shoulders lifted, then dropped with a deep sigh. "Where should I meet ya after my lesson?"

Chino stood in the shadowed doorway of the *sala*, watching Abby with her children. At one end of a low table, Susanna sat on a small stool, patiently practicing what her mother called her letters. Rosy mouth puckered in deep concentration, chubby fingers clutching a pencil, the little girl moved her hand across a piece of paper with slow deliberation. At the opposite end of the table, Abby and Teddy sat close together on the floor. An opened book lay in front of them. As Abby moved her finger across one of the pages, Teddy read aloud. When he stumbled over a word, she corrected him in a gentle voice, then gave him a nod and a smile of encouragement to continue.

Though the love and devotion Abby showed her children caused a pleasant warmth to settle over Chino, the scene also caused a strong pang of longing. A longing, not only for the family he'd lost, but for the missed opportunity to learn to read and write.

A corner of his mouth lifted in a smile. If Nighthawk could hear his thoughts, he would be amused. His friend had tried repeatedly to get him to become a student of Father Julian in Tucson—the White Eyes priest who had taught Nighthawk. But Chino had always refused. Knowing how to read and write the words of the White Eyes had never been important to him. Not once in his life had he felt less of a man because he did not have such knowledge.

Until now. Ever since Abby came into his life, his thoughts seemed determined to walk a path they had never traveled—a path he would be wise to avoid.

He released a compressed breath. Thoughts of

learning to read and write were foolish. There could be no future for two people from such different lifeways. Abby might desire him, but she hadn't stopped hating all Apache for killing her husband. She couldn't change who she was, any more than he could.

He pushed away from the doorframe, then quietly moved down the hall.

Abby had been aware of Chino's presence from the moment he'd stopped in the doorway of the *sala*. Though she'd taken care to sneak only an occasional peek at him through her partially lowered eyelashes, she'd seen the longing in his gaze while he watched her work with her children. Then the next time she looked at him, something had changed his wistful expression to one of raw despair. The need to go to him warred with the common sense telling her to stay put. Before a victor in her inner battle could be declared, she snuck another peek at him, only to find the doorway empty.

"Momma! Momma, what's wrong?"

Teddy's voice broke into Abby's troubled thoughts, bringing her back to the present. She turned to look at her son, managing a smile. "Nothing's wrong. I was just thinking."

" 'Bout Mr. Whitehorse?"

Abby blinked, her smile fading. "Why would I be thinking about him?"

He flashed her an impatient look. "I know he was watchin' us."

"Yes, he was," she said, casting a glance toward the doorway. "I wonder why."

"Maybe he wanted to see what yer teaching me."

"Do you think so?"

One of his shoulders lifted in a shrug. "Maybe." He looked down at the reader lying on the table. "Do I hafta keep reading?"

"What?" She cleared her throat, dismayed at how easily she'd been distracted. "Yes, we'll finish this page. You can start from—" she pointed to the place in the reader—"here."

Somehow she managed to keep her mind focused enough to help Teddy finish his reading lesson. After getting him started on some addition and subtraction problems, she checked Susanna's progress on practicing the alphabet, then sat quietly while her children worked. But her mind was anything but quiet, her thoughts centered on Chino.

He was such a complex man. Nothing like what she imagined an Apache would be. Fierce warrior, yes, but so much more. All the more reason, she supposed, for the strength of his appeal. That and the chemistry between them. She only had to look at him and her pulse quickened, the heat started to build in her belly, then slipped lower where it became an insistent throb. Squirming in her chair, she tried to concentrate on something else, but had little success.

149

She knew she had to stop thinking of Chino Whitehorse as anything other than the man who would help save her ranch. Continuing to allow herself to think of him in any other terms would only result in heartache. She drew a shallow breath, then released a soft sigh. Yes, that was exactly what she should do, especially given the fact that he had a wife. She just needed to try harder. Squeezing her eyes closed, she offered a quick prayer to ask for the strength to carry out what would surely be a difficult task.

Abby put Teddy and Susanna to bed that evening, then went out onto the ramada. Cesar and Chino sat in their usual seats, discussing the white stallion.

"I watched you work with him today," Cesar said. "He is *muy terco*."

Chino chuckled. "Yes, he is pigheaded. But he is beginning to accept me. Soon, he will know I am his friend, that he can trust me."

"You have much patience."

"Patience is the only way to work with one that is *muy terco*, sí?"

"Sí. Sí. You are right."

As Abby moved to take a seat, she smiled at the easy banter between the two men. She drew a deep breath of the warm evening air, contentment washing over her along with a satisfying sense of family. Wouldn't it be wonderful if every evening could be like this? Her lips flattened at the direction of her thoughts. *Well, it can't be, dammit! So stop these silly notions about*—Cesar's voice ended her mental scolding.

"Have you given this pigheaded horse a name?"

Chino nodded. "Egusi."

"Egusi," Abby said, trying out the strange word. "So what does it mean?"

"It is Apache for 'he is smart.' "

"He is that," she replied. "Guess that's more flattering than naming him Pigheaded."

They all chuckled, then Chino said, "There are other horses in your herd that have blue eyes."

"Yes," Abby said. "Surprising, isn't it? I remember Alan telling me the man who sold him the horses said blue eyes are pretty common in this breed. To me, that makes them even more unique. And I hope it will be more of a reason for people to buy them."

"I have never seen finer horses," Chino said. "They should bring you a good price."

"Sí," Cesar said with a nod. "Chino is correct. Your horses are *magnífico*. People will pay *mucho* money to own one."

Abby smiled. "I hope both of you are right.

Their conversation shifted to other things; then after a while Cesar pushed to his feet. "It is time for this old man to seek his bed."

Chino started to rise. "I also should—"

Cesar made a motion for him to sit down. "It is

still early for young people like you. Stay and keep Abby company. She needs to be around someone her own age."

"Cesar," Abby began, "Maybe Chino has—"

"Buenas noches," Cesar said, talking right over Abby's attempted protest. *"Dios mediante,* I will see you in the morning."

"Yes, God willing," Abby said with a sigh. "Sleep well."

She dropped her head onto the back of her chair, then looked at Chino. "If there's something you need to do, you don't have to stay. But first, I'd like to ask you a question."

When he tipped his head in acknowledgment, she said, "I saw you this afternoon while I was teaching the children, and I . . . um. . . . Well, I figured watching me with Teddy and Susanna must've brought back memories of your son. So, I wanted to ask if you'd like to help with my children's lessons."

Chino lifted a hand to finger one of his earrings, but didn't answer immediately. Finally he said, "I do not want to intrude."

"You wouldn't be, I promise. You can help Teddy with his arithmetic, if you'd like. Men are usually better with figures than women."

"I cannot teach him."

"Sure you can. He loves spending time with you."

When he didn't respond, she said, "If you don't want to help him with arithmetic, you can work on his reading. He's getting much better. Would you rather do that?"

His hand stilled on his earring. "I told you," he replied in a stiff voice. "I cannot teach the boy."

"But, why? You're already teaching Teddy, so I don't understand. Would helping him with his numbers and reading remind you too much of your son? Is that it?"

"I did not teach my son what you teach your children."

Abby studied him for a few moments, wondering at the anger and hurt she heard in his last statement. Then everything clicked into place. Leaning forward in her chair, she reached out to place a hand on his knee. "I feel so stupid for not realizing it sooner. You can't read, can you?"

His silence answered her question.

"Chino, I'm sorry," she said, her voice cracking. "Your English is so good that I never stopped to think—" She swallowed the sudden lump of tears in her throat. "I didn't mean to embarrass you. Please say you'll forgive me?"

He shoved her hand off his leg, then rose. "There is nothing to forgive."

"If you want to learn to read, I'd be happy to teach you."

He crossed his arms over his chest. "I have lived twenty-eight years. That is too old to learn to read the words of the White Eyes."

"No, it isn't. People are never too old to learn."

He didn't respond for a few moments, and although the shadows were too heavy for her to see his face, she could feel his intense stare. Finally, he said, "For me, it is too late."

"But why? Reading will give you the knowledge to find new opportunities, the chance to improve your life."

"What do you care what happens to me when I leave here?"

"I do care, Chino." When his only response was a grunt, she said, "Will you tell me about your plans for the future?"

"I have no plans."

Abby frowned. "What about your wife? Once you leave here, don't you plan to resume your life with her?"

Another long silence passed, then she heard him release a deep sigh. "That is not possible. She is . . . gone."

"Gone? I don't understand."

"My wife is—" he drew a shuddering breath— "with our son." The whispered words sounded as if they'd been ripped from his throat.

Abby gasped, then jumped to her feet and moved closer to him. She had to fight back more tears before she could speak. "I'm so sorry. I had no idea." She wanted to touch him, but his posture was so stiff, so forbidding that she didn't dare. Instead, she curled her hands into tight fists, digging her nails into her palms. The pain was tiny compared to what the man in front of her had endured.

When he didn't respond, she cleared her throat, then said, "I won't ask if you want to talk about her, since I'm pretty sure I already know your answer. But I will say again, if you ever change your mind about learning to read, my offer is still open."

He stared down at her for a moment, then gave a curt nod, before turning on his heel and leaving the ramada.

Abby watched until he disappeared into the darkness, then dropped back into her chair, her heart aching for him. And for herself. Each of them had lost a spouse, the person they'd loved and expected to spend many years with, the person who'd shared their dreams for the future.

Then unbidden, another thought popped into her mind. Now that she knew Chino had lost his wife, the barrier of his marriage had disappeared. Though such a selfish thought filled her with shame, another emotion bubbled up inside her. Hope.

The strength of her attraction and her desire for Chino still astounded her. She'd loved Alan, believed there would never be another man in her life, that no one could take his place in her heart. But Alan was gone, and though she would always love him, lately the intensity of those feelings had begun to pale. Since the moment she'd met Chino Whitehorse, everything in her life had begun to change.

Not only had she accepted the help of a hated Apache, she found him incredibly attractive, and even more surprising, she wanted more from him than friendship. That she wanted an intimate relationship with any man, more specifically with an Apache, still amazed her. But amazing or not, there was no doubt in her mind. She did.

However sure she was of her feelings, half of that hoped-for relationship remained in question: Chino's willingness to participate. Though certain the desire sizzling in her veins wasn't all one-sided, she needed to find out exactly how deep his attraction to her went. Then all that would remain would be getting him to realize what she already knew. There could be more between them—much more—than working together to save the Flying M. That shouldn't be a difficult task.

Unless memories of his wife were too strong.

Chapter Ten

Chino moved to the corral holding Egusi. Though his gaze was focused on the white stallion, his thoughts were not.

With each day he spent on the Flying M, his original sense of belonging had intensified. There was something about the ranch that spoke to a place deep inside him. As he'd told Abby, the Apache had a strong affiliation with the land of their grandfathers, so perhaps that was the reason the valleys and mountains made him feel as if he belonged here. Or maybe it was the herd of fine horses, animals he had loved since childhood. Then his mind hit on another possibility. He tried to push it away, but the idea refused to heed his silent command. Perhaps the source of his sense of belonging was Abby.

He could not deny the strength of his attraction to

her, an attraction he felt certain was mutual. But her appeal went far beyond the physical. Her independence, her determination, her gentleness as a loving mother, even her sharp tongue, all enhanced his attraction to her.

For a moment, he allowed himself to consider staying permanently. He imagined what sharing his life with Abby would be like—the satisfaction of working with horses, the joy of being part of a family again, the laughter, the passion.

A blistering wave of heat swept through him, making his groin ache with a throbbing need. Though he'd desired his wife, she had never made his body react with the white-hot hunger clawing at him now. Shifting to ease the discomfort, he turned his thoughts away from the pictures he'd conjured in his mind. He couldn't stay, no matter how appealing the idea was. There could be no future for them—an Apache with nothing to offer a woman, especially a White Eyes woman who hated his people.

Though he didn't want to think about leaving the ranch, the horses or Abby's children, and especially not about leaving Abby, he forced himself to consider his options. He soon realized there was only one answer. When the time came, he would ride away, no matter how difficult.

His conversation with Abby of a few evenings earlier replayed in his mind. What he'd told her, that he had no plans for the future, was true. From that moment two years ago, when he'd realized he would not be joining his wife and son in the Spirit World, he had refused to consider what lay ahead of him. He had only one goal, satisfying the burning need in his heart, the need to avenge the deaths of his loved ones.

But now, with the end of his quest for revenge in sight, for the first time, he found himself thinking about his future. What would he do? Where would he go?

Returning to the White Mountain Reservation was not an option. He refused to live in the horrible conditions his people were forced to endure there. But if not the reservation, then where? There weren't many places where an Apache would be welcome, so his choices were few. Glancing around the valley that cradled the ranch house of the Flying M, he had to close his eyes against a sharp pain in his chest, a pang of longing for a place like this.

He'd saved nearly all the money he'd made over the past two years, working at whatever odd jobs he'd been able to find. Perhaps he would buy land and start his own ranch. With Egusi, he could—He snorted, then opened his eyes.

To think he could buy land was foolish. He would never find someone willing to sell to a red devil. He blew out a deep breath, fury roiling in his belly at the way the government of the White Eyes had treated his people. They had broken every promise they had made the Apache, taken away land that had been their home for many generations, then forced them onto a reservation and treated them like animals.

Shaking off his anger, he shoved aside thoughts of making plans for his future. When the time came, he would make a decision. But for now, he had to concentrate on Neville Warner. He had to make sure Abby's ranch didn't fall into the man's hands, had to make sure the deaths of his wife and son were avenged.

Once he'd accomplished those goals, then he would decide which path his future would take.

The pounding of feet on the hard ground pulled him from his thoughts. He turned to see Teddy racing toward him.

More than a week had passed since the boy had started running each morning. Already his strength and stamina were much improved.

Teddy slid to a halt beside Chino. "I'm not too late, am I? Momma was helping me with my cipherin'."

"No, you are not late. We have plenty of time for your lesson."

"Good," Teddy said, the anxiety in his expression easing. "I didn't wanna miss learnin' about—" He looked up to meet Chino's gaze and his mouth turned down in a frown. "What is it yer gonna teach me?"

"How to survive."

Teddy snapped his fingers. "Yeah, that's it." His frown disappeared for a moment, then returned. "What's survive?"

Chino cleared his throat to cover a chuckle. "It is what you must know to take care of yourself." Seeing that the boy still didn't understand, he said, "If I were riding across a valley, far from any ranches, and my horse became hurt or became frightened and ran away, then I would need to know how to take care of myself. How to survive."

"I get it. Yer gonna teach me stuff like what plants not ta eat 'cause they'll make me puke?"

"Puke?"

"Yeah," the boy wrinkled his nose, "get sick to my stomach. You know what that means, don't ya?"

"Ah, yes," he replied, smothering a grin, "I know. Plants you can eat is part of what I will teach you." He started toward a stand of mesquite. "Come. We will start your lesson."

As they walked to the other side of the ranch yard and passed through the trees, Teddy kept up an endless string of questions.

Chino patiently answered each one, both amused and pleased by the boy's unending curiosity. Each day he spent time with Abby's son, the ache in his chest for the loss of his own son eased a little more. Teddy possessed a quick mind, a strong will and an eagerness to please—all qualities Chino admired, qualities any father would be proud to see in his son.

While Chino explained how to find water and which plants had edible roots or fruit, he felt a strange sensation in the flesh of his outer thigh. Though the shaking wasn't as strong as those he'd experienced in the past, this, too, had to be a message from the Spirits, and he would not ignore the warning.

One hand absently rubbing his thigh, he scanned the valley. The constant wind caused the grass to undulate in ripples, and ruffled the leaves of the mesquite trees. Nothing looked amiss, nor did he hear anything that might signal trouble. Still, he remained even more alert than usual, continually checking for any sign of impending danger.

As Chino and Teddy approached the house, Marita stepped onto the ramada to wait for them.

"It is about time," she said. "I was going to send Cesar to find you two. Supper is ready."

"Great," Teddy said, darting past her. "I'm starved."

"Wait, *niño*." Her stern voice stopped Teddy in his tracks. "You are forgetting something, sí?"

He turned toward her. "Sorry, I forgot."

"You are forgiven. Now go wash your hands." She looked up at Chino. "Both of you. Pronto."

Chino did as he'd been instructed, then joined the others at the table.

During supper, Abby had trouble keeping her gaze off Chino. Not that he did anything different to snag her attention, but she couldn't seem to stop herself from looking at him. Even after he caught her staring and gave her a quizzical look, she had difficulty keeping her eyes focused on anything but him.

She tried to concentrate on Susanna's happy chatter about the kittens and Teddy's glowing report on what he'd learned that day, but nothing would divert her attention entirely from Chino. Her reaction to the man grew stronger each day, so strong that she wasn't sure how much longer she could go on without acting on her attraction to him. Now that she knew he was a widower, that wouldn't be so wrong, would it? What harm could come from two adults finding pleasure in each other's company?

She cast a quick glance at Marita, then at Cesar. No doubt they would not agree with her logic, but she didn't care. She just—Laughter jarred Abby from her musings. She lifted her gaze, half expecting to find all eyes focused on her. Relieved not to be the subject of everyone's amusement, she managed a smile, hoping no one had noticed her lack of attention.

After she tucked her children into their beds, she went outside. The wind had nearly died, and the sky was a swath of purple velvet with a thousand twinkling stars. As she stepped out from beneath the ramada, she saw movement to her left, the silhouette of a man emerging from the shadows. Chino.

Her pulse quickening, she drew a steadying

breath. "I thought you'd gone to bed," she said, wishing she didn't sound so breathless.

"I wanted to talk to you."

"Why? Did something happen?"

"No," he replied, then lowered his voice to add, "not yet." He motioned across the yard. "Walk with me."

Abby nodded, realizing he wanted to get away from the house before telling her more.

As he led her toward the barn, soft moonlight cast everything around them in a pale silvery glow. He stopped by the corral nearest to the barn, but didn't speak.

Finally Abby said, "What did you want to tell me?"

"I received a warning today," he replied, turning toward her. His brow furrowing, he added, "I think it was a warning."

"Another muscle tremor that something bad is going to happen?"

He nodded, then ran a hand over his outer thigh. "I felt a shaking in my leg. But not as strong as before."

"So you're not sure what the tremor means?"

"No, but I cannot ignore any warning the Spirits send me. I did not want to worry you—" he lifted a hand and brushed a strand of hair off her cheek— "but I thought you should know."

Abby's pulse kicked higher, his touch sending a curl of heat through her body. "Yes," she said, needing every ounce of concentration she could muster to speak. "I'm glad you told me. I'll be sure to be even more—" Drawing a quavering breath, she caught her bottom lip between her teeth.

"What is it?" His brow furrowing again, he gave her a quizzical look. "Are you—"

"I want to kiss you," she blurted out, her breath catching in her throat. *Oh my God, did I actually say the words out loud?* From the shocked look on Chino's face, she had. Though her cheeks burned with embarrassment, she had no intention of apologizing, or retracting her declaration. Instead, she would use his momentary shock to her advantage, even though she knew he would view her behavior as forward. That didn't matter; all she wanted was to feel his lips beneath hers.

Before he recovered enough to voice a protest, she stepped closer, rose onto her toes, and captured his mouth with hers. She felt his body stiffen, but she didn't retreat. With a soft moan, she slid her arms around his neck, pressed her breasts against his chest, and deepened the kiss.

Several seconds passed before she realized he wasn't participating. Easing her mouth from his, she dropped back onto her heels, then withdrew her arms and took a step away.

When he didn't speak, she glanced up at him. The moonlight sharpened the planes and angles of his face, accentuating his strong jaw, prominent cheek-bones and slightly hooked nose.

She swallowed her disappointment, then said, "The first time I kissed you, I know I surprised you, but I thought you wouldn't mind if I . . . if we . . ." She blew out a deep breath. "Obviously I was wrong."

"I did not mind."

She tipped her head to one side. "You don't have to say that to make me feel better. I can tell when a man doesn't mind being kissed, and that's definitely not the impression you gave me. In fact, your reaction was more like you didn't want me touching you."

He moved his head slowly from side to side. "That is not true. I did like you touching me." His voice was a low rasp. He hesitated, then said, "I do not know how to kiss you."

Abby's eyes widened. "You never kissed your wife?"

"Not the way you kissed me."

"I know you said the Apache consider kissing very personal, but I still thought you and your wife must have . . ." She pursed her lips and gave him a long, considering look. "Would you like to learn?"

He stared at her for a moment. "You are offering to be my teacher?"

"Who else?" she replied, then grinned. "Even if I

could talk Marita into it, she's a little too old for you, don't you think?"

He grinned back at her. The moonlight caught the dimple in his left cheek, sending her pulse into a wild rhythm. "She would not like hearing you call her old."

"Marita would say I spoke the truth, as you're so fond of saying. Besides, she knows I love her and mean no disrespect."

He nodded, his smile slowly fading. Lifting a hand, he touched a fingertip to her chin. "Will you give me my first lesson now?"

Abby wished the light were better. Even the bright glow of the moon didn't allow her to look deeply into his eyes, to probe their depths for the heat she'd glimpsed there before. His voice and his touch told her he wasn't immune to her, but she would have liked the reassurance of seeing desire smoldering in his eyes.

"Yes," she finally said in a murmur. Once again she closed the distance between them and lifted her hands to his shoulders. "Put your arms around me."

He followed her instructions, resting his hands lightly against her back.

"Good." She smiled up at him. "Now, the first thing you need to know is, there are all kinds of kisses." As she spoke, she brought her face closer to his. "There's the soft little hello peck, like—" she demonstrated—"that. Then there's the teasing kiss, for when you're in a playful mood." Starting at one corner of his mouth, she nibbled on his lips, working her way to the opposite corner with slow, deliberate precision.

When she broke contact, she reveled in the fact that his breathing was as uneven as hers. Looping her arms around his neck, she slid her hands into his long hair and clutched the thick, silky strands with her fingers. "And then there's the passion kiss," she said in a throaty voice. "The one that takes your breath away and makes your knees weak. The one that sets your heart to pounding so hard you're afraid it will leap from your chest."

She looked up at him, noticing his flared nostrils and hooded eyes before focusing on his mouth. "Ready?"

He drew a shuddering breath, released it slowly, then gave her a nod. Pressing her lips to his, she let her eyes drift shut. With a groan, she leaned more fully against him, moving her mouth over his with growing urgency. Even though this man wasn't skilled at kissing, his lack of experience did nothing to prevent a wildfire of need from igniting in her belly and surging through her body.

She changed the angle of her kiss, pulling his bottom lip into her mouth, sucking on the soft flesh, giving it a gentle nip with her teeth. His moan sent her desire soaring higher and prompted her to plunge her tongue between his lips.

He gasped, his spine going rigid, his fingers digging into her back. Several seconds passed before he snapped out of his momentary shock. Moaning again, he widened his stance, and hauled her even closer, his arms tightening around her like iron bands.

Suddenly, her role as teacher seemed to slip away. No longer was he the recipient of the kiss, but a full and eager participant. He rubbed his mouth over hers, returning the teasing thrusts of her tongue with growing skill, giving back exactly what he got, and then some.

A wave of triumph washed over Abby. She was thrilled to have broken through to the passionate male she'd suspected lay in wait beneath Chino's cool, always-in-control exterior.

When she finally pulled her mouth from his, their ragged breathing was loud in the otherwise still evening. She couldn't tell if the pounding against her ribs was from her own heart, from his, or their combined heartbeats.

She slowly opened her fingers and let his hair slip from her grasp, then eased back in his arms a little. Blowing out a deep breath, she smiled. "Well, I must say, you're an excellent student. That was one powerful kiss."

"You have much skill as a teacher," he replied with a grin, his teeth a bright flash of white.

Although she couldn't see the crinkles at the corners of his eyes, she was certain they were there. Warmth unfurled in her chest and surrounded her heart, an unmistakable sensation she'd experienced only once in her life. When she realized the direction of her thoughts, she quickly shoved such an unthinkable notion aside. No, she couldn't allow herself to fall in love with Chino Whitehorse. She couldn't deny that she found him physically attractive, or that she desired him, but there could be nothing more. Anything else would be impossible. He was Apache, a fact she never would be able to overlook.

She pulled her arms from around his neck and stepped out of his embrace. "It's getting late," she said, keeping her gaze averted from his, "so I'll say good night." Not waiting for him to respond, she turned and hurried toward the house.

Chino watched her walk away, wondering at her abrupt change. In the blink of an eye, she'd gone from the heat of a blazing campfire to the coolness of a mountain stream.

He sucked in a lungful of air, which was still heavy with Abby's scent. Immediately, his head filled with images of their last kiss. A passion kiss, she'd called it. Yes, she had spoken the truth. Closing his eyes, he recalled every moment of that kiss. Her taste. The sound of her moan. Her breasts crushed against his chest. Her thighs pressed to his, her belly cradling his swollen manhood.

A tortured groan escaped his throat. Opening his

eyes, he huffed out a breath, and willed the ache in his groin to ease. Knowing it could be a long time before he would be able to sleep, he decided to take a walk.

He'd gone only a few yards when he heard the sound of a horse approaching. Slipping into the shadows, he waited for the horse to come into view. Soon a lone rider came around the hill to the north and headed toward the barn. Recognizing the gray horse as Nestor's, he stepped into the open and waved a hello.

Nestor jerked so hard on the reins that the gray sat back on his hocks, whinnying in protest, the flecks of sweat on his neck glistening in the moonlight.

Chino ignored the urge to tell the man he should not treat horses so harshly, especially one that obviously had been ridden hard. Instead he said, "You found the cattle?" Since the day Nestor had returned to report half the herd was missing, Abby had insisted he check them more frequently.

Nestor dismounted, tossed the reins over the gray's head, then started toward the barn. "Sí."

"All of them?"

Nestor stopped and turned toward Chino. "Sí."

When the man offered nothing more, Chino said, "You have been gone many hours. There was trouble?"

"No. No trouble. I went into town." He pointed to

171

a package tied behind his saddle. "There were some things I needed at the mercantile."

Chino didn't mention that the mercantile had been closed for hours. Instead, he said, "Señora Madison will be relieved to know the cattle are safe."

"You will tell her in the morning, sí?"

"She may have questions. You should speak to her."

"I will not see her in the morning. I have . . . uh— There is something I must do."

Chino stared at him for a moment, then said, "I will tell her what you said."

Nestor nodded his thanks, then continued on to the barn.

Chino watched until man and horse disappeared through the door. Heading in the opposite direction, he considered seeing if Abby was still awake so he could tell her what Nestor had said about the cattle. He glanced at the house and saw the soft glow of lamplight in the window of the room he knew was Abby's.

He gave his head a shake. No, it would be better if he kept his distance from her. If he hadn't suspected it before, tonight's kissing lesson revealed a truth he could no longer ignore. He was losing the battle over his attraction to her. And even more disturbing, he suspected his heart had begun to care for her.

172

Chapter Eleven

The following morning, Chino rose earlier than usual. His unsettling discovery of the night before had made his sleep restless. He bathed in the creek, offered his morning prayers to Ussen, then headed for the main house.

He found Marita already in the kitchen. As he closed the door, she turned toward him.

"Buenos días," she said, offering him a bright smile. "The morning is beautiful, sí?"

"Sí," he replied, returning her smile.

"The coffee is ready. You would like a cup?"

He nodded.

He accepted the cup from Marita with a murmured, *"Gracias."* Taking a sip, he glanced toward the door to the hall. "Where is everyone?"

"The *niños* are still asleep," she said, dropping a

tortilla onto a hot griddle. "Cesar is bringing water from the creek, and Señora Abby is getting dressed. She will be here soon."

The words had barely left her mouth when Abby stepped into the room.

"Ah," Marita said. "There she is." She wiped her hands on her apron, then poured another cup of coffee and handed it to the younger woman. "Señor Whitehorse has been waiting for you."

"He has?" Abby's gaze shifted to meet his.

Chino's eyes narrowed. In spite of the sudden bloom of color on her cheeks, she looked tired, as if she, too, had not slept well. Not wanting to think about what that might mean, he stepped closer. "I must talk to you."

She stared at him for several seconds, then said, "We can go into the *sala.*"

As soon as they were alone, Abby said, "I sensed you didn't want to speak in front of Marita. So, what's this about?"

"Nestor."

"He's back?"

"Yes. Last night."

"Good," she said, releasing a sigh. "I was afraid he hadn't returned because there was another problem with the cattle."

"No, I asked. He said all the cattle were there."

"Well, that's a relief," she replied; then her brow furrowed. "But why are you telling me this? He could have told me himself at breakfast."

"He will not be at breakfast. He said he had something he had to do." He paused, hoping she would say she knew where Nestor had gone that morning. When she didn't, he said, "You know where he went?"

"No," she replied with a shrug, "but he rides out early lots of mornings."

She took a sip of coffee, eyeing him over the rim of her cup. "Is something else bothering you?"

"I asked Nestor if he was late because of a problem. He said the cattle were fine. That he went to town to buy something at the mercantile." When Abby made no comment, he continued. "He did not return until many hours after the mercantile closed. Arivaca is not far, but his horse had been ridden hard."

"Maybe he couldn't find what he wanted in Arivaca and rode over to Tubac. That's a long ride from here."

Chino dipped his head in acknowledgment of the possibility, then after another pause, he said, "He has been gone other evenings? To visit someone?"

"He's returned to the ranch late many times. As far as visiting someone, I'm not sure—" Her eyebrows arched. "Ah, you're talking about a woman?" At his nod, she said, "Not that I know of. At least he's never mentioned a woman. But even if he does visit one occasionally, I doubt he'd share that information with me."

"You are probably right. But there is still something that troubles me. You said you do not pay him wages, so how does he buy from the mercantile?"

Abby shrugged. "Maybe he has money saved from before he came here. Or maybe the mercantile owner allowed him to buy on credit."

Chino nodded but made no reply.

After a few moments, Abby said, "Why all the curiosity about Nestor? Surely you don't still have doubts about him." She waved her hand in a dismissive gesture. "That's ridiculous. I told you, he's been a godsend to me and this ranch. He does the work of two men around here. We couldn't make it without him."

He inhaled a deep breath, released it slowly. "Perhaps I was wrong. But to protect you and your horses, I must look at everything."

"I understand," she replied, flashing a smile. "Now that we've settled that, how about some breakfast?"

Again Chino nodded, suddenly wishing he could begin every day with the warmth of her smile. Scolding himself for allowing such thoughts to intrude into his mind, he waited until she started back toward the kitchen, then followed. As he reached the *sala* doorway, the flesh on the outside of his thigh began to shake. He stopped, his full concentration on the shaking muscle. The tremor lasted only a few seconds, but this time, there was no mistaking the message. Something bad was going to happen.

His first thought was Abby's horses—that the animals once again faced danger. Though he didn't want to alarm her, he felt she needed to be told.

In the kitchen, he swallowed the last of his coffee, set down his cup, then grabbed a tortilla from the plate by the stove. Moving close to Abby, he said, "I need to check the horses."

"What? But you haven't—" Her eyes widened, then she lowered her voice to say, "Another tremor?"

He nodded. "It was much stronger."

"Will you stay with the herd?"

"Only if I find something that tells me the horses are in danger."

"Should I go with you?"

"No. Stay here. If there is trouble, I will fire two shots with my rifle."

"Okay, but please—" she grabbed his forearm and squeezed—"be careful."

Chino stared down into her pleading eyes, wishing he dared kiss her. But Marita was in the room, and he heard Cesar pouring water into the olla outside the door. Instead, he settled for a brief touch of his fingers on her hand. "I will."

Rather than taking the time to saddle his horse, he rode bareback, urging the bay into a gallop. As he drew near the valley, he slowed the horse to a walk and circled to approach the herd from the west, just in case someone had been watching him and knew his pattern.

He entered the valley with great caution, then pulled back on the reins and scanned the herd. Several heads came up, ears swiveling toward him, but neither their behavior nor his own keen instincts warned him of another human's presence. Just to be certain, he waited a few minutes more, then finally moved closer. He untied the sorrel mare's tether, then moved the stake to a new area of tall grass and reattached the rope tether. Again he waited. The other horses drifted closer to the mare, then continued to graze, relaxed and giving no sign of an intruder.

Satisfied whatever bad thing the shaking in his thigh foretold wouldn't involve the herd of horses, he started back to the house.

As he rode into the yard, he could hear the wail of a child crying. Fear clutching at his belly, he slid off his horse and ran toward the barn.

Inside one of the stalls, he found Abby trying to console her sobbing daughter.

"What happened?" he asked, crouching beside Abby.

"One of her kittens is missing."

Susanna sniffed, wiped her nose on the sleeve of her dress, then threw herself into Chino's arms. "Find my kitty, peeze," she managed to get out before she burst into another round of tears, which quickly soaked the front of his shirt.

Chino thought his heart would break from the sound of the little girl's sobs. He held her close, one hand rubbing her back in a soothing motion. "Shh, do not cry, *sha*. Which kitten is missing?"

She sniffed again, then pushed away from his chest. "The pwetty gray one," she said, then hiccupped, "with white paws." She tipped back her head and looked up at him with glistening green eyes. A lone tear trickled down one plump cheek. "Do you 'member dat one?"

"I remember," he said, using his thumb to wipe away the tear. "Go back to the house with your mother. I will look for the kitten."

She released a shuddering breath, then moved away from him. " 'Kay." Turning to Abby, she held out her hand. "Come on, Momma. Papa Chino is gonna find my kitty."

Abby glanced up and met his gaze, obviously as startled as he by what her daughter had called him. "Chino will look, sweetheart," she said, dropping her gaze to Susanna. "And I know he'll try really, really hard to find your kitten, but he may not be able to."

Susanna sighed, then bobbed her head. "I know. Some mean, ol' animal mighta got my kitty."

"Yes," Abby replied in a raspy voice, "that's right." She glanced again at Chino, then led her daughter from the barn.

Chino released his horse in the corral and started looking for Susanna's missing kitten. He checked the barn first, even though he was certain the girl, and probably Abby as well, had already looked there. Then he went out into the yard, methodically checking everywhere he thought a kitten might hide.

When he found no sign of the missing feline near the barn or the house, he widened his search. As he passed the front of the house, he saw Abby watching him through one of the windows. When he gave her a quick shake of his head, she closed her eyes for a moment, then turned away from the window.

A short time later, he started back to the house. Abby must have seen him coming, because he'd barely stepped beneath the ramada when the back door opened and she emerged.

He waited until she shut the door before saying, "Where is Susanna?"

"Sleeping. She wore herself out crying." Abby moved closer, studying his face. "You found the missing kitten?"

A muscle jumping in his jaw, he nodded.

"Oh God," she said, the hope in her eyes dying. "I tried to prepare her for this. Told her wild animals get family pets all the time. But she's still going to be devastated."

Unable to stand seeing her in pain, he pulled her into his embrace.

She wrapped her arms around his waist, and

pressed a cheek to his chest. As she drew a deep breath, her breasts pushed more firmly against him, making him momentarily forget the reason for her being in his arms. Her scent teasing his senses, he smoothed her hair with one hand.

After a few seconds, he said, "I found it near the creek. Close to where Susanna plays with the kittens."

Abby groaned. "A coyote?" Then before Chino could respond, she added, "No, that doesn't make sense. Coyotes don't make a kill then leave the carcass behind."

"No, a coyote did not torture and kill the kitten. Another animal did. One on two legs."

"Two legs?" Abby pushed herself away from him so she could meet his gaze. "What are you saying?"

"Only a man," he said, his voice dropping to a fierce whisper, "could do what I saw."

"Do—" she drew a deep breath—"what?"

He shook his head. "It is not something you would want to hear." Swallowing the bile rising in his throat, he tried to put the picture of Susanna's kitten from his mind. Yet he knew he'd never forget the gruesome scene he'd found.

She stared up at him, her shoulders rippling with a shudder. "But who . . . who would do such a thing?" She gasped, grabbing his arms, her fingers biting into his flesh through the fabric of his shirt. "Where Susanna plays by the creek is less than fifty feet from here. How could someone get that close to the house without us knowing?"

Chino shook his head again. "I do not know. I will go back. Look for his trail. He tried to cover his tracks, but he might have been careless."

Abby bobbed her head in agreement, then loosened her grip and let her hands slip from his arms. "Okay. What did you do with the . . . um . . . remains?"

"Buried. Under a tree on the other side of the creek."

She squeezed her eyes closed for a second, then released a long sigh. "Thank you. I'd hate for Susanna to see—Susanna!" A moan sounded in her throat. "What am I going to tell her? I've always told my children the truth, but this time I don't know if I can."

"Children must know they will face sad times. Apache children are taught this, because our life-way is a hard one." He lifted a hand to touch Abby's cheek. "Your daughter is very young, and very smart. She will know if you do not speak the truth."

"Yes, that's true." She sighed again. "There were originally five kittens in the litter. One died the day after they were born, and Susanna was heartbroken. I tried to tell her that sometimes baby animals aren't strong enough to survive, and to remember she still had four other kittens to play with." She rubbed a hand over her eyes. "But what will I tell her this time?"

Chino was silent for a moment, then finally said, "Tell her the kitten passed to the Spirit World to be with a little girl who did not have one."

"Do you think that's a good idea? I mean, I hate to make up something just to ease her sorrow." When he didn't reply, she said, "You would approve, if that's what I told Susanna?"

"Why would I not approve?"

"Because it's not the truth, and I know how strongly you feel about speaking the truth."

"You do not think it is possible?"

"What? That God wanted the kitten in heaven for a little girl who didn't have a pet of her own?" At his nod, her brow furrowed. "When I was a child, my mother used to read the Bible to me. I remember being awed by what God could do. So I guess it's possible that He had plans for the kitten."

He trailed his fingers down her cheek. "Yes," he murmured, touching a fingertip to the indentation in her chin. "It is possible."

"You're sure you won't be upset with me if I don't tell Susanna the entire truth?"

He shook his head. "Tell her the kitten has passed to the Spirit World to play with another little girl. That is enough truth. She does not need to know more."

She swallowed hard. "As soon as she wakes up, I'll talk to her."

He gave her a nod, touched her cheek again, then dropped his hand to his side.

Abby moved away from Chino, crossed her arms beneath her breasts and stared out across the ranch yard. She couldn't believe what was happening, couldn't understand why she'd suddenly lost control of everything in her life.

Several minutes passed before she spoke. "What happened to Susanna's kitten was the bad thing your muscle tremor predicted, wasn't it?"

"Yes," he replied in a tight voice.

"And you think Warner is behind this?"

"I am sure he is."

She drew a deep breath, then released it with a huff. "So now what do we do?"

"Keep your children close to the house, unless you are with them."

She swung around to face him. "What! Are you saying my children could be in danger?"

He nodded, his mouth compressed to a grim line.

"I don't understand," she said, shaking her head slowly. "Warner ordering one of his men to torture and kill a kitten is despicable enough, but for him to make my children a target—Well, I just don't want to believe he's capable of doing something that—"

"He is capable."

The hardness in his voice took Abby by surprise.

Moving closer, she studied his expression: the dark eyes blazing with anger, the tightness of his jaw. "What do you mean?"

"He has ordered other children to be killed."

"How do you know that?"

His eyes bored into hers as he said, "I told you about the day I was shot. That four of us were traveling to the Chiricahua Reservation when Warner and his men found our camp. I did not tell you the others were my wife, her brother and my son."

"Oh, Chino," she said with a soft gasp, "don't tell me, Neville—"

"He ordered his men to 'kill the thieving red devils. Even the kid.' "

"Oh, dear God." Her voice dropped to a whisper. "You saw your wife and son shot." Shocked to the core by what he'd revealed, she swayed on her feet. To keep herself from falling, she reached for him, clutched his arm. "No wonder you hate him so much."

A fierce scowl settled on his face. "Now you know why I have sworn revenge."

Steadier now, she uncurled her fingers from his arm, then reached up to push a strand of hair off his cheek. "Neville Warner has to be the most vile, loathsome man that ever drew breath." She narrowed her eyes. "And if I have my way, I'll be the one to make sure the son of a bitch pays. I want him to pay for what he did to you and for what he's trying to do to me and my children."

He blinked, surprise registering in his expression. Then as he stared down at her, she watched the last of his anger fade from his dark eyes, only to be replaced by something much more potent. The unmistakable spark of desire.

"So beautiful," he said, his voice gentle. "So fierce." His mouth curved into a smile, flashing his dimple. "Like a mother *indui*, a mountain lion, protecting her cubs."

Abby couldn't respond. The sudden humming in her ears, the wild pounding of her heart, the heat swirling low in her belly, robbed her of the ability to speak. Even her mind seemed unable to function. The only coherent thought she had was her desperate need to kiss this man.

As soon as the idea popped into her head, she reacted before she could consider her actions. Shoving her fingers into his hair and fisting her hands in the silky strands, she gently tugged his face closer to hers.

His eyes widened, but he didn't resist her advance or try to pull away. When her mouth touched his in a light brushing kiss, she heard his quickly indrawn breath, followed by a soft, throaty moan.

She needed no further encouragement. Rising on her toes, she placed her mouth more firmly atop his, and pressed herself against him from breast to thighs. He widened his stance, wrapped his arms around her and pulled her closer. Through the layers of her skirts, the hard ridge of his aroused manhood pushed against her belly.

She broke contact long enough to whisper his name, then reclaimed his mouth in a kiss that went beyond anything she'd ever experienced. Need hotter and more intense than any she'd known careened through her body, pooling in the damp flesh between her thighs. Desperate for more, she pushed her tongue into his mouth, reveling in his responding groan.

He lowered his hands to grip her bottom, began moving his hips in a thrusting motion. With each forward thrust, he rubbed his swollen flesh more firmly against her belly, increasing the throbbing ache between her thighs. Her fingers tightened in his hair, her own hips moving to match his rhythm.

He groaned, then jerked his mouth from hers. "Enough." His voice was breathless and raw with the same need that had Abby's head spinning and her blood sizzling.

Though she nearly said, "No, not nearly enough," she held her tongue. Instead, she blew out a deep breath, then opened her fists and let the heated silk of his hair slip from her grasp.

She took a step back, looking up at him, watching him struggle to compose himself. His chest was heaving, and his eyes still simmered with desire.

Pleased by his reaction, she ran a fingertip over his mouth, still wet from her kiss.

"I don't know what came over me," she said, her voice unsteady. "I've never behaved like this. Never felt like this. But I'm—" she sucked in another deep breath, then released it slowly—"I'm not sorry."

Neville Warner sat back in his chair, elbows resting on the leather arms, fingers steepled under his chin. "It's about time you checked in," he said, watching a man enter his office.

The man shrugged. "It could not be helped."

Warner made a snorting sound, then said, "You delivered my latest . . . message . . . to Abigail Madison?"

"Yesterday," the man replied, dropping into one of the chairs on the opposite side of the desk.

"And?"

"She is nervous, I think."

Warner leaned forward in his chair, then slapped his hand on the top of his desk. "Nervous isn't good enough. I'm paying you a helluva lot of money to make sure she agrees to sell me the Flying M. But none of the things you suggested has helped. Taking half her cattle, shooting at her horses, killin' one of her brat's pets. Not one of them has gotten me one damn inch closer to owning that land. Land I need for running my cattle, dammit. Do you hear me?"

When the man opened his mouth to respond, Warner made a slashing motion with his arm. "Shut up and let me think."

Several minutes passed while the only sound in the room was the soft ticking of a clock. Finally, Warner wrapped his knuckles on his desktop, then smiled.

"It's time to stop playing games."

The other man stared at him for a moment, stroking a thumb down one side of his mustache. His eyes narrowing, he said, "You have a plan?"

"Yeah, I got a plan. But first I'm gonna pay one last call on Abigail Madison. If she refuses—" his smile broadened—"well, you may get the chance to earn a big bonus."

The man's eyes lit up at the mention of more money. "Before you make the trip, there is something you should know."

"That right?" Warner replied. When the man nodded, he said, "Well, out with it."

Chapter Twelve

Late in the afternoon, two days after the ordeal with Susanna's kitten, Abby walked beside Teddy toward Egusi's corral.

"I don't see why you hafta come with me," the boy said to her, shooting a glare in her direction. "I ain't a baby."

"No, son, you're not," Abby replied, inwardly wincing at his grammar, but determined not to correct him. He was already upset over her insisting she accompany him to the corral. "I wanted to watch Chino work with the horse, too, and I thought you wouldn't mind if I walked with you. But I won't stay if you think I'll be in the way."

Teddy's brow wrinkled with a scowl. "If you stay, ya gotta be really quiet. Egusi don't like lotsa noise."

"Ah, I see," Abby said, biting her lip to stop a

smile. "In that case, I'll be very, very quiet. Egusi won't even know I'm there."

Her son gave her a sharp nod. "Okay, you can stay." He raised one hand and shook a finger at her. "But if you upset Egusi, Mr. Whitehorse is gonna be really mad at you."

"I understand," she replied, once again fighting to maintain a serious expression. "And thanks for letting me stay."

When they arrived at the corral, Chino was already inside, approaching the white horse with measured steps.

As he moved closer, he spoke to the stallion. Abby couldn't make out his words, though she suspected he spoke Apache. When she whispered the question to Teddy, he responded with a quick nod followed by glare that plainly said, "Shush."

Chino stopped beside the horse, then slowly lifted his hand toward the stallion. As he touched the strong neck, Egusi's hide quivered. The stallion stomped a hoof once, made a snuffling sound, then settled down.

Abby watched as Chino rubbed the horse with slow and deliberate movements, fascinated by the contrast of his bronze hands moving over the stallion's white hide. A contrast repeated in the image that popped into her head—those same hands gliding over another pale body. Hers.

She pressed her knuckles against her mouth to stifle a gasp. A tingle raced up her spine, making her shiver.

She tried to breathe normally, tried to watch him work without imagining herself as the recipient of Chino's competent ministrations. But every place he touched the horse—neck, withers, legs—she felt heat in a corresponding part of her body, her flesh quivering just as Egusi's had.

By the time Chino finished working his magic, methodically moving his hands from head to rump on both sides of the stallion, Egusi was totally relaxed. The horse stood with his head lowered, his eyes closed in a half-doze. And Abby was on fire.

The blood thundered through her veins, her legs weak and shaking, the place between her thighs damp and throbbing. She clutched the top rail of the fence to keep herself from sliding to the ground.

Chino gave the stallion a final pat, then turned and walked over to where she and Teddy stood outside the corral.

Abby drew what she hoped would be a calming breath, then managed a shaky smile. "What—" Embarrassed by the raspiness of her voice, she cleared her throat, then started again. "What were you doing just now?"

"Momma!" Teddy said, with a dramatic roll of his eyes. "That's how ya gentle a horse."

"Is that right?"

"Yeah." He looked up at Chino. "Tell Momma that's what you were doin'."

He smiled at the boy, then lifted his gaze to meet Abby's. "Yes, that is how I gentle a horse."

She looked over at the dozing stallion, then back at Chino. "And rubbing your hands over its body that way—" she couldn't stop another shiver from shaking her—"really . . . um . . . works?"

She saw something flare in his dark eyes, but he looked away before she could put a name to that brief flicker.

"I have gentled many colts with my hands," he said. "Never a horse as old as this one. Or as stubborn," he added with a quick smile. "He will be more difficult."

"For a horse who's spent his entire life running free, I'd say convincing him to let you touch him like that is pretty remarkable. You've made excellent progress, if my opinion means anything."

"Yes, it does," he replied, meeting her gaze again, his stare holding her transfixed.

As she looked into his eyes, she noticed the flicker again, the same flare of heat she'd seen moments before. But this time, she had no trouble recognizing its source. Desire, hot and potent, smoldered in the depths of those dark, hypnotic eyes. But as she continued staring at him, she watched his usual cool demeanor slide back into place.

She pushed aside her disappointment, licked her

suddenly dry lips, then said, "I . . . um . . . have some work to do, so I'll leave Teddy in your care."

Her son turned toward her, his face clearly showing his displeasure. "I can take care o' myself."

"I know you can, son. That's not—" She glanced up at Chino, caught his nod. "Never mind. I'll see both of you later."

After brushing a hand over Teddy's head, she turned and started toward the house.

Abby spent the rest of the day thinking about the desire she'd seen in Chino's eyes and his method of taming horses. Especially the latter, although again her mind replaced the horse, conjuring images of Chino's hands rubbing over her. But rather than slow, easy touches meant to relax and tame, the strokes of his hands became caresses, meant to stoke the fires of her desire.

Though only the daydreams of a woman who hadn't been with a man for more than two years, they were shockingly real. And by evening, the fantasy had replayed in her head so many times that her body literally quivered with need.

As she sat on the ramada after the others had said their good-nights and departed, she tried to think of something besides what her imagination insisted on calling up at every opportunity. But each time she managed to grasp another topic to occupy her mind,

Chino pushed it aside. Heaving a sigh, she gave up and allowed the images full rein.

Then abruptly, imagining him touching her wasn't enough. She rose, intending to go to Chino, to turn her fantasy into reality. He wasn't immune to her. She knew that from his arousal during their last kiss, as well as the desire she'd seen burning in his eyes that afternoon by Egusi's corral. But would he be willing to do more than kiss her, to share a night of passion? Shocked by the direction of her thoughts and determined to put them out of her mind, she crossed the ramada, then jerked open the door with more force than necessary.

She drew a steadying breath, then went inside the house and eased the door closed behind her. In her bedroom, she took a seat on the stool in front of her dressing table. After removing the pins from her hair, she picked up her brush. Soon the rhythm of brushing her hair relaxed her tense muscles, and as always, lulled her into a dreamy state. Immediately, images of Chino filled her mind.

Her hands paused in their task. Staring at her reflection in the mirror over her dressing table, she wondered what was wrong with her. How could she spend so much time thinking about a man who should be the last one she'd consider in intimate terms? He was Apache, and although he hadn't fired the shot that killed Alan, he was still one of them. For that alone, she should hate him with every breath she took, and she had when they'd first met. But soon afterward, her initial hatred had started to shrivel, and somewhere along the way, she now realized, had met with a silent death.

Though she accepted the surprising revelation without so much as a twinge, she couldn't help wondering what had brought about such a drastic change. Perhaps Cesar's statement about there being good and bad in all people had stuck in her subconscious, allowing her to view Chino in a different light. Though she acknowledged that Cesar's words might have contributed to swaying her opinion, she was certain getting to know Chino was the biggest factor in the demise of her hatred. He was like no man she had ever met. Aside from being physically attractive, he possessed a combination of traits she deeply admired—everything she could ever want in the man she loved.

Abby jerked as if she'd been struck. Squeezing her eyes closed for a moment, she took a calming breath, then exhaled slowly. When she'd regained at least a portion of her composure, she forced herself to consider this second stunning revelation.

She groaned, dropping her hands into her lap. *It can't be true! I love Alan.* But in spite of her efforts to convince herself that her feelings for Chino had not traveled the length of the emotional spectrum, the answer remained the same. Her initial hatred of him had somehow undergone a complete transformation. In spite of the love she still had for her dead husband, she was falling in love with Chino White-horse.

As unthinkable as the idea seemed, and as much as she tried to find reason to dismiss her conclusion, one thing made her finally acknowledge the truth. She never would have considered offering herself to Chino unless she had strong feelings for him.

But now that she had accepted her growing love for him, what should she do about it?

That question nagged at her while she finished brushing her hair, then bent to remove her shoes and stockings. Wiggling her toes, she stared at her bare feet, once again lost in thought. Finally, she released a deep breath, then rose from the stool.

Chino lay on the bed in the bunkhouse, wearing only his buckskin trousers. As he rolled the bead of one earring between his thumb and fingers, he contemplated Egusi and how the stallion was responding to his gentling efforts. With any luck, by the time he was ready to leave the Flying M, the horse would trust him completely. And if the training went as he anticipated, he also might be riding the horse by then.

Before Chino fully enjoyed the pleasure of that thought, another intruded. Leaving the Flying M. He didn't want to think about leaving Teddy and Su-sanna, who had stolen his heart from almost the moment he had met them. Knowing he'd never see the children again would give him great pain, but leaving Abby would be far worse. After the deaths of his wife and son, he'd thought he would never have to face another such devastating loss. Then the Spirits sent him to the Flying M, where he met the White Eyes woman who made him question everything he knew.

Just thinking about leaving Abby caused an ache in his chest. But once he'd dealt with Neville Warner, there would be no reason to stay on the Flying M. Not even the knowledge that his heart had begun to care for her. She wouldn't want an Apache in—

A noise outside the opened window jarred him from his thoughts. Straining to listen, he caught the faint swishing of fabric, the soft tread of someone walking across the hard ground. Pushing himself up onto one forearm, he slipped a hand beneath the pillow and wrapped his fingers around the handle of his knife.

Frozen in place and holding his breath, he watched the door slowly swing inward.

"Chino?" His keen hearing had no difficulty picking up the soft whisper.

When he didn't answer, the door cracked open a little more.

"Chino, are you awake?" This time the words were spoken in a slightly louder whisper.

"Yes," he replied, releasing his grip on his knife and sitting up.

The door opened, then immediately closed again. In the darkened bunkhouse interior, Chino could make out Abby's pale face, the faint outline of her light-colored dress but nothing more.

He rose, moved to the table, then struck a match and held it to the wick of the oil lamp. Turning toward Abby, he said, "Why are you here?"

The lamp cast a small circle of weak light on the floor, revealing her bare feet peeking out from beneath the hem of her dress. He narrowed his eyes, but he still couldn't make out her expression.

He heard her draw a deep breath, heard her swallow. She took a step toward him, then another. Though her face remained in partial shadow, he saw the way she rubbed her hands on her skirt. Wondering at the reason for her nervousness, he moved closer.

He reached out to touch her arm. "What is—" His breath hissed between his teeth. "You are trembling."

"I know, I . . ."

"Did something happen?"

Abby shook her head. "No," she said, inwardly wincing at how her voice quavered over the word. "Nothing's happened." She tried to smile, not sure her efforts were a success. "But I'm hoping something does."

He frowned. "I do not understand."

She needed a minute to pull herself together. She

hadn't been this nervous since the first time with—
Shoving that thought aside, she lifted a hand to toy
with a strand of his hair. "I came here to see you."
She released his hair, touched her fingers to his
mouth, then ran a fingertip over his bottom lip.

He didn't respond, his only reaction a slight stiff-
ening of his spine.

She glanced up, met his intense stare. "You're not
going to make this easy for me, are you?"

Again he didn't reply. Clearly confused, he gave
her a helpless look.

She dropped her hand away from his face. "Okay,"
she said, the heat of a blush creeping up her cheeks,
"I came here to ask you to—Damn, this is harder
than I thought." She drew a deep breath, then let it
out slowly. "It's been a long time since my hus—
since Alan died. I have needs. Needs only a man can
satisfy." She paused, waiting for her words to sink
in, then added, "Do you understand what I'm saying?"

His eyebrows arched. "You want to share my bed?
For us to be . . . together?"

"Yes, that's what I want."

"Why do you ask this of me?"

"Because I need you, the way a woman needs a
man." Unable to resist touching his mouth again, she
traced the outline of his upper lip. "I enjoyed kissing
you, and I'm pretty sure you enjoyed it, too. I know
we would be good together." She replaced her fin-

gers with her mouth for a quick kiss. "I want you, Chino, and I think you want me, too."

When he made no reply, her face flamed even hotter. "I guess I was wrong," she said, lowering her head and taking a step back, "I'm sorry if I—"

"No." His fingers circled her wrist in a gentle but firm grip. "You were not wrong."

Her gaze snapping to his, she gave him a quizzical look.

"You were not wrong," he said again. "I do want you."

She stared at him, searching his eyes for confirmation. There was no mistaking the banked fire of desire, but there was something else as well. "I sense you're not telling me everything?"

He released her arm, his chest expanding with a deep breath. For the first time, she noticed he wore some sort of necklace. What appeared to be a round piece of leather, suspended from a narrow thong tied around his neck, rested on his chest. The unusual medallion lay just above an angry-looking scar—a permanent reminder of his brush with death. She lifted her hand to touch the puckered skin, but his voice stopped her.

"It is true. I want you. But it is not a good idea."

Her gaze flew from his chest to his face. "Why? If it's what we both want, what's the harm?"

"I do not want you to think there can be more between us."

Though Abby knew he was right, the love growing in her heart rebelled at hearing the words spoken aloud. She knew he wanted nothing permanent, that he would leave eventually, that she would have to be content with whatever time they had left. Yes, she knew all of that, but that didn't stop the ache in her chest.

She needed all her willpower to ignore the pain and force her lips into a smile. "Don't worry. I won't expect anything more."

He stared at her, his expression grim.

For a moment, the previous warnings she'd given herself returned, sounding an alarm that not controlling her need would be a mistake. But she ignored her inner voice; she intended to continue down the path she'd chosen. Desperate to lighten the mood, she managed a chuckle. "You look like you're going to war, not planning to take me to your bed."

His face remained somber. "You are sure?"

"Yes, of course." When he didn't look convinced, she traced a mark above her left breast with one finger. "Cross my heart." Seeing he didn't understand, she added, "That's part of an Anglo saying. 'Cross my heart and may I die, if I so much as tell a lie.' "

He continued to stare at her for several more seconds. "That means you—"

"Yes, I speak the truth. Now do you believe me?"

The corners of his mouth curved upward. He carefully brushed a wisp of hair away from her face, then picked up a strand from where it lay on her shoulder and rubbed it between his fingers. "You are not like any woman I have ever known."

Abby wanted to ask if that was good or bad, but decided she really didn't want to know. Instead she smiled. "And you're like no man I've ever known." When he continued playing with her hair, she said, "Aren't you going to kiss me?"

A chuckle rumbling in his chest, he tucked the strand of hair behind her ear. "So impatient."

"Yes," she said, moving closer, "I am." She rose onto her toes, touched her tongue to the corner of his mouth, then gave his lower lip a quick nip with her teeth.

He jerked away from her, then threw back his head and laughed, the rich sound increasing the love growing in Abby's heart—the heart she prayed was strong enough to survive his leaving. Refusing to think about that eventuality, she took his hand and started toward the bunk.

He pulled his hand free. "Let me turn down the—"

"No, leave it."

When he didn't move, she glanced up at him. The heat in his eyes had spiked upward. She gave another tug, and he didn't resist.

Abby stopped beside the bunk, then reached for the buttons on the front of her dress. She couldn't believe her actions of the past several minutes. She'd never acted with such brazen intent. But then, she'd never wanted a man as much as she did Chino.

When the last button popped free, she pulled the garment over her head and tossed it aside. Her petticoat soon followed. Clad in only her underclothes, she stretched out on her side on the narrow bed, then lifted a hand toward him in invitation.

After the briefest of hesitations, Chino complied and lay on his back in front of her.

As she wiggled closer, he slipped a hand beneath her and wrapped his arm around her, bringing her camisole-covered breasts into contact with his bare chest, and her thighs against his. Lifting her gaze, she smiled, then dipped her head and kissed him.

Chino groaned, pulling her more firmly against him, one hand clamped around her waist, the other fisting in her hair.

She deepened the kiss, urging his lips apart, then slipping her tongue inside. Emboldened by the tightening of his embrace and another of his groans, she shifted so she lay atop him. Her belly brushed the hard ridge of his aroused flesh, and his hips bucked upward, sending her already inflamed desire into another realm.

Her pulse hammered against her temples; the throbbing ache low in her belly intensified. The flesh between her thighs grew moist. Wrenching her mouth from his, she sucked in a lungful of air, then reached for the hem of her camisole. "Help me with this," she said, trying to tug the garment up with one hand. "Please. I want to feel your skin against mine."

Chino's heart pounded so hard, he could barely hear her words. His hand shaking with need, he had trouble removing his fingers from her hair. Finally, he freed his hand then grabbed the other side of the camisole's hem, and helped her pull it up and over her head.

As she tried to shake the stray locks of hair off her face, her breasts bounced just inches above his face.

His throat went dry, his heart pounding even harder. He swallowed hard, unable to stop looking at the creamy globes with their tightly puckered coral tips.

Abby went still above him. Realizing she was watching him, he forced his gaze from the temptation of her breasts to her face.

Though she didn't open her mouth, he clearly heard her say, "Kiss me there." Wondering if the desire raging through him had somehow affected his mind, he blinked several times.

Before his senses cleared, she changed positions again so that she sat astride his hips. Placing her hands on the bed on either side of his head, she leaned forward, then whispered, "Please."

Chapter Thirteen

Abby's bold offer ignited the fire simmering in Chino's veins. Lifting his hands to cup her breasts, he pressed his lips to the creamy flesh.

Her eyes closed as a moaned "Yes" came from her throat. Encouraged by her reaction, he kissed the opposite breast, then ran his tongue over its hardened peak.

"More," he heard her say in a breathless whisper. "Please, more."

Chino wasn't highly experienced when it came to intimacies between men and women, yet instinctively he knew what Abby wanted. He circled each nipple with another slow swirl of his tongue, then pulled one tight bud into his mouth and suckled.

She gasped, the tug of his mouth sending a scorching burst of heat through her body. Easing away from him, she pushed herself back into a sitting position. "I can't take this any longer," she said, surprised at the huskiness of her voice.

His eyes widened. "I hurt you?"

The concern on his face plucked at her heart. "Yes," she replied. "But not in the way you mean."

"I do not understand."

"The hurt I'm feeling is an ache." She smoothed the furrows in his forehead with her fingertips. "An ache, deep inside, for us to be together." Seeing understanding dawn in his eyes, she smiled, then lowered her hand to the waistband of his trousers. "Do you need help getting out of these?"

The bed shook with his chuckle. "If you will move, I can do it."

She climbed off him, then untied the ribbon of her drawers and let them slide to the floor. After adding the garment to the pile of her other clothes, she turned around just as Chino straightened from removing his trousers.

Her breath caught in her throat. He was spectacular. The perfect bronze-skinned warrior, fiercely proud in his nakedness. Her gaze moved from the wonderful angles and planes of his face to his wide shoulders, then down the rest of his magnificent body. Past his smooth, well-muscled chest—marred only by the puckered scar—to his flat stomach and narrow hips. Skipping over his manhood for a moment, she finished her perusal, noting the strong thighs and calves of his long legs, and ending with his well-formed feet. Then she allowed her gaze to travel back up to the proof of his desire. Jutting forward from a thatch of black hair, his fully aroused sex twitched under her silent regard.

She shivered, forcing herself to look elsewhere. Wetting her lips, she reached out to touch the leather medallion on his chest. "What is it?"

"Later," he said in a rough voice. Pulling her against him, he wrapped her in his arms, then tumbled the two of them onto the bed.

He ignored her screech of surprise, rolling her onto her back and pushing her legs apart. As he lifted his hips in anticipation of joining his body with hers, Abby said something his desire-fogged brain couldn't understand. Intent on his purpose, he started to thrust forward, but before his manhood did more than brush the damp flesh he desperately needed to plunge into, she spoke again, louder this time.

"Chino!"

The tone of her voice finally penetrated his mind, and he froze. Drawing a shuddering breath, he lifted his head and pinned her with an intent stare. "You said you wanted us to be together. You have changed your mind?"

"No. But not like this. Not for our first time together."

He scowled. "If we join our bodies, that is not being together?"

"Yes, but it shouldn't be like two rutting animals. That's no way to—"

He pushed himself up onto his knees and started to move off her.

"Chino! What are you doing?"

"I cannot do what you want. I do not know any other way."

Abby frowned. "I don't understand what you're trying to tell me."

A flush worked its way up Chino's neck. He couldn't meet her gaze. "I have never been with a White Eyes woman. I do not know how they . . . do . . . this. All I know is how to be—" his voice dropped to a gruff whisper—"a rutting animal."

Abby inhaled with a soft gasp. "Oh, Chino. That's not what I meant. I wasn't calling you an animal. I just meant I didn't want our first time together to be rushed." She managed a shaky laugh. "Actually, on second thought. If it's been as long for you as it has me, our first time could be really quick."

She stroked his cheek with the backs of her knuckles. "Do you understand?"

Several seconds passed while he mulled over her words. Finally, he settled on his side next to her, then released a deep breath. "Yes, I understand. But I am not sure what you want me to do."

She brushed his hair over his shoulder, then

pressed a kiss to his chest. "All I want is for you, for us, to take everything real slow and easy. Make this last as long as we can. Do you think you can do that?"

He gave her a nod. "I will try," he said, though he didn't sound sure of himself.

"I know you will. And so will I. But don't worry if taking this slow doesn't work. The second time it definitely will." Seeing his eyes widen at the mention of a second time, she grinned. "I'm thinking it'll probably be more than twice. So if you have to have more than a couple hours' sleep, you'd better tell me now."

He opened his mouth to reply, then snapped it shut. The shock on his face made Abby bite her lip to hold in a laugh.

She waited, but when he made no effort to speak, she said, "Can I assume you're not objecting?"

His chest rose, then fell with a deep breath. "Yes."

The timbre of his voice sent her pulse into an even faster gallop. Looping her arms around his neck, she whispered, "Kiss me," then pulled his face down to hers.

Chino did as she asked, kissing her just as she'd taught him, nibbling and sucking on her lips, pushing his tongue into her mouth and mimicking what another part of his body longed to make a reality.

Everything Abby taught him quickly became second nature, his hands touching and gliding in much the same way as when he soothed a wild horse. Only running his hands over Abby's silky skin was not meant to sooth or tame. He wanted to excite her, to fire her passion, to make her wild with desire. But pushing her need higher also took his own to greater heights. Though nearing the point of exploding, he managed to hold back by concentrating on Abby.

He kissed her throat, her shoulder, the upper swell of her breast, then moved his lips to the rosy tip. As he circled one puckered nipple with his tongue, she moaned, arching to press her breast closer against him. Complying with her silent plea, he closed his lips around the tight peak and pulled it into his mouth.

"Touch me," she whispered, grabbing his wrist and pushing his hand lower.

His fingers skimmed over the smooth silk of her belly, then eased through the triangle of coppery curls. When he reached the damp folds of her sex, he heard her sigh his name. Smiling against her breast, he rubbed his fingers over the slick flesh, moving with slow deliberation.

"Yes, there," she said, lifting her hips to bring his fingers in better contact with her most sensitive spot.

He released her nipple and raised his head so he could look at her face. Her eyes were slitted, her mouth open, her breathing labored. Fascinated, he rubbed her again, then again, intuitively knowing how to touch her. Her hips moved in concert with every stroke of his fingers. Just watching her, listening to her soft pants, and knowing he was the source of her obvious pleasure, not only stroked his ego but sent his own desire even higher. He never could have imagined wanting a woman as much as he wanted this one. He clenched his teeth, calling on every self-control technique he knew to keep himself in check.

Just when he thought he'd lost the battle, Abby gave a sharp gasp, then her hips pushed against his hand in a faster and faster rhythm. Sobbing his name, she arched up one last time, then dropped back onto the bed and went still.

She opened her eyes and met his gaze, the green flecks glowing in the soft lamplight. "Guess I didn't listen to my own advice, huh?" she said in a breathless voice, then flashed him a smile.

For a moment, Chino's powerful need became secondary to the warmth twining around his heart. Refusing to consider the reason for the sensation in his chest, he returned her smile. "Did you try to take it slow?"

"Yes, but obviously, not very well."

"You tried. That is the important thing."

Abby nodded, her throat nearly closing with another surge of love for the man beside her. Shifting slightly, she felt his swollen manhood nudge her thigh.

Her lips curving in another smile, she slid her

hand between them and wrapped her fingers around him.

His breath hissed through his teeth, his hardened flesh jerking against her hand.

A second gentle squeeze of her fingers, and he needed no further encouragement.

In one swift move, he rolled atop her, parted her legs, then flexed his hips and plunged into her. He heard her draw a quick breath, then exhale with a contented sigh. He knew exactly how she felt. Being inside her, their bodies joined in the most intimate of embraces, made him complete, as if he had found what had been missing in his life. The indescribable moment stole the air from his lungs. Wanting to savor the sensation just a little longer, he tried to hold himself perfectly still.

But his body's craving for relief had other, more urgent plans. Though he tried not to rush, his initial slow rhythm soon gave way to a much faster pace. And when she wrapped her legs around his hips, pushing him even deeper, there was no way he could slow down. Bracing himself on his forearms, he pumped into her welcoming heat again and again, until he was gasping for breath, his skin damp with sweat. Then with a groan, he drove his hips forward one final time. Thousands of bright lights exploded behind his closed eyelids, their intensity as strong as his own explosive release.

His breathing ragged, his arms and legs weak, he

managed to open his eyes. Stunned by what he'd just experienced, he blinked several times, trying to clear the fuzziness from his mind.

When he met Abby's gaze, the look on her face threatened to close his throat. Calling on all the strength he had left, he swallowed hard, then shifted his weight so he could lift one hand and brush a strand of hair off her flushed cheek.

"I also did not listen to your advice," he said, his voice raspy.

She smiled. "That's okay. At least you tried."

"I do not think it is okay," he replied, with a shake of his head. "I did not try very hard."

Her eyebrows arched, and then she burst out laughing. When her laughter died, she wiped her eyes and said, "Well, like you told me, trying is the important thing."

Chino couldn't respond. The emotions filling his chest and pushing up to clog his throat wouldn't allow him to speak. As much as he didn't want to face the truth, he couldn't avoid it any longer. His heart had begun caring for Abby.

He eased away from her, though the narrow bed didn't allow him to move far. As he rolled to one side, she shifted positions so that he ended up on his back, holding her in his arms.

They lay that way for a long time, letting the night air coming in through the window cool their sweat-dampened bodies. Finally she stirred enough to kiss his jaw, then let her head fall back onto his shoulder.

"Penny for your thought," she said.

He exhaled with a whoosh of air. "You speak in riddles again."

"Sorry. Sometimes I forget—" She cleared her throat. "I asked what you were thinking about."

When he didn't respond, she said, "It's okay if you were thinking about your wife."

Again he remained silent.

"I was thinking about Alan. Wondering what his reaction would be if he knew what we just did, if he'd be upset. And you know what? I don't think he'd mind."

"Why do you think that?"

"I loved my husband, and we had a good life together. But Alan was a lot older than I, and we both knew he'd probably go first. Though we never expected him to die when he did, or how he—" She exhaled a deep breath. "Anyway, from the beginning, he tried to prepare me for life after he died. Teaching me how to run this ranch, how to take care of everything to make sure our children always had a roof over their heads. But he also used to tell me he didn't want me to be alone. That he wanted me to be happy."

She kissed the hollow between his neck and shoulder. "And you make me very happy."

Chino chuckled, lifting a hand to smooth the wild tangle of her hair. "And I am happy."

Abby smiled, snuggling closer. "Good."

Another few minutes passed in silence, then she said, "What was her name?"

His hand tightened in her hair. Forcing his fingers to relax, he sighed, then said, "I cannot speak her name."

"It's still too painful for you. I understand. That's how I was when—"

"That is not the reason. My people do not speak the name of someone who has passed to the Spirit World."

"You don't say their name out of respect. Is that what you mean?"

"No. To keep the person's ghost from appearing."

"What?" Abby pushed herself up onto one forearm, and stared down at him. "Did you say ghost?"

He nodded. "The Apache have a great fear of ghosts."

"Why? What are you afraid of?"

"Ghost sickness."

Abby's mouth dropped open. "I think you'd better explain that to me."

"My people believe a person's spirit does not pass to the Spirit World at the moment of death. It remains in the area as a ghost. Relatives must prepare the body for burial, but touching the body means they are in danger of getting ghost sickness."

"I know preparing a corpse for burial is not something anyone wants to do, but getting this 'ghost sickness' from touching a dead person! That's just plain ridiculous."

Chino didn't reply, but directed a scowl at her.

"Have you ever had ghost sickness?"

"Once. I helped bury my mother."

"What was it like?"

"I was weak and afraid of the dark. My head hurt. My chest felt numb."

Abby thought the symptoms sounded more like grief than an actual illness, but kept that opinion to herself. Instead, she said, "So how did you get rid of the sickness?"

"A medicine man in our band performed a cleansing ceremony."

"And, let me guess, this ceremony cured you?"

When he opened his mouth to respond, she held up a hand. "Stupid question. I know about you and the truth." She looked at him for several seconds, then said, "How long does a ghost stay around after a person dies? Your wife died two years ago, so wouldn't her ghost have joined her by now?"

"It is possible. But I cannot risk calling her ghost back."

"By saying her name?"

"Yes, or whistling at night."

"What's wrong with whistling at night?"

"Apache children are taught never to whistle at night. It calls to ghosts who will whistle back and scare them."

Abby shook her head, slightly dazed by what Chino had revealed about the Apache life-way. "Well," she said at last, "that sure tops my mother warning me about bugbears hiding in the woods." Seeing he didn't understand, she added, "It's not important."

She leaned closer, her mouth just inches from his. "I think," she said in a soft whisper, "that it's time to try slow and easy." She pressed a quick kiss on his lips. "That is, if you've recovered enough."

He blinked, then a chuckle rumbled in his chest. "Yes," he replied, "I have recovered." Sliding a hand beneath her hair to cradle the back of her head, he pulled her closer.

"Slow and easy," he murmured before capturing her mouth in a breath-stealing kiss.

This time, no longer blinded by their initial urgency, slow and easy worked. For Chino, who had never made love to his wife more than once in one night, the leisurely pace was both an education and an incredible experience.

As much as he'd wanted Abby the first time, what he'd felt then was nothing compared to the need building in him now. Mesmerized by the woman who touched and kissed him in ways that both shocked and excited him, he was helpless to do anything more than lie on his back and enjoy her incredible skill. Her hands and mouth soon taught him there were many levels of desire. Most he never had imagined, let alone experienced.

His senses dangerously close to the limit of their endurance, he reversed their positions, flipping her onto her back. Hoping to temporarily cool the wild-fire of need sizzling in his veins, he became the one doing the torturous kissing and stroking. Her moans and soft gasps told him his efforts were having the effect he wanted. But they also caused something he hadn't anticipated. Increasing her desire drove his even higher. Using every shred of concentration he could gather, he slowly fanned the banked fire of her need, coaxing the first flicker to burst into flame, then expand into a blazing inferno.

Her response quickly wore down his self-control. When his restraint nearly reached the snapping point, he shifted their positions again and slid into her body with one swift stroke.

He sucked in a quick breath as the tight clench of her inner muscles pushed him closer to the edge. For several seconds, he held still, fighting the urge to seek immediate relief from the pleasure-torment. His heart was pounding like the thundering hooves of a thousand horses.

He finally exhaled a long sigh, then began moving his hips. Trying to ignore the instant return of his white-hot lust, he forced himself to take gentle, lazy strokes. They fit together perfectly, as if they'd been made for one another. Refusing to consider the implications of that thought, he focused on Abby's flushed face, gauging her reaction.

Though he tried to maintain the steady, unhurried pace, to make sure Abby made the journey with him, soon his body stopped obeying his mental commands. His need was too great to hold back any longer. With the severing of the last thread of his self-control, slow and easy became fast and frenzied.

Chino fought the encroaching blackness long enough to pray that Abby would join him, then gave himself over to the mindless darkness of his body's quest for release. His hips pumping harder and faster, he thrust into her as far as he could, nearly withdrew then plunged back into her moist heat.

Somehow his mind cleared enough to hear Abby gasp his name, then her back arched—welcome signals that she had reached the pinnacle just ahead of him. As her body convulsed, squeezing his hardened flesh even more, he gave a guttural cry, then exploded in a series of intense throbs. Totally drained, his arms weak and trembling, he collapsed atop her, pressing his face against her neck.

Abby felt as if she were floating, her body limp and weightless in the aftermath of spent passion. As her breathing slowed to normal, her mind whirled with the magnitude of what had just happened. Making love with Chino went far beyond anything she'd expected. She realized she wasn't falling in love with him. She already had.

Not wanting to think about that and what would happen to her love when he left, she blinked away a sudden spurt of tears. When she could trust her voice, she said, "Didn't I tell you slow and easy would be good?"

She felt his chest expand with a deep breath. As he exhaled, he pushed himself up onto his forearms, then lifted his head. His eyes sparkling, he gave her a crooked smile. "More than good."

Abby thought her heart might burst. The strength of her love for this man nearly overwhelmed her. Determined not to think about her feelings for Chino, or what the future held, she promised herself to think only of the present. To enjoy whatever time they had together. She had the rest of her life to deal with losing another man she loved.

Chapter Fourteen

Chino awoke slowly, his mind and body sluggish in responding to the light pouring through the bunkhouse window. Surprised he'd slept so late and so soundly, he extended his arms and legs in a lazy stretch. The slight pull of well-used muscles gave him another surprise. Then memories from the night before came flooding back, supplying the reason for his sound sleep and his tight muscles. Abby.

As he headed to the creek to bathe, he recalled every minute he'd spent with Abby—the softness of her mouth, the scrape of her teeth on his lip, the eagerness of her touch. His manhood stirred at the thought of Abby's hands moving over his body, searching out the places that pushed his desire even higher. He still couldn't believe how he'd reacted. The self-control he'd been taught to maintain at all times, the cornerstone of being Apache, had left him in a flash. Desire, wild and hot, had overtaken him so completely that he'd been unable to think of anything except wallowing in the sensations Abby created in him.

The night he'd spent with her, sharing the passion that exploded between them, was like none he'd ever experienced. He recalled the taste of her, the hardened tips of her breasts. The scent and texture of her skin. The slick heat between her thighs. Recalling his reaction to all those things, another surge of desire slammed into him. Never had he behaved with such boldness. Not even with his wife.

He sucked in a quick breath, then stumbled to a halt. Heart pounding, he waited for the sharp sting of grief. But rather than the usual twisting pain in his chest, he felt only a gentle ache.

He frowned. His heart had cared deeply for his wife, so why did thinking of her no longer make him feel as if he'd been slashed with a knife? Especially after spending an intimate night with another woman.

Disturbed by the direction of his thoughts, he frowned more deeply. No, he told himself, the answer that came to mind wasn't possible. What he'd felt after the first time with Abby couldn't be real. The flood of emotion was a natural reaction to satisfied passion, nothing more. Wasn't it? Or had his heart, as he'd thought the night before, truly begun to care for her? Unwilling to contemplate an affirmative answer, he gave his head a shake to chase away the troubling thoughts, then resumed his trek to the creek.

He needed to concentrate on keeping Abby's horses safe and making sure she held on to the Flying M. He couldn't afford to waste his time thinking about a woman who could not have a permanent place in his future—a future that at best remained uncertain. Once he had accomplished what his visions had sent him here to do, Abby would no longer need him, and he would be free to leave, though he still didn't know where he would go, or what he would do.

For the past two years, he'd lived every day with only one goal in mind—fulfilling his quest for revenge. Beyond that, his only plan for the future was to live out his years in solitude, with no commitments, no responsibilities. Now the prospect of such a lonely existence no longer held any appeal, but filled him with bone-deep sadness.

Abby tried to talk herself out of going to Chino two nights later. She knew the consequences of her actions. Knew that continuing an intimate relationship would result in more heartache when he finally left the ranch. But she also knew life was too precious to waste—a lesson she'd learned when Alan died. Therefore, she planned to take advantage of whatever time she and Chino had left. There might never be another man in her life. One she desired as much as she did Chino. One who would capture her heart just as he had done. Living in such a remote part of Arizona Territory made that a very real possibility. So she wanted to tuck away as many memories as she could, memories to pull out and relive in the years ahead.

She drew a deep breath, then exhaled slowly. In spite of her misgivings, she left the ranch house and started across the yard. The glow of lamplight in the bunkhouse window served as a beacon, drawing her to the man she could no more stop wanting than she could stop the sun from rising every morning.

She cracked open the door, then whispered his name.

"I am here."

Her pulse quickening at the sound of his voice, she entered the room, closed the door behind her, then turned to watch him rise from his bunk.

He moved closer. "It is late. I thought you would not come."

She lifted her gaze to meet his. "I considered it," she said, surprising herself with her honesty. "But I can't stay away from you." She lifted a hand to touch his mouth, then trailed her fingertips across a high cheekbone and down the cord on one side of his neck. His answering shiver made her smile. "And unless I'm badly mistaken—" she rose onto her toes and gave him a quick kiss—"I think you feel the same way about me."

"It is true," he said.

Her gaze shifted to the leather medallion hanging around his neck. "I keep meaning to ask about this—" she touched a finger to what looked like a horse painted on the leather disk—"but something always distracts me."

His eyes widened, humor dancing in their dark depths. "I do that?"

She gave him a playful punch on the arm. "Of course, you do. You're one powerful distraction, Mr. Whitehorse."

He touched a finger to her chin. "You think that is so?"

She nodded. "It is true."

He smiled at her choice of words, then shifted his hand to brush a wisp of hair off her face. "You are also a distraction for me."

"Well, before all this distracting gets out of hand," she replied in a thick voice, "will you tell me about the necklace?"

His smile slowly fading, he stroked a finger over her cheek, then moved his hand to clasp the leather medallion. "Yes, I will tell you."

He remained silent for a moment, then said, "I wear this to ask the Spirit of my horse power to protect me."

"Hmm, sort of like a good-luck charm, I guess."

She watched him idly rub his thumb over the front of the medallion before saying, "So what's it supposed to protect you against?"

"Evil spirits. Ghosts."

Her eyebrows rose, but rather than commenting on his response, she nodded at one of the white beads dangling from his ears. "Is that also the reason you wear earrings?"

He shook his head. "Apache ear strings are not for protection. Our ears are pierced when we are in our cradle boards by our mother or grandmother. They do this to make us grow faster and hear sooner so we will obey quicker."

"Really?" Abby swallowed the urge to laugh, then cleared her throat. "What about other Apache men, do they wear a necklace to protect them?"

"Some do. Like this, with a painted symbol of their power source, or made from animal teeth or claws. Some Apache wear a small deerskin pouch around the neck, or at the waist. It is a medicine bag."

"What's inside?"

"Could be many things," he replied with a shrug. "Things that have special meaning. A blue stone, the one White Eyes call turquoise, the root of the plant that prevents sickness and something that connects them to their power source."

"Give me an example."

"If a man's power source is the eagle, his medicine bag might have a feather or claw from an eagle."

She nodded, once again realizing the vast differences in their cultures. Yet despite the disparities, they possessed some of the same values, values she deeply admired—willingness to work hard, loyalty to family, love of horses. Surely, such common ground would be enough of a base for a man and woman to build on, to create a life together.

A sudden lump filled her throat. She had to stop letting her mind wander into territory she should avoid. Nothing would be gained by thinking about a future with Chino, a future that could not be. Too bad she couldn't control the dictates of her heart, then she wouldn't have—Chino's voice pulled her from her melancholy thoughts.

She blinked several times, then looked up to see his brow furrowed and his eyes filled with concern. Ignoring the tightness in her chest, she released a shuddering breath. "I'm sorry, what did you say?"

"I asked if something is wrong."

She shook her head, forcing her lips to curve in a smile. "No, just woolgathering."

"What is woolgathering?"

Abby chuckled, his confusion chasing away the last of her gloomy mood. "It means daydreaming."

"Ah." He nodded, then brushed another lock of hair off her face. "Your daydreams were not good dreams. I saw sadness in your eyes."

"It was nothing," she replied, grabbing his wrist when he started to withdraw his hand. With her gaze locked on his, she brought his hand to her mouth. The heat swirling in the inky depths of his eyes mesmerized her as she swiped the tip of her tongue across his palm, slowly, deliberately. Rewarded by the surprised catch in his breathing, she repeated the action.

A growl rumbled in his throat. "If you are playing a game," he said in a whisper, "I do not know the rules."

She stared at him a moment longer, then dropped his hand. "No, it's not a game," she said, hoping her expression didn't reveal the truth. In fact, she was playing a game, a very dangerous game of the heart, one she had no chance of winning. Pushing that thought aside, she managed a smile. "I was just having some fun. But if you'd like to play a game. I'm sure I can think of something. One we'd both enjoy."

He crossed his arms over his bare chest. "What kind of game?"

"Oh, I don't know. Maybe, a contest to see which of us can undress the fastest."

One eyebrow arched, he glanced down at his trousers and bare feet, then returned his gaze to her face. "There must be something wrong with your eyes. You could not win such a game."

She lifted a shoulder in a shrug. "Who said I wanted to win?"

He stared at her for several seconds, then burst

out laughing. "I have never met a woman like you."

"I hope that's good."

"Yes," he replied, picking up a strand of her hair. "It is good." Rubbing her hair between his fingers, he swept his gaze over her. The hunger in his eyes devoured her in a lazy perusal from her face to her toes, and then back again. He released her hair, then whispered, "Very good."

Her pulse thundering in her ears, Abby swallowed hard and tried to ignore the sudden flood of love rushing through her veins. Tilting her head to one side, she said, "So, are you ready to play my game, or not?"

With a chuckle, he took a step back. "If that is the game you want to play, I am ready."

"Okay, then on the count of three, take off your clothes."

A smile teasing his mouth, he nodded.

"One. Two. Three."

Abby turned her back, then reached for the buttons on the front of her blouse, working each free as quickly as she could. When she got to the bottom button, she snuck a peak over her shoulder. Chino had tugged off one leg of his buckskin trousers and was working on the opposite leg. She cast a quick, appreciative gaze over the flexing muscles of his bare bottom while shrugging out of her blouse. Her pulse quickening, she freed the button of her skirt and shoved the fabric down over her hips in one smooth motion.

As she stepped out of the garment, Chino said, "I win."

She straightened, then slowly turned around. "You don't mind if I check, do you?"

He frowned. "What is there to check? You can see I am naked. That means, I—" The furrows in his brow disappeared. "Ah, I understand." He widened his stance, shoved his hair over his shoulders, then relaxed his arms at his sides. "You did not care about winning, because you wanted to look at me this way."

She acknowledged his statement with a slight nod and a smile. Taking her time, she looked at him, drinking in his male beauty with her eyes, her mind and her heart. "Turn around," she managed to say in a less-than-steady voice.

His eyebrows lifted, but he said nothing as he followed her instructions.

After several seconds, Abby drew a deep breath, then released it slowly. "You were right. You definitely won."

He turned back, his eyes sparkling with humor. "You are sure? You do not want to look some more? To make sure of my victory."

Though Abby longed to say she could never look at him enough, she kept that thought to herself. Instead, she said, "That's not necessary. I'm convinced."

With swift movements, she dispensed with the rest of her clothes. "No more games," she said, holding out a hand to him. "Come, lie down with me."

Chino didn't hesitate, but placed his hand in hers, then let her lead him to his bed.

As they stretched out on the narrow bunk, he wrapped his arms around her and pulled her against him. The sensation of her breasts pressed to his chest, their hardened tips burning into his skin, started a buzzing in his head and a wild pounding of his heart. He nuzzled the side of her neck, then the delicate skin on the underside of her jaw, before settling his mouth over hers.

She groaned, eagerly participating in the kiss. Wiggling closer, she pushed her hips forward, capturing his hardened flesh between their bodies. Her fingers grasping handfuls of his hair, she rubbed her belly against him, each move slow and deliberate.

This time he groaned, the erotic gliding of her silken skin on his aroused flesh almost more than he could bear. His hips flexed of their own accord, his manhood throbbing with the need to once again claim her as his.

He tore his mouth from hers. "Enough."

She shifted positions, rising onto her knees then bending to press her lips to the base of his throat. In a series of kisses, she moved to his chest, leaving a trail of fire wherever her lips touched. She laved her tongue over one of his nipples, making him jerk as if he'd been shot.

She stopped instantly. "Did I hurt you?" she asked, her voice low and slightly breathless.

Unable to speak, he managed to move his head in a negative response.

"Good." He could hear the smile in her voice. "Because I've just begun."

He sucked in a deep breath, trying to prepare himself for more of her torture-pleasure. And as her tongue dipped into his navel and her fingers encircled his hardened sex, he squeezed his eyes shut, his hands curling over the sides of the bunk.

She kissed his belly, her hand sliding up, then down his aching flesh. When her hand stilled, he relaxed, certain he would have to endure no—His breath hissing through his teeth, he went rigid.

Certain he had to be mistaken, he lifted his head. He blinked, then stared in shock at Abby's head bent over his groin, her hair spread across his thighs in a bright tangle of reddish-brown. Before his mind fully accepted that her tongue had indeed touched the tip of his manhood, she took him into her mouth.

He gave a strangled gasp, his hips jerking upward in reaction to the fire of need roaring through him. A moan rumbled in his chest, his head fell back onto the bed and the blood pounded so hard in his ears that all other sound faded. He lay powerless, caught in the snare of her intimate onslaught.

Nothing in his past experience had prepared him for the incredible pull of her mouth, the indescribable swirling flick of her tongue. Though he willed himself to remain still, his body refused to obey. Soon his hips began moving, driving his need even higher, pushing him closer and closer to the release his body craved.

When he could take no more, he grabbed her arm and managed to force a croaked, "Stop," through his dry throat.

Abby went still at his command. She slowly released him, then straightened. Shaking her hair off her face, she wiped the back of one hand over her mouth and met his gaze.

"What's wrong? I thought you liked—"

"I did like what you—" He huffed out a breath, releasing his grip on her arm. "I made you stop because I was close to—" A muscle worked in his jaw. "I have never done . . . that, and I did not know what—" He couldn't find the words to discuss such a personal subject.

She stared at him for several seconds, then gave him a gentle smile. "I understand. I didn't mean to make you uncomfortable. I just wanted to give you pleasure."

When he didn't respond, she said, "Did I do something that isn't allowed by your people?"

"I know of nothing in our life-way that forbids what you did." He flashed a quick smile. "I am glad there is not."

"Me, too."

He lifted a hand and stroked her cheek. He longed to tell her what was in his heart, that he was beginning to care deeply for her, but he did not speak the words. She might desire him, but he knew that was temporary. Her need eventually would lessen, and her hatred of his people would return. Then, she would push him away—just as the White Eyes continued to push all Apache away.

He was forced to face another bitter truth. In spite of his growing feelings for Abby, there could be no permanent place for him in her life. Once he had fulfilled the directives of the Spirits, he would ride away from the Flying M. But when he did, he feared his heart would be left behind.

He tightened his jaw. He was Apache, trained to withstand great physical pain without making a sound. He had endured much pain, survived when he thought it wasn't possible, and he could do it again. Closing his eyes, he offered a quick prayer to the Great Spirit, asking for the strength he needed to survive without Abby.

Several seconds passed, then he opened his eyes and met her gaze. Hoping to ease the concern he saw on her face, he said, "Do not worry. I am fine."

Abby drew a shuddering breath. "You looked like

235

you were in pain. Are you sure you're okay?"

At his nod, she said, "And you're truly not upset because of what I did?"

"No."

She stared at him a moment longer. Satisfied with his response, she smiled. "Well then, is there any reason why we can't continue?"

"I do not know of a reason."

"Just what I wanted to hear." She shifted positions until she lay stretched out beside him, then nuzzled his neck. "Hmm, I love the smell of your skin. The scent makes me so—I don't know how to describe how it makes me feel."

Chino wrapped an arm around her waist, holding her close to his side. Using his other hand, he toyed with her hair. "Your scent makes me feel like I drank too much of the White Eyes' whiskey."

She smiled against his neck. "Drunk! Yes, that's it exactly."

His chest shook with silent laughter. "Again, you surprise me. I have not seen you drink whiskey."

"I don't as a general rule. Alan used to say a shot of whiskey now and then strengthens the blood, so it was always around. Sometimes I would have a drink with him, but I only drank too much one time. We were celebrating our arrival here at the ranch. Believe me, the way I felt the next morning cured me of overindulging."

"Yes, escaping with whiskey is not worth the aching head, the sickness."

Though Abby wanted to ask if he'd used whiskey as an escape, she didn't, not wanting to bring up what surely must be a sensitive subject, especially when there were more pleasant ways to spend their time together.

She shifted again, this time moving so she lay atop him. "I have a better idea for escape." She wiggled her hips, rubbing her belly across his arousal. Feeling the responding twitch of the hardened flesh caught between their bodies, she wiggled her hips again.

He groaned, then pushed his pelvis upward, grinding his manhood against her.

She smiled. "So you have the same idea, huh?"

"Yes," he whispered, grasping her bottom to hold her more firmly in place.

Abby braced her hands on his chest, then pulled her knees up so that she sat astride his thighs.

"Hmm, I like this," she said. Wrapping her fingers around his manhood, she adjusted her position, then took him into her with one quick downward movement of her hips. She gave a soft gasp, her eyes drifting closed. Holding perfectly still for several seconds, she allowed herself to savor the incredible pleasure rippling through her.

When she opened her eyes, she found Chino staring at her, the banked fire of need making his eyes shine like polished stone in the lamplight. Holding his gaze, she began moving in a slow, easy rhythm. Each time she lifted then lowered her hips, the fire in his eyes burned even hotter.

He cupped her breasts, and brushed a thumb over each tightened nipple, causing a moan to vibrate in her throat. Then abruptly, he released her breasts and clutched her hips, taking control of the thrusts of their bodies. He pushed into her as far as possible, then dropped his hips while lifting her with his hands so that he nearly withdrew. With each successive stroke, he increased the pace.

The heat simmering between her thighs turned into a wild throbbing. The pressure continued to build, becoming more insistent, more consuming. Then she was there, approaching the pinnacle of her release. Digging her fingers into his arms, she pushed against him harder, faster, desperate to reach the top.

"Chino, please," she said in a raspy whisper.

When he didn't react, she grabbed his hand and moved it toward where they were joined. "Please," she said again. "Touch me."

His fingers sliding over the damp flesh between her thighs, he found the sensitive bud. Continuing the thrusts of his hips, he stroked her with his fingers.

She moaned. Yes. Yes. Her breathing harsh, her pulse pounding in her ears, she scaled the final peak and sailed over the edge. As her release began, one powerful spasm after another racking her body, she gave herself over to mind-numbing pleasure.

"Chino," she said in a gasping whisper, "I love you, Chino."

When the spasms finally stopped, she inhaled a shuddering breath, then collapsed onto his chest.

Chapter Fifteen

Something teased the back of Abby's mind. Something important. Something she needed to remember. But the fuzzy thought remained trapped on the fringe of her brain, hopelessly tangled in the hazy afterglow of her release. Before she could clear her senses enough to figure out the puzzle, Chino flipped her onto her back, spread her thighs and pushed his straining sex into her.

Now that she was filled with him, her legs wrapped around his hips, the need to capture an elusive memory lost its importance. She focused her full concentration on the man poised above her.

Gone was the gentle lover. He became fierce, almost wild, using all his strength and energy to pump into her with an intensity that bordered on desperation. She thought her climax had wrung her dry, that her body couldn't possibly respond again so soon. But she was mistaken. Almost immediately, the heat started to build again, quickly escalating to a throbbing ache. She came alive beneath him. Becoming as wild as he, she thrashed her head from side to side, pushing her hips up to meet each of his downward thrusts, clawing at his back.

Then she was flying again, gliding on the wings of another release. She cried out, her voice trailing away on a low, keening sob.

He responded with a groan that sounded like it had been ripped from his throat. Head thrown back, he pushed into her again, then twice more before his hips bucked forward a final time. He went still, nostrils flared, breathing ragged. Gasping her name, he shook with the force of his release. With one powerful throb after another, he spilled his seed deep inside her.

After several seconds, he inhaled a quavering breath and tried to move. His arms shook with the effort then collapsed, pitching him forward to sprawl atop her. He groaned, trying again to move.

"Stay," she murmured.

"I will hurt you."

"No, you won't."

Though he made no further protests, he shifted one hand enough to curl his fingers around a strand of her hair. "So soft," he whispered.

Abby smiled, reveling in the warmth of his breath

241

on her neck, the pleasant crush of his body, the dampness of his skin. She couldn't imagine a better feeling than lying this way with the man she loved. Loved! Oh, dear God, that was the memory her mind had tried to dig up.

She'd told Chino she loved him. Though she'd had no plans to confess her love, hadn't meant to say the words, they'd slipped out in a moment of passion. There was no point in chastising herself. What was done, was done. Still, in spite of having allowed her heart to rule her tongue, she wondered if she should do something, or say something.

Maybe she should retract her declaration, tell him she didn't want to give him the wrong impression, that she simply got carried away. No, she couldn't do that. Even if she were willing to lie to him, retracting her words would only draw attention to the admission she'd made. And raise questions she didn't want to answer.

Maybe she could pretend she hadn't said anything and hope Chino had been so caught up in their lovemaking that her words hadn't registered.

Yes, that seemed the best course of action—one she hoped wouldn't be a mistake.

Over the next week, Abby's life settled into a routine. Her days were the same as always: She rose at dawn, taking care of her normal load of chores and continuing her children's lessons. Her added responsibility to her daily pattern was keeping watch for anything unusual, anything to signal that Warner had made another move. But after the sun went down, she sought out Chino. For a few hours every evening, he took her mind off the problems facing them, making her forget everything but enjoying the sensual journeys they made together.

Although she hadn't thought it possible, each day she loved him more. At first, her growing feelings for Chino disturbed her. She worried that she was somehow tarnishing the love she'd had for her husband. Alan had been her first love, and he would always hold a special place in her heart. But she'd come to realize that since she'd lost him she'd matured, grown into a woman capable of more than she'd ever imagined. Now she was ready for a different, much deeper kind of love, and a man who was the other half of her soul. Chino Whitehorse.

She'd never given any serious thought to the idea of destiny, that the path a person took in life was predetermined. But now she was intrigued by the possibility that she'd been destined to meet and fall in love with Chino. And more intriguing, if that was true, could there be a future for them?

Though her heart cried yes, the logical part of her mind gave a different answer.

Early one afternoon, Abby had finally succeeded in getting Susanna to take a nap, when Teddy's voice echoed through the house.

"Momma. Momma. Come quick."

She left the bedroom door cracked, then hurried down the hall. "Teddy, not so loud," she said in a low voice. "I just got your sister to sleep.

"Sorry," he said, his bottom lip sticking out.

She ruffled his hair. "It's okay, son. Now what's all the excitement about?"

"Someone's coming."

Abby's heart gave an extra thump. "Could you see who it is?"

Teddy shook his head. "They're too far away. But one of the horses looks like the one that Mr. Warner rides."

Warner! Just thinking the name caused a bad taste in her mouth. "Did they see you?"

"Don't think so. I was waitin' under the tree in front, cuz Chino's gonna show me how to make rope outta rawhide. Anyways, when I saw the horses comin' up the road, I came in here to get ya."

"You did the right thing, sweetheart. Do you know where Chino is?"

"In the barn, getting the rawhide for my lesson."

"Okay. I want you to go out onto the ramada. Marita is there. Stay with her until I get back."

He frowned. "But what about my lesson?"

"It'll have to wait until later. Now do what I told you."

The boy looked like he was going to voice another

protest, but changed his mind and stomped toward the rear of the house.

Once Abby heard the back door open and close, she drew a deep breath to steady her nerves, then marched outside.

She moved to the center of the yard and stopped, watching the approaching riders. Teddy was right. There was no mistaking the horse in the lead, Neville Warner's black-and-white pinto.

The four men halted their horses twenty feet away. Abby swept her gaze past Warner to the others. One she recognized from a previous visit. The other two didn't look familiar. Returning her gaze to Warner, she watched him look around the ranch yard, then urge his horse forward. He stopped a few feet away, dismounted, then walked toward her.

Though Abby longed to shriek her outrage at him, she forced herself to remain calm.

"What can I do for you, Mr. Warner?"

He pushed his hat off his forehead with a thumb, revealing the pinched expression on his face. "I told you before, Abby, call me Neville."

"All right . . . Neville, what the hell are you doing here?"

"Come, come, Abby, is that any way to speak to a friend?"

"You're not a friend, Neville, and if you came to make another offer to buy the Flying M, you rode a long way for nothing. My answer is still no."

Anger flashed in his eyes. A muscle ticked in his cheek. He took a deep breath, obviously trying to regain his composure. "You're speaking in haste again, my dear, which is a foolish thing to do."

Though Abby's skin crawled at his endearment, she bit back the retort she longed to make. Instead, she said, "It doesn't matter how many times you come here, how many times you extend your offer. Get it through your head, I have no intention of selling my ranch. Not now. Not ever."

Warner's face flushed a deep red. "You're more of a fool than I originally thought," he ground out, his voice quivering with rage. He looked toward the barn, then back at her. "Where is he?"

"Who?"

"Don't play the innocent with me. I know ya got a pet red devil around here. He ain't much help to you if he's off hiding someplace, afraid to show his face."

Abby's heart leaped to her throat. How could he know about Chino? "Who's on my ranch is my business."

Warner rocked back on his heels. "So, ya aren't denying it." His mouth twisting with what could only be described as an evil grin, he said, "Must be he's crawling between yer legs." He scratched his chin. "Guess I should have thought of that. A young, comely widow, with no man to take care of her needs. Needs I could've satisfied."

Before Abby could overcome her shock and form a reply, he moved closer. Leaning forward until his face was just inches from hers, he said, "But it's too late for that now. I wouldn't touch a woman who'd been used by a filthy savage." He took a step back, then brushed a hand over the front of his shirt, as if ridding himself of something dirty.

The very idea that being close to her had somehow soiled his clothes pushed Abby's temper a notch higher, but by gritting her teeth, she managed to hold it in check. Lifting her chin, she said, "You're not welcome on my ranch, Mr. Warner. I want you to leave. And this time, do not come back. Ever."

"Oh, I'm leaving, all right. But not before I say my piece. I warned you the last time I came here that things have a way of changing. So let me give some more advice—advice you'd be wise to accept. You'll be making a mistake, a big mistake, if you don't agree to sell me the Flying M." He glanced around the ranch yard again, then added, "If you don't, the consequences could be—" his lips curved in a mocking smile—"severe. Real severe."

Not waiting for her reply, he turned, nodded to his men, then mounted the pinto.

Abby watched them gallop away, her temper nearing the boiling point. The nerve of that man! When the riders were out of sight, she sucked in several deep, calming breaths. Closing her eyes, she willed her anger to cool. She had to get herself back in control before the children saw her.

When she opened her eyes, Chino stood in front of her, his gaze riveted on hers. Not surprised by his silent approach, she gave him a weak smile. "Did you hear any of that?"

He nodded, his lips pressed into a thin line.

"What a pathetic excuse for a human being. Damn that man's soul to hell. If he even has a soul."

"What will you do?"

Her chin came up. "Well, I'm not giving in to his threats. The only way he'll get this ranch is over my dead body."

Chino stepped closer, her words sending a shiver of alarm racing up his spine. Touching her cheek with his fingertips, he said, "Do not say that. If something happened to you, I could not—" Shocked that he'd nearly admitted he could not survive the death of another woman his heart cared for, he cleared his throat, then said, "I could not bear to see your children lose their mother."

Abby grasped his hand and pressed a kiss to his palm. "Don't worry, I won't do anything stupid. My children lost one parent, and I have no intention of letting them become orphans." Dropping his hand, she turned to look in the direction Warner had taken.

After a moment, she said, "I wonder how he found out about you."

"Someone saw me. Maybe the one who shot at the horses."

"Yes, maybe." She scanned the surrounding hills. "Or maybe he's got someone watching the ranch." Her eyes narrowed, her fingers curling into fists. "Just the thought of someone spying on us makes me so furious I could scream. If I find out who's responsible, he'd better hope he never crosses the sights of my rifle."

"If I find him first, you will not need your rifle."

The harshness in his voice brought Abby's gaze back to his face. Though she wanted to ask what he would do, his fierce expression warned her off. "Well," she said at last, "we have to find out who he is before either one of us can do anything to stop him."

Chino nodded, then said, "I must find Teddy, so I can begin his lesson." He raised one hand, showing her the strips of rawhide she hadn't noticed before.

"I told him to stay on the ramada with Marita."

He nodded again, then started to walk away.

"Chino?"

He stopped and turned back to her.

"Will you come to my room tonight?" When his eyebrows lifted, she said, "After Warner's threat, I won't feel comfortable leaving the children alone in the house."

When he didn't respond, she gave him a pleading look. "Please. I need you with me tonight."

He stared at her long and hard, then finally said, "I will come."

Neville Warner galloped into the yard of his ranch headquarters, then jerked his horse to an abrupt halt in front of the barn. Dismounting, he tossed the reins to the stable boy. He yelled for his men to follow him into the house.

A few minutes later, he sat behind his desk, a bottle of whiskey in front of him. After pouring the amber liquor into a glass, he looked at the men standing on the opposite side of his desk.

"We need to make some adjustments to my strategy." He tossed back the whiskey, gritting his teeth against the burning in his throat. "No damn Injun-loving woman is gonna stand in the way of me getting what I want."

"We saw no *indio, jefe,*" one man said.

"I guarantee," Warner replied, splashing another healthy dose of whiskey into his glass, "he was there. But one filthy savage ain't gonna stop me. I need the Flying M for my cattle, and I aim to have it."

"More cattle will be here in a few weeks."

"Dammit, I know that!"

He sat back in his chair, sipping the whiskey and contemplating the situation. Finally, he said, "It's time to stop pussyfooting around. Show the Madison woman I'm dead serious. And if that savage gets in the way—" he grinned—"I got no objection if he . . . let's just say, disappears."

The other men smiled, then one said, "You have a plan, *jefe?*"

"I got an idea." He downed the last of his whiskey, then leaned forward to reach for the bottle. "But I need to think on it a spell. Get on back to the bunkhouse. I'll send for ya once I work out the details."

Abby stood at her bedroom window, staring out at the Arizona night, at the stars studding the blue-black sky. Normally, she loved to look at the night-time sky. But that night she found no joy in the twinkling stars. Fear clutched at her insides. Fear that she would be unable to keep the Flying M.

A whisper of sound pulled her from her musings. Turning, she saw Chino enter the room, then close the door.

Before he could take more than a step, she rushed to him. A tiny sob escaped her throat as she threw herself against him.

He staggered back a step, his hands automatically grasping her waist. "What is wrong?"

She drew a shuddering breath. "Nothing," she said, her face pressed to his neck. "I'm just glad you're here."

"I told you I would come to you."

"I know. I can't stop thinking about Neville Warner, about what he said. But now that you're here, I feel . . . I feel like everything will be all right."

She lifted her head, then leaned back so she could meet his gaze. "You probably think I'm being silly."

He shook his head. "You are many things. But you are not silly."

A weak smile curved her mouth, and she eased out of his embrace. "I knew you'd cheer me up."

"I will do much more," he replied, his eyebrows arched, "if you are interested."

The last of her anxiety slipping away, she moved back into his arms. "Oh, yes," she said, running her hands up his chest, then around his neck, "I'm definitely interested." Rising onto her toes, she pressed her mouth to his.

The fire simmering in her blood flared to life, setting Abby's body ablaze with quivering need. Deepening the kiss, she pressed closer, tightened her arms around his neck and rubbed her breasts against him.

With a groan he grabbed her shoulders and gently set her away from him. When she opened her mouth to protest, he silenced her by reaching for the button at the neck of her dress.

She blinked with surprise, then grabbed his shirt and tugged the fabric from the waistband of his trousers.

They needed only a few moments to pull off their clothes, then fall onto Abby's bed. Rolling and twisting, sighing and gasping, they kissed and touched, stoking the flames of need higher and higher.

Soon touches and kisses weren't enough for Abby. She became desperate for more, desperate to have the last of her fears erased. Only Chino could give her those things. She clutched at him, nipped him with her teeth, ground her hips against him.

Chino understood Abby's bold behavior. It was a natural reaction to her encounter with Warner, an attempt to forget his threats, to calm her fears, by seeking a physical bond. Her desperation sent his own desire to new heights, drove him to return her fevered kisses, her frenzied caresses, with an intensity that soon rivaled hers.

Her breathing harsh, she shoved him onto his back and positioned herself atop him. She joined their bodies in one swift move, then went still, a growl ripped from her throat.

Then she started moving, wild and demanding. She rubbed herself against him, riding him, pushing him to increase the pace. He grasped her waist, meeting her stroke for stroke in a coupling that quickly became frantic and fierce, nearly bordering on violent.

Her fingers digging into his arms, she continued her passionate assault, then sucking in a sharp breath, she abruptly froze for a heartbeat. Gasping his name, she arched her back and slid over the edge, her body quaking with the first spasm of her release.

Chino clenched his jaw, tried to hold back. But

the strong contractions of her inner muscles were more than he could bear. Closing his eyes, he thrust his hips upward once, twice. Then with a deep groan, he pushed up a final time, giving himself over to the powerful throbs of his climax.

When the pounding in her ears quieted, somehow Abby found the strength to move. She eased off Chino and rolled onto her back beside him.

After several minutes, she stretched, drew a deep breath, then exhaled with a sigh. "I wonder if this is rare."

"What do you mean?"

"This passion between us." She turned her head, watching him lever himself up onto a forearm. "It's like magic. I just have to look at you, touch you—" she shivered, though not from cold—"and I'm on fire."

He trailed his fingers along her arm. "It is the same for me."

She studied him in silence for a moment, then said, "It wasn't this way with Alan. I mean, we were very compatible in the . . . um . . . intimate part of our marriage. But nothing like what I feel with you."

"It is true," he said, bending to run his tongue over one erect nipple. "What we share is rare."

"Yes," she murmured, dismayed to feel tears stinging her eyes. Determined not to think about a future without Chino Whitehorse, she blinked away her tears and managed a smile. "I wish we could go to the creek."

"Why?"

"A quick dip in the water would feel wonderful right now." She sighed. "But we can't leave the children alone."

"You can go. I will stay here."

"Thanks," she replied, her heart swelling with another surge of love. "But if we can't go together, I'd rather not go at all."

Chino got out of bed, then started toward the door.

"Where are you going?"

He looked over his shoulder, and smiled. "I will not be long."

"But what . . ." His naked form disappeared through the doorway, leaving her alone to speculate on the reason for his sudden departure.

Chapter Sixteen

By the time Abby had slipped on a robe and returned from checking on Teddy and Susanna, Chino was back in her bedroom.

He stood in the middle of the room, arms crossed over his chest. A bucket sat on the floor near his feet.

"What's this?" she said, stepping into the room and easing the door shut behind her.

"You could not go to the creek." He indicated the bucket. "So I brought some of it to you."

Her eyebrows rose. "You did that for me?"

He nodded. "It is not the same as taking a bath in the creek. But the water will cool you."

She stared at him, her lips curving into a slow smile. "You truly are an extraordinary man, Chino Whitehorse."

He gave her a considering look. "You are using sweet words so I will help you?"

She blinked with surprise, then tipped back her head and laughed, her mood more carefree than she could have imagined a few hours earlier. Wiping the moisture from her eyes, she said, "I don't know. Are you saying you'd be interested in helping me?"

He shrugged, his eyes glowing with an emotion she wished she could read. "It is possible."

She pursed her lips into a mock pout. "Only possible, hmm, that's not very encouraging." Loosening the tie of her robe, she took a step toward him. "I'll have to think of something to make the idea—" she let the robe slide off her shoulders—"more appealing."

His gaze moved over her, lingering on her breasts and the triangle of hair between her thighs. He swallowed, then lifted his head and looked into her eyes. "Come here," he whispered in a raspy voice, unfolding his arms and wiggling his fingers at her. "Let me wash you."

Her shoulders rippling with a shiver of anticipation, she stepped closer.

She watched him bend to pick up a cloth, dip it in the bucket then squeeze out the excess water, fascinated by the flexing of muscles beneath the bronze skin of his back and arms. When he straightened and reached for her, the chaotic pounding of her pulse against her eardrums drowned out all other sound.

At the first touch of the wet cloth, she sucked in a sharp breath, shocked that the creek water had the opposite effect from what she'd expected. Rather than cooling her, it set her on fire.

He washed her arms and shoulders, then spent a great deal of time on her breasts, before finally moving to her belly. Little sizzles of desire danced over her body. A dull throb started between her thighs. She bit her lip to keep from crying out, but a whimper escaped.

If he was aware of how his ministrations affected her, he gave no sign. His expression remained impassive, although she could tell by the hard set of his jaw that his teeth were clenched.

He dipped the cloth in the pail again, then knelt in front of her. Beginning at the side of one hip, he ran the cloth down the full length of her leg. At her ankle, he started the return journey, this time on the inside. When he reached her inner thigh, her breath caught in her throat. Would he really wash her *there?*

The question had barely formed in her head when his hand inched higher. He brushed the cloth over her, with slow, infinite care. She bit down harder on her lip. The incredible intimacy of the moment was like nothing she'd experienced, sending her desire leaping even higher. Her knees threatening to buckle, she put her hands on his shoulders to keep herself from collapsing.

She whispered his name, hoping he'd hear the desperation in her voice, but he ignored her. He continued to rub the cloth over her in the same torturous, lazy pace, until she wanted to scream her frustration.

By the time he finally tossed the cloth into the bucket, her entire body hummed with the need he had stoked to astonishing heights.

He brushed several curling wisps of hair off her face, his eyes blazing with a heat as hot as the one coursing through her veins.

She wet her lips, and saw the tick of a muscle in his jaw. When she started to speak, he shook his head and pressed his fingers to her mouth.

In one efficient move, he lifted her into his arms, carried her to the bed, then eased her down onto the mattress.

She stared up at him, momentarily stunned by the depth of the emotions raging through her. Her heart overflowed with love for this man. She had never thought she would fall in love again, especially not the overwhelming love she felt for Chino. But she'd been wrong. Not only were her feelings for him deeper than she could have imagined, but her love also continued to grow stronger each day.

As he stretched out beside her, she tangled her fingers in his hair and gently tugged his face closer to hers.

She touched her mouth to his, softly, innocently at first. Then she kissed him harder, pulling his lower lip into her mouth and suckling. As she released him, she nipped the plump flesh with her teeth, causing him to gasp and then immediately retaliate.

He caught her lower lip between his teeth, gave her a quick nip to match the one she'd given him, then used his tongue to soothe the spot.

She groaned, and tried to pull him back to her. But he resisted, lifting his head to meet her gaze.

For several seconds, he stared at her, that same mysterious emotion again glowing in his eyes. Finally, he lifted a hand and touched her chin, then trailed his fingers along the side of her neck, between her breasts and down to her stomach. Halting his hand's sensual journey, he said, "I want to taste you—" he pushed his hand lower, through the curls at the apex of her thighs until a blunt fingertip nudged the bud of flesh—"here. The way you tasted me."

Her eyes widened, from both his shocking words and the increased throbbing his touch created. Before she could find her voice, he spoke again.

"It would give you pleasure?"

Her already pounding heart thumped even harder. "I . . . I'm not . . . I mean, I don't know, because I've never . . ."

The glow in his eyes intensified at her admission. "Then I will be the first."

"Yes, but you don't have to—"

A brief kiss halted her words. "I know I do not have to do this," he said, easing her legs apart. "I want to."

Abby swallowed hard, then managed a nod.

He shifted his position, so he knelt between her thighs. He leaned forward to kiss her again, this time on the inside of her knee. Then his lips inched higher. Pressing kisses along the way, his mouth moved closer and closer to the throbbing flesh between her thighs.

Her fingers digging into the mattress, she tried to prepare herself for the moment when his mouth touched her there. The warmth of his breath fanned over her inner thigh, his tongue tracing a pattern of moist heat on her skin. She moaned a protest.

He whispered something, words her fuzzy brain couldn't understand. As she opened her mouth to ask what he'd said, he opened the folds of her sex, his touch light, gentle. Whatever she'd started to say flew from her mind. She held her breath, both anticipation and frustration building at the delay.

When his tongue finally found her, the air exploded from her lungs, her hips arching up. At the second rasp of his tongue, she clenched her teeth, lips clamped shut to keep from crying out.

He pushed her legs farther apart, then settled his mouth over her for the most intimate of kisses. Somehow she heard his moan over the pounding of her pulse, felt the vibration against her, and his reaction pushed her desire even higher. He resumed caressing her with his tongue, lapping repeatedly before sucking the hard kernel of flesh.

This time Abby couldn't hold back a cry of joy. Shocked that he instinctively knew how to touch her, how to bring her such incredible pleasure, she could do nothing more than tighten her grip on the mattress and rock her hips to match his rhythm.

His assault continued, mixing the fiery flick of his tongue with the gentle suckle of his mouth, driving her to a level she'd never attained before. Feeling as if liquid flame had replaced the blood in her veins, scorching her from the inside out, she thought she might die if she didn't find relief soon.

Her muscles tense, her nerve endings screaming, she concentrated on attaining what her body craved. The pressure between her thighs continued to build, increasing the throbbing ache, lifting her closer and closer to her peak.

Then abruptly she was there, the first tremor catching her by surprise. With a sharp gasp, she dug her heels into the mattress, her hips frozen in place for an instant. Then she began to move, riding the powerful spasms racking her body. Not certain she could survive the intensity of her climax, she moaned her ecstasy.

When the final shudder passed, she loosened her grip on the mattress and went limp with exhaustion.

She drew a quavering breath, then exhaled with a contented sigh, the words, "I love you, Chino," echoing in her head. Though she longed to say them out loud, she managed to keep the declaration locked inside. She knew hoping for a day when she could declare her love aloud was pointless, that continuing to do so would only set herself up for additional heartache. Yet she couldn't convince her heart to stop nurturing a seed of hope—no matter how small.

Though aware Chino had moved and now lay on his side next to her, she couldn't summon the energy to open her eyes. But when his fingers touched her face, she managed to turn her head enough to brush her lips over his hand.

"You are all right?" he whispered, pushing himself up onto a forearm.

The concern in his voice prodded her to find the strength to lift her eyelids. "Yes," she said, her voice raspy. "I'm marvelous." Though moving required all her concentration, she raised a hand to push his hair over his shoulder. "And you . . . well—" she sighed again—"you're beyond description."

"That is good?"

She smiled up at him. "Absolutely." She touched his mouth, then withdrew her hand and allowed her eyelids to drift closed once more.

For a long time, Chino stared at Abby, pondering the powerful emotions filling his chest. When he'd pleasured her with his mouth, something had happened to him. Inside. He felt closer to her than at any other time, as if she had become a part of him. The experience chased the last of the doubts from his mind. Until he took his final breath and passed to the Spirit World, his heart totally and irrevocably belonged to this woman.

Although he now accepted what he knew was meant to be from the moment he and Abby met, he knew such acceptance changed nothing. Though he wished it could be different, he'd been given no sign that his future could be with this woman. So as soon as he made sure her horses and ranch were safe, he would leave. And hope he would find a way to forget what could not be.

Abby stirred beside him, bringing him back to the present. He watched her stretch, then open her eyes and flash him a quick smile.

As he returned her smile, she looped her arms around his neck and pulled him down beside her.

"Tell me about your childhood," she said, snuggling closer.

"What do you want to know?"

"Where you were born. What you did as a child."

He didn't respond immediately. Then after drawing a deep breath, he said, "I was born in mountains my people call Land of Standing-Up Rocks. The White Eyes call them the Chiricahua Mountains."

She ran her hand over his chest in a lazy circular

pattern. "A place with such an intriguing name must be beautiful."

"Yes. It is like no place I have seen." He smiled, remembering the many strange rock formations, the beauty of the peaceful valleys. "My band spent much of every summer near the place of my birth, so our women could gather nuts and berries."

"I remember you said your band went to Mexico for part of the year. Wasn't it hard moving around all the time?"

"No. That has been our way since the Apache first walked the earth. When we were free, all bands moved their camps to find game, to gather food. That is how we survived, until—" Chino drew a breath, trying to control his sudden bitterness—"the White Eyes came. They said we had to live on reservations. They would not allow us to continue the ways of our grandfathers."

"Tell me about living on the reservation."

"Why do you what to know?"

"Because—" she sat up so she could look into his eyes—"I want to understand what it was like for you."

Chino studied her for a moment. Finding only open curiosity in her expression, he finally said, "When the White Eyes came to the homeland of the Coyotero, our leader saw the superior weapons of the soldiers. He had heard of the—"

"Wait! Who are the Coyotero? I thought you were a Chokonen."

"I am. My wife was Coyotero. When two Apache marry, it is our way for the man to live with the band of his wife. Her band of Coyotero lived to the north of the Chokonen homeland, near *Sierra Blanca*—White Mountain."

Abby considered that, then nodded. "Go on."

"Our leader had heard of the trouble between the White Eyes and other Apache bands, and did not want this for his people. He did not care for the White Eyes, but he accepted their presence in our homeland and agreed to live at peace on what became the White Mountain Reservation.

"Life was not too difficult at first. Then many of our people died from a White Eyes sickness, and there was trouble. That is when the White Eyes in Washington said all Apache on the White Mountain Reservation should move to the south, to San Carlos. This was a bad idea. The White Eyes did not understand why some bands refused to move. There are many Apache bands. Not all are friends. Some are enemies. But our leader still wanted peace, so he agreed to move.

"San Carlos was crowded. Life was not good there. Many Apache were not happy. Some left."

"But you decided to stay?"

"I thought of leaving. Of taking my wife and son and joining other Apache in Mexico. But others who had been at San Carlos longer told me a story I could not forget. The year before we moved there, there was trouble. Some Apache left the reservation. Soldiers were sent to find them." He couldn't suppress a shudder. "The soldiers brought back their heads. Displayed them for the other Apache to see."

"Oh, God," Abby murmured, bile rising in her throat. "That's despicable."

He nodded. "Whenever I thought of leaving, I would remember what the others told me. About what the soldiers did—" He shuddered again. "I would not risk that happening to my family. I decided to stay at San Carlos."

"Things must have improved. Otherwise, how did you get permits to travel off the reservation?"

"Our agent, John Clum, tried to understand our life-way. He came to care for us. Tried to make life better for us. Many Apache came to respect him. He selected men, trained them to be what he called his Apache Police to keep peace at San Carlos. One of his police was Keja, brother of my wife. He was a man John Clum came to trust. To get permits to travel to the Chiricahua reservation, one of the Apache police had to travel with us. I chose Keja." He squeezed his eyes closed for a moment, gathering his thoughts. "I was a fool to take my family from San Carlos. I should have stayed. Maybe then I would not have killed them."

267

"What are you saying? You didn't kill your wife and son. Neville Warner's men did."

"I did not fire the gun that killed them. But I am to blame for their deaths. It is the responsibility of an Apache man to protect his family." His voice dropped to a tortured whisper. "I failed."

"Chino, that's ridiculous!" She clutched his arm, her nails biting into his skin. "You can't blame yourself. There's no way you could've known Neville Warner and his men would find your camp, or what he'd do to you and your family."

Chino remained silent for a long time. Then finally he said, "What you say is true. But it does not take away the pain—" he lifted a hand and touched his chest—"here."

Abby swallowed hard, deeply touched by another example of his love and dedication to his family. "Of course it doesn't. The pain of losing your wife and son will always be with you. But you can't continue to blame yourself, because it will destroy you."

He lifted his hand and stroked her cheek. "Again you show me," he murmured, "how wise you are. You are a special woman."

"Even though I'm a White Eyes?" she said, keeping her voice light, teasing.

He smiled. "Yes."

"Good," she replied, returning his smile. "Because I think—" she slid down beside him—"that's enough talk for one night." Bending down to brush her lips over his, she said, "What do you think?"

His response was a deep groan and a hand clasped to the back of her head to hold her close.

She kissed him eagerly, her spent passion abruptly flaring back to life.

As Abby used her lips and her hands to reignite his desire, the last of Chino's painful memories faded. Soon, the only thoughts left in his head were of the woman kissing him, touching him, and his need to bury his rock-hard manhood inside her, to let the raging fire in his blood consume him.

He rolled her onto her back, settled between her spread thighs and thrust into her, catching her gasp in his mouth. She locked her legs around his hips, driving him deeper, pulling him closer to the glorious relief awaiting him.

Not ready to reach the zenith just yet, wanting to draw out the pleasure singing in his veins a little longer, he changed his pace, slowing his frantic strokes to an easy, unhurried rhythm. With the gentle flexing of his hips, he pushed himself as deep as possible then nearly withdrew. The scent of their passion filled his nostrils, making him dizzy. The incredible glide of his flesh repeatedly sliding into her heat stole his breath. The clenching of her inner muscles caused his thundering heart to pound even harder. Soon his overwrought senses could take no more, and his control snapped.

He thrust into her again and again, panting, straining, the pressure continuing to build. Just as he thought he couldn't survive another second of the need clawing at him, he reached the pinnacle. A feral moan rumbling in his chest, he exploded.

A long time passed before he was able to move. Totally drained, his muscles shaking with exhaustion, he managed to roll onto his side. When some of his strength returned, he hauled Abby up against him so she lay with her back pressed to his chest. In a matter of seconds, sleep claimed him.

Chino dreamed of sunlit days in the Coyotero camp. The days before San Carlos. He saw his wife watching their son play, laughter shining in her dark eyes. Sensing his presence, she turned. Her laughter fading, she stared at him for a moment, then raised her hand and waved.

The dream changed. No longer did he see his wife and son. Instead, he saw himself on the Flying M.

He was working with Egusi, getting the horse used to the feel of a saddle on his back. Then he headed to the house and the woman waiting for him. Abby met him at the door, big with his child, the green flecks in her eyes sparkling with happiness and love. Just looking at her made his heart sing. Sweeping her into his arms, he nuzzled her neck, inhaled her heady scent.

She laughed, the sound filling him with indescribable joy. He lowered his head to kiss her, but before his lips touched hers, she disappeared, a flash of darkness momentarily blocking out all light.

A shiver of dread raced up his spine. His heart slamming against his ribs, he waited for the next scene to begin.

Chapter Seventeen

The horses' heads came up, their nostrils flared, testing the air. Something had disturbed their peaceful grazing, made the mares whicker for their foals to stay close. The sound of pounding hooves drifted to the valley, followed by the whoop of human voices. The horses jostled against each other, their hides quivering with anticipation, with growing fear.

Five riders burst into one end of the valley, kicking their mounts for more speed. The sun glinted off their black hair, reflected off the barrels of their rifles. Headbands of various colors bisected their foreheads, their faces adorned with bright splashes of paint in a variety of patterns. At least two also carried a bow and arrows.

As the men raced into the center of the herd, they

started another series of wild whoops, shooting bullets and arrows into the air.

Some of the horses whinnied in fright, eyes wild, their delicate hooves moving in a nervous dance. Others reared, trumpeting their displeasure, pawing the air. The lead mare ran in circles, pulling on the rope tether, desperate for freedom. When the rest of the herd bolted, scattering in all directions, the mare became more frantic to break free, jerking harder and harder on the stake. Her struggles tightened the rope even more, cutting into the flesh of her neck, but she didn't stop.

Finally, the earth gave. She'd won the battle. Tail raised in triumph, she raced away, dragging the rope and bouncing stake behind her.

As the mare galloped from the valley, the riders stopped. They talked among themselves for several moments, then one pulled another arrow from his quiver. He notched the arrow in his bow, drew and fired, sending the arrow into the churned-up ground. Hooking the bow over his saddle horn, he turned and gave a signal to the others. Then he jabbed the heels of his moccasins into his horse's sides and raced away. The rest followed suit, each choosing to flee in a different direction.

Chino awoke with a start. Uncertain what had awakened him, he rubbed a hand over his face, then sat up and glanced around. He frowned, momentarily disoriented by his surroundings. Why was he in Abby's bedroom?

Then he remembered the previous night. He turned to look at Abby, her features relaxed in sleep. Knowing he had eased her worries—even for a few hours—sent a deep contentment through him. His gaze skimmed over her flushed cheeks, her kiss-swollen lips, and the fascinating dent in her chin. Recalling the latest in the list of first experiences he'd shared with this remarkable woman, he smiled. As the intimate details of their night together came rushing back, his blood heated at the memory of touching her, tasting her. But more surprising than his physical reaction was the sensation filling his chest, a warmth surrounding his heart. Then he remembered something else from the night before. The discovery that his heart belonged to Abby, that he loved her.

He pulled his gaze from her, turning to stare out the window at the sky. The first tentative streaks of pink signaled dawn would soon arrive. In spite of his love for Abby, he knew nothing had changed. Once the horses were safe—The horses!

Another memory surfaced. He'd been dreaming about Abby, about their having a future together, living on her ranch, having a child. But then the dream had changed. He closed his eyes, trying to concentrate, to remember. It had something to do with the horses.

His eyes snapped open. The last part hadn't been a dream. He'd had a vision—a message from the Spirits. That was what had awakened him.

He must have made some sort of sound, because Abby stirred beside him.

"Chino," she said, her voice thick with sleep, "what's wrong?"

He hesitated. He knew he had to tell her about the vision, but he didn't want to say anything until he could remember all of what the Spirits had shown him. He took a deep breath, eased it out slowly, then turned to look at her. His heart swelling with another surge of love, he said, "I must leave now. You do not want your children to find me here."

She frowned, but finally nodded.

He smoothed a tangled strand of her hair, then smiled. "Go back to sleep, *lika.*"

She yawned, closed her eyes and immediately fell asleep.

Chino slipped out the rear door of the house. But he didn't go to the bunkhouse. Instead he sat beneath a mesquite tree, and once again contemplated the increasingly light sky. He cleared his mind of everything, concentrating only on remembering the vision. As the images began appearing in his mind's eye, he watched the scene unfold, carefully observing and listening, committing everything to memory.

He went over the vision again and again, making sure there was nothing he'd missed, and trying to answer a question nagging at him. Something troubled him about what the Spirits had shown him. There was something that wasn't right. Something that didn't fit. After going over the vision several more times, he realized the riders were the source of his uneasiness. But he couldn't pinpoint exactly what bothered him.

Though he knew the answer had to be there, for some reason his mind failed to solve the mystery. By the time he gave up trying, the sky had lightened even more, casting the valley in a pale, golden-pink glow. The sun would soon be up.

He exhaled with a sigh. He knew he should go to Abby, should tell her about his vision. She deserved to know what the Spirits had shown him. But considering his uneasy feeling about the vision, maybe he should wait until the Spirits spoke to him again, or at least until he figured out what troubled him. Though that seemed the wise choice, he also knew how important Abby's horses were to her. She would want to know about any possible threat to the herd, regardless of his uneasiness.

Uncertain about which path to take, he pushed himself to his feet. He would bathe and offer his morning prayers, asking for guidance in making his decision.

By mid-morning, Chino had decided what to do. He would tell Abby about the vision—at least part of it.

The part he found troubling he would not reveal, not until he found the answers he sought. But once he'd made his decision, finding an opportunity to speak to her proved difficult. Something or someone kept interfering with his plans.

First Susanna ripped a hole in her favorite dress and insisted, with a wail and a stomp of her foot, that the dress be mended right that minute. Marita was busy washing clothes, so the task fell to Abby. Then Cesar came in to ask what she wanted him to plant in a new section of garden, a decision apparently put off too long, which now had to be made right away. Cesar had just left when Teddy appeared at Chino's side, announcing it was time for another of his Apache lessons.

Chino nodded at the boy, accepting the fact that his conversation with Abby would have to wait.

A short time later, he sat beside Teddy in the barn, watching the boy's small fingers work strips of leather into rope. Though it was only the second time Teddy had tried braiding the rawhide, he was good with his hands and already showed signs of becoming proficient at the task.

He watched the boy work, his thoughts drifting again to his latest vision. If only he could find answers to his nagging questions. His musings came to a halt when Teddy spoke.

"Can I ask ya something else about when you was a little boy?"

Chino smiled. Every time he and Teddy were together, the boy kept up a steady stream of questions—except when he worked with Egusi. Teddy knew that was the one time Chino insisted on total quiet. Hoping to keep his amusement out of his voice, he said, "What do you want to ask?"

"Did ya ever play games?"

"Apache children play many games."

"Like what?"

"When I was a boy, I spent much time playing arrow games with my friends."

Teddy's hands halted. "Arrow games? How'd ya play them?"

"One game was to see how far each boy could shoot an arrow. Another was to see which boy could shoot through a hole in a target. The game I liked best used a target of twisted grass. We would throw it into the air and try to pierce the grass with our arrows before it touched the ground."

"I bet that was really hard to do."

Chino shrugged. "It takes much practice with a bow."

"What'd ya get if you won?"

"The arrows the other boys used in the game."

Teddy nodded, then shifted his attention back to braiding the rawhide. After a minute, he said, "Would ya teach me how to shoot an arrow that good?"

The boy's question sent a pang of regret through

Chino's chest. Even if he started teaching Teddy to shoot a bow and arrow, he wouldn't be around when the boy improved enough to hit twisted grass thrown in the air. As much as he wanted to witness that day, he knew he wouldn't. But how could he refuse the boy's request without hurting his feelings?

He inhaled a deep breath, then released it slowly. "I need to ask your mother before I agree to teach you."

"You always gotta ask her," Teddy muttered, his lower lip poking out.

"Parents know what is best for their children. It is right for me to ask your—" He went still, the flesh on the outside of his thigh starting to shake. Holding his breath, he waited for the severe shaking to subside. When the tremor finally stopped, he got to his feet.

"Come with me to the house," he said. "I must speak to your mother."

Teddy looked up at him, surprise and hope shining in his eyes. "Are ya gonna ask her about teaching me to shoot a bow and arrow?"

Chino shook his head. "That will have to be another time."

The boy's hopeful expression turned to a frown. "But I just started working on my rope."

"It is important."

"Can't I stay here 'til you get back?"

"No. After I speak to your mother, I must check the horses."

The boy stared at him for several seconds, then huffed out a breath. "Then, can I bring the rope with me?"

At Chino's nod, Teddy gathered the strips of rawhide, got to his feet and followed him to the house.

After settling Teddy on the ramada, Chino found Abby in the kitchen, helping Marita make bread.

"Hi," she said, looking up from the table where she was kneading bread. She flashed a bright smile. "Beautiful day, isn't it?"

"Yes," he replied, stepping closer, noticing the extra-bright green flecks sparkling in her eyes. He knew what he had to say would extinguish those sparkles, but he couldn't wait any longer. "I must speak to you," he said in a low voice. "It is important."

Her smile fading instantly, she gave him a nod. "Of course." Giving the dough a final pat, she reached for a towel. As she wiped her hands, she glanced over her shoulder. "Marita, can you finish the bread by yourself?"

"Sí, sí. I can do."

Once he'd followed Abby into the *sala*, she turned to meet his gaze, then said, "What's this about?"

"Your horses. Last night, I had another vision."

He watched the color drain from her face, and just

as he'd expected, the sparkle in her eyes flickered out.

"What—" her throat worked—"what did you see?"

"Five men on horseback chasing your horses from the valley."

"Were any of them hurt?"

"Only the lead mare. The rope cut her neck when she pulled on the tether to get free. The men fired their weapons into the air. But they did not try to hurt the horses."

She squeezed her eyes closed for a second, then released a deep sigh. "That's all they wanted to do? Scare my horses into running from the valley?"

He shrugged. "That is all the Spirits showed me. Once the horses ran off, the men also left the valley, riding in different directions. Then the vision ended."

Abby mulled over his words, then said, "When do you think this will happen?"

"Soon. While I was in the barn with Teddy, I had a shaking of the flesh in my leg. That is why I—" He went still.

"Chino?" She grabbed his arm. "What is it?"

"Another shaking of my flesh. Much stronger than before. We must get to the valley. Now."

The words had barely left his mouth before Abby turned to leave. "Give me a few minutes," she said. Stopping in the doorway, she looked back at him.

"Will you saddle my horse while I change and tell Marita where we're going?"

At his nod, she disappeared down the hall.

Chino led the horses from the barn a short time later. Just as he finished securing his rawhide bag behind his saddle, Abby joined him. She slid her rifle into its scabbard, then mounted her gelding. When she turned to look at him, he'd already swung onto his horse.

Her lips pressed into a firm line, she gave him a nod, then started the chestnut forward. Chino touched his heels to the bay. Leaning over the sleek neck, he pressed the horse for more speed. The bay stretched out into a gallop, racing away from the ranch yard, Abby and her gelding only a stride behind.

In a matter of minutes, Chino's bay crested the hill overlooking the valley. Drawing back on the reins, he brought his horse to a sliding stop. Abby pulled the chestnut to a halt beside him.

She gave a soft gasp. "Oh, God, we're too late."

Other than one last swirl of dust, churned up by the hooves of fleeing horses, the valley was empty.

Chino reacted first, kneeing the bay forward so he could get a closer look.

At the base of the hill, he dismounted, then squatted to study the ground. Though his vision had shown him five riders scattering the herd, he searched for confirmation. But with the turf so torn up, it was difficult to tell.

"Chino. I found something."

He looked up to see Abby standing twenty yards away. A quick glance at the ground by her feet sent his pulse into an erratic beat. He straightened, then started toward her, trying to prepare himself for her reaction to what she'd found.

As he reached her side, he glanced again at the ground, then lifted his gaze to meet hers. No longer did he see apprehension for her herd clouding her eyes. Now he saw only the turbulence of seething anger.

"Did you know?" she asked in a shaky voice.

Chino sighed. There was no point in denying it. "I knew. The Spirits showed me two men with bows. I saw them shooting arrows into the air. And this one." He pointed to the arrow Abby had found, the shaft partially buried in the chewed-up earth. "After they chased off the herd, the leader shot the arrow into the ground, then signaled the others to leave."

"So you knew they were Apache, but you didn't bother to tell me?"

"I knew they carried bows and arrows. But I was not sure who they were."

She glared at him. "Not sure. Well, that's certainly convenient, isn't it?" Not waiting for him to respond, she said, "And I suppose there was nothing else in your vision to tell you Apaches did this?"

He frowned, remembering other pieces of the vision. Headbands, painted faces, moccasins. Her reaction was the reason he hadn't mentioned those things before. Choosing his words with care, he said, "The Spirits do not always tell me everything."

"Yeah, something else that's real convenient." She paced away from him, her hands clenched into tight fists, then turned and stomped back. "Did you really have a vision about this latest attack on my herd? Or did you know about it some other way?"

"If I did not have a vision, how would I know what happened here?"

"Maybe you know the men who did this. Maybe you helped plan it. Maybe you're in cahoots with Warner after all."

"I had a vision," he said, his jaw rigid. "You know it is my way to speak the truth."

"So you keep telling me," she replied, staring at him through eyes growing colder by the second. After several seconds, she said, "Okay, let's say you had a vision. But the question is, when. Was it last night, or was it days, even weeks ago?"

"I told you, the vision came to me last night."

"My guess is, it didn't. I bet the only reason you told me today was because you had no choice. Because you knew it was about to happen. Even at that, you waited to tell me until you were sure we had no chance of reaching this valley before my horses got scattered from here to kingdom come."

"If the Spirits had sent me the vision before last night, what reason would I have not to tell you then?"

She made a sound, somewhere between a laugh and a snort. "Well, I think that should be obvious." When his only response was a quizzical look, she huffed out a breath. "So we could continue our nightly . . . activities."

A muscle jerking in his jaw, he crossed his arms over his chest. "If that was my plan, there would be no reason to tell you about the vision at all."

Her eyes narrowed, and then she started pacing again, obviously thinking about his last statement. Finally, she turned back. "Okay, I'll give you that one. But are you still going to stand there and claim you didn't know the men were Apache?"

He scowled, deciding to tell her everything. "The Spirits showed me men with painted faces, wearing headbands and moccasins, carrying bows. At first, I thought they were Apache, but something was not right." He bent and pulled the arrow from the ground. "I could not—" His brow furrowing, he studied the arrow. Suddenly, what had bothered him about the vision clicked into place. After a moment, he said, "The men were not Apache."

She gave him a look of disgust. "Need I remind you, the only ones using arrows in these parts are renegade Apaches?"

"No, there are others. The men who did this. Their

faces were not painted in the way of the Apache."

"What do you mean?"

"When Apache warriors prepare to fight the enemy, their faces are painted in the way of their band. One band of Chiricahua, the *Chihende,* wear red paint, here." Using two fingers, he drew an imaginary stripe across the bridge of his nose. "Apache to the west, the *Binii edinende,* wear many small dots of white on their faces. A band to the east, the *Guulgahende,* paint a large circle, here and here." He touched one cheek, then the other. "The men who did this did not wear the same paint. They are not Apache."

"Face paint is enough to convince you?"

"It is enough," he said with a nod. "But this—" he straightened, then held the arrow toward her—"is more proof. This was not made by Apache."

Her eyebrows lifted. "How can you be sure?"

"The feathers are wrong."

She touched one of the feathers. "What's wrong with them?"

"The feathers of Apache arrow face the same direction. They are attached one at a time with a piece of wet sinew. Then another piece of sinew is wrapped around all three feathers." He twirled the arrow between his fingers. "These feathers do not face the same direction. They were not tied to the shaft in the correct way."

He waited several seconds, then said again, "This was not made by Apache."

Abby stared at the arrow in Chino's hand, her mind slow to grasp everything he'd just told her. Lifting her head, she met his gaze. "So what are you saying? The men were pretending to be Apache?"

He nodded. "After the Spirits sent me the vision, there was something that did not seem right. I went over the vision many times, but I could not find an answer. When I saw this arrow, I knew what had disturbed me. The men carried bows and arrows, wore headbands and moccasins, painted their faces. They did all this to make them look like Apache. But they are not."

"Then whoever sent them," Abby said in a quiet voice, "wanted me to think Apaches did this."

"Yes."

"But why? If Warner is behind this, why would he have his men dress up like Apaches?"

"So you would not suspect he sent the men, or—" he swallowed hard, then shrugged—"to turn you against me. To make you think I am involved."

Abby looked away, unable to stand the pain she saw reflected in his eyes. Sickened by the realization that she'd done exactly what he'd described, she moved closer. Laying her hand on his arm, she said, "Chino, I'm sorry. I should have known you—" He shook off her hand.

"It is better this way," he said, taking a step back.

"I don't understand. What's better this way?"

His chest rose, then fell with a deep breath. "We knew what was between us would end." A muscle ticking in his jaw, he added, "It is better that it happened now."

Abby gasped. "Chino, don't say that. I'm sorry about accusing you of being part of this. I didn't mean to make you angry. It's just that when I saw the arrow, I—"

"I let myself think you trusted me. Let myself forget how much you hate Apache." He pinned her with a fierce glare. "I will not forget again."

Chapter Eighteen

Abby's heart pounded with fear as Chino's last words echoed in her head. Much as the admission pained her, she'd brought this on herself. For a moment, she had suspected him of being involved with the men who'd scattered the herd of horses. She'd seen that arrow sticking in the ground, and in that instant, her old hatred reared its ugly head. If she'd taken the time to think through everything that had happened, she would have known he wasn't involved. Then she wouldn't have spewed those accusing words at him. Unfortunately, the damage was done.

She reached a shaking hand toward him. "Chino, please, listen to—"

He brushed past her, heading for his horse with stiff strides. Avoiding her gaze, he grabbed the bay's mane and jumped into the saddle in one fluid motion. "I will look for tracks."

Abby swallowed the words she'd started to say, knowing he was in no frame of mind to listen. Drawing a steadying breath, she said, "I thought you said the men split up. What good will it do to follow one of them?"

He gathered the reins into his hands, still refusing to look at her. "I do not plan to follow any of the riders. The Spirits showed them leaving without taking any of your horses. I want to see if this is true." Staring straight ahead, he started his bay forward.

His coldness caused a crushing pain in her heart, as if an enormous stone were pressing down on her chest. Telling herself he would listen to her once his temper cooled, she tried to ignore the pain and concentrate on another concern. Her horses. "Chino, wait!"

Her call brought him to a halt. He didn't turn around, but waited for her to speak.

"We need to start rounding up the horses before they get any farther away."

He shifted in his saddle, but still didn't look at her. "Go back to the house," he said. "Get Nestor to help you. After I check for tracks, I will meet you back here."

"Where should we take the horses? They're going to be too skittish to come back here for a while."

"The pasture behind the barn. There is not as much grass, but the creek is close."

Not waiting for her to reply, he started his horse forward again. This time, Abby didn't stop him.

A full minute passed before she could make herself move. Then with a deep sigh, she grabbed her reins and mounted the gelding.

On the ride back to the house, she struggled not to give in to the urge to cry. She'd certainly made a horrible mess of things. But there was no time to feel sorry for herself. Blinking away the last of her threatening tears, she lifted her chin. She had work to do—get the horses rounded up and settled in a new pasture. That had to be her first priority. Only after she'd accomplished that task could she think about tackling the more difficult one: figuring out a way to earn Chino's forgiveness.

Although she acknowledged the truth in what he'd said—they both knew their relationship would end—she couldn't bear the thought of what they'd shared ending on such a bitter note. And she couldn't allow him to ride away thinking she didn't trust him. Or worse, that she hated him.

Since discovering she'd fallen in love with Chino, she'd tried not to think about the day he would leave. And in spite of knowing what lay ahead, she'd foolishly harbored a secret hope that they could have a future together. But after what had just happened between them, that hope had taken a severe and most likely fatal blow.

As the ranch house came into view, tears once again burned her eyes. She loved the Flying M, but it would never be the same once Chino Whitehorse rode away for the final time.

Chino found no evidence that any of the horses had been taken and was waiting for Abby and Nestor when they rode into the valley.

"How do you want to do this?" Abby asked, after stopping her horse near his.

"I want to find the lead mare." He pointed south. "She went that way. You and Nestor should start to the north."

Abby nodded and started to turn her horse when Nestor spoke.

"There is a better way."

She glanced at the man beside her. "What?"

"We can find more horses if we ride in different directions."

"That does make sense," she said, turning to look at Chino. "What do you think?"

Chino studied Nestor, pondering the man's suggestion. Though splitting up would save time, he wasn't sure he wanted to agree. He hadn't received a sign from the Spirits, a warning of impending danger. But for reasons he couldn't explain, the idea of Abby and Nestor splitting up made him uneasy. In spite of his concern, he found nothing suspicious in the man's expression. And without a valid reason, voicing disagreement would raise questions he couldn't answer.

Finally, he said, "I agree. We will search in different directions."

"I will go to the north," Nestor said.

"Okay," Abby replied, "then I'll head west."

Chino nodded. "If there is trouble, fire two shots."

Abby and Nestor indicated they understood by nodding, then swung their horses around, heading in different directions.

Chino watched them for several seconds, hoping he hadn't made a mistake. After whispering a prayer to the Great Spirit to protect the woman he loved, he reined his horse toward the south, then touched his heels to the bay's sides.

More than an hour passed before Chino found the lead mare. Several other members of the herd, the yellow mare, her foal, two grays and a pinto, grazed nearby.

He stopped a good distance away, waiting to see if one of the horses would sound the alarm. When none of them gave him more than a brief glance, he started forward at a slow walk, noting how the lead mare stood with her head down, her sides heaving, his eyes narrowed. Checking the area, he quickly realized what had happened.

Though Abby touted her horses' hard feet as an

asset, the characteristic hadn't proven to be a benefit
for the mare. She'd started across a rocky patch of
ground, having no problem with the terrain, but the
stake had got caught between the rocks. The mare's
attempts to pull free had only succeeded in wedging
the stake more firmly in place, leaving her worn out,
a fresh trail of blood trickling down her neck.

He inched the bay forward. When the mare didn't
react, he moved a few feet closer, then stopped. After
pulling a container of salve from the bag tied behind
his saddle, he carefully slid to the ground. As he approached on foot, he crooned to her in Apache, hoping she wouldn't bolt and hurt herself more severely.

Her head came up. Swiveling her ears toward him,
she looked at him through dark eyes clouded with
pain and confusion.

"Do not be afraid," he told her in Apache. "I will
not hurt you."

She took a step sideways, warily watching him
move closer.

He continued a soft litany of words, keeping his
pace painfully slow until he stood beside her. Careful
not to make any quick moves, he lifted a hand toward her muzzle.

She tossed her head, but finally lowered her muzzle to snuffle his palm.

"You know my scent," he murmured into her ear.
"You know I will not hurt you."

The mare nickered, then bobbed her head, making Chino smile.

He quickly examined her neck, relieved to find she wasn't seriously hurt. Though her injuries were mostly rope burns—painful but not serious—two deeper grooves in her flesh continued to ooze blood. After applying a thick layer of salve to each wound, he returned to his horse to retrieve a rope hackamore.

Though unsure if the mare would allow the hackamore, he didn't want to risk additional injury by leaving the tether rope around her neck. At first she fought him, jerking her head away or sidling out of his reach. But finally, through patience and gentle persuasion, he earned her trust.

After removing the rope from around her neck, he cut a section to use as a lead. He secured one end to the hackamore, then mounted his horse and looped the other end around his saddle horn. When he began the task of leading the mare to the herd's temporary home, the other horses followed as he'd expected.

By the time Chino and the six horses arrived at the pasture by the barn, the sun was well past its zenith. He hobbled the mare not far from the creek, checked her wounds again, then moved back to watch her. She appeared uneasy in her new surroundings, but soon settled down, lowering her head to graze.

As he mounted his horse to go look for more of

the herd, Nestor rode in with four horses. When the man drew even with him, Chino said, "Did you see more than these four?"

Nestor pulled his horse to a halt. "Sí. Six or seven. But they run away when they see me."

"You are going back to look for them?"

Nestor nodded. "The horses are probably far away by now. Maybe too far to get back with them before dark. I will get my bedroll and have Tía Marita pack some food, then I will leave."

"The horses are nervous. Be more careful when you find them, or they will run again."

Anger flashed in Nestor's cold eyes, but he didn't reply. Instead, he pressed his lips into a flat line, gave Chino a curt nod, then jerked on the reins and jabbed his spurs into his horse's sides. The gray whinnied in protest, which earned the animal another fierce jab of the spurs. That time, the sharp rowels drew blood.

Chino curled his hands into fists, fury at Nestor's behavior surging through him. He longed to follow the man, grab him by the scruff of the neck and tell him such cruel treatment of horses would not be tolerated on the Flying M, but he didn't. Though certain Abby would agree, he had no right to speak for her. Keeping his expression purposely bland, he watched until Nestor disappeared around the barn.

* * *

Abby worked throughout the remainder of the day, taking only enough time to refill her canteen or grab something to eat whenever she brought in more horses.

As she approached the pasture with two more horses, full darkness had begun to settle over the ranch. With clouds obscuring the nearly full moon, she knew the rest of the search would have to wait until morning.

She saw to her horse, then headed for the house, barely able to put one foot in front of the other. Her physical exertion, coupled with her mental anguish over the situation with Chino, had worn her to the point of near total exhaustion.

She waved away Marita's attempt to get her to sit down at the table. "I'm too tired to eat."

"It is no good," Marita said, clucking her tongue. "Not to eat."

She patted the older woman's arm. "I'll be fine."

"If you not eat, you will be *muy mal.*"

"You worry too much, Marita." She managed to summon the strength to smile. "I won't get bad sick." Ignoring the older woman's frown, she said, "Have Chino and Nestor returned?"

"I have not seen either of them."

"Okay. Well, I'll go check on the children, then I'm going to bed."

"Sí, señora. Sleep well."

Abby nodded, then headed down the hall.

A few minutes later, Abby slid into her bed with a sigh. She stretched out on the mattress and had nearly fallen asleep when she heard something outside. Her exhaustion melting away, she rose and went to the window.

Someone had gone inside the barn, though the distance and lack of moonlight prevented her from telling if it was Nestor or Chino. She continued to watch the barn, and soon the man emerged and started across the yard toward the house.

As he drew closer, she squinted in an effort to penetrate the darkness. When she made out the flutter of long hair, her breath caught in her throat. Heart pounding, her body humming with anticipation, she kept her gaze on him, afraid if she looked away, he would disappear. But rather than proceed to the house, he veered away. Toward the bunkhouse.

She slumped against the window, pressing her forehead to the glass. "Oh, Chino," she whispered in a shaky voice, "please, don't let it end like this."

With a fist pressed to her mouth to hold back a sob, she pushed away from the window, then stumbled across the room and dropped onto her bed. Curling onto her side, she squeezed her eyes shut and prayed for sleep to come quickly.

But her prayers were not answered. There was a crushing ache in her chest, and tears streamed down her cheeks and soaked her pillow. A long time passed before she was finally granted the sanctuary of sleep.

The next morning, Abby awoke with gritty eyes and a pounding headache. She forced down the food Marita pressed on her, kissed her children, then rode away from the ranch yard. Alone. According to Marita, Chino had risen even earlier, given her a message for Abby, then left. And since Nestor's horse wasn't in the barn, apparently he'd also ridden out.

That was fine with Abby, since she wasn't fit company anyway.

As she rode to the valley where the horses had been, then started to the northwest—exactly as Chino had directed in the message he'd left—she thought about his vision. In particular, his explanation about why the men who'd chased away her horses weren't Apache.

She didn't doubt that the raid had been carried out on Neville Warner's orders. But why would he have his men dress like Apache? Was Chino correct? Had he wanted to drive a wedge between the two of them? If that had been Warner's goal, he'd succeeded—due in large part to her own stupidity. Her stomach cramped at the memory of the pain she'd seen on Chino's face. Pain she had caused.

He certainly understood the reason behind her accusations. The anguish and grief of losing a spouse. He'd lost not only his wife, but had also endured the death of a child. So he wasn't immune to grief, and just like her, continued to suffer its effects. He still hated those responsible for his loss, just as she hated the ones who'd taken Alan from her.

Alan. Thinking his name stirred up a mixture of conflicting emotions. Gratitude for the years they'd had together. Sadness at the loss of a man who had been both friend and husband. Anger that his life had been cut short, and that Teddy and Susanna would grow up without a father. If only he hadn't ridden out to check on the cattle that day, then maybe he wouldn't have crossed paths with the Apache raiding party and he'd—

Abby jerked on the reins so sharply, her horse sat back on his hocks, nearly unseating her. "Sorry, boy," she said, running her hand over the gelding's neck. "I just had a really disturbing thought."

For a long time, she sat perfectly still, staring straight ahead yet not seeing the land she loved so much. Could she be correct? Had her hatred for Alan's killers been misplaced?

If the men who'd run off her horses weren't Apache, as Chino claimed—and she believed him— perhaps the same thing had happened two years earlier. Though that time, they'd had a more lethal purpose in dressing like Apaches.

Her stomach twisted in a knot again, only this time with white-hot fury. Had Neville Warner been so hell-bent on getting the Flying M that he'd actually hired someone to kill Alan? And what about the other ranchers he'd bought out? Maybe those sales hadn't been voluntary after all, but the result of coercive tactics. She knew he wanted more land to run additional cattle—he'd made no secret of his ambitious plans for his Warner Land and Cattle Company—but had he forced the owners into accepting his sales offers? Had he ordered someone murdered for his own personal gain? Was he truly capable of something that despicable?

The answer sent an icy prickle down the length of her spine. Yes, the more she thought about Neville Warner, the more she was convinced her instincts were right. During his last visit to her ranch, his true colors had begun to surface. But at the time, she hadn't realized his vile nature went far beyond the glimpse he'd revealed. The man was evil clear to the bone.

With sudden clarity, she knew he was behind the string of bad luck, the unfortunate accidents, the tragic incidents—including the so-called Apache raid that took Alan's life—that had plagued the area over the past several years.

The problem was, she had no proof.

Pressing her lips together with determination, she sat straighter in the saddle, then touched her heels to the gelding. As her horse moved forward, she made herself a solemn pledge. Even if she needed the rest of her life, she would find out who was to blame for Alan's death. And if the finger of guilt pointed at Neville Warner, she would make sure he paid for his crime. Paid dearly.

While searching for her missing horses, one more question nagged at her. What would Warner try next in order to get her to sell the Flying M? Goose bumps rising on her arms, she didn't have to ponder the answer for long. Anything. Without a doubt, the man would do anything to get what he wanted.

Armed with the knowledge that she now knew the true nature of the enemy she was up against, she pushed herself harder, determined to do everything possible to prevent Neville Warner from winning.

Chino rubbed a hand over his face, weary from a long day in the saddle searching for the missing horses. He'd found another eight horses, but after taking the last of them to join the others, he guessed about that same number were still missing from the herd.

He'd caught a glimpse of Abby only once. She had brought in some horses and was heading back out when he approached the barn from the opposite direction. For a moment, he'd considered catching up with her, but decided against the idea just as quickly.

There was no point in telling her he understood her doubts about him, or that he was no longer upset with her. She'd nurtured her hatred of those she thought responsible for killing her husband, just as he'd done with those who killed his wife and son. He couldn't condemn her for feeling an emotion that had controlled his life for the past two years. He knew the accusations she'd thrown at him were a natural reaction to seeing an arrow stuck in the ground where her herd of horses had grazed. But if he went to her and made such an admission, he feared he would give her hope—false hope that they could resume their relationship—and he didn't want to put her through the pain of his rejection.

He snorted, forcing himself to face the truth. He wasn't refusing to continue their relationship because of the pain *she* would feel. He was doing it to prevent his own pain. Because if he touched her again, made love to her again, he wasn't sure he could survive the pain of another—this time final—break between them.

He swallowed hard, trying without success to dislodge the lump wedged in his throat. Letting Abby think he was still angry with her was for the best.

Twilight had begun to settle over the ranch by the time Chino rode toward the barn. For once, his search had come up empty. He hoped Abby and Nestor had been more successful. Any horses the three of them hadn't found by now were probably too far away to—

The sound of Abby's voice calling him pierced his tired brain. He looked up and saw her standing in front of the house. She called his name again, lifted

303

her hand in a wave, then started toward him at a run.

His mood lifting, he urged more speed from the exhausted bay. As he closed the distance to Abby, he allowed himself to dream of coming home to this woman each day, of having her greet him with such enthusiasm whenever he returned.

Then he pulled his horse to a halt, slid to the ground and saw Abby's face. His romantic daydream shattered into a thousand pieces.

"Chino," she said between gasping breaths. "Thank God you're back." She grabbed his arms, the coldness of her fingers penetrating the fabric of his shirt.

He shifted his gaze from her hands to her agony-filled eyes. Somehow he forced words through his tight throat. "What is wrong?"

She swallowed hard. "It's Teddy." She sucked in a quavering breath, then swallowed again. "He's—" Her voice broke. "He's gone."

Chapter Nineteen

Chino shook off Abby's hands, then pulled her into his arms. Squeezing his eyes closed, he murmured, "When?"

"We're not sure. Sometime this afternoon."

He eased out a deep breath, then held her away from him. "I must see to my horse. He worked hard today." He lifted a hand to smooth the tangle of her hair. "Go back to the house. I will be there soon."

She nodded, then turned and retraced her steps.

Chino watched her for several seconds, the shuffle of her feet and the slight slump of her shoulders increasing the ache in his chest. His mouth pressed into a grim line, he sighed, then led his horse to the barn.

A few minutes later, he entered the back door of

the house. Abby, Marita and Cesar were at the table, all sitting as still as stone.

As he started toward them, Marita turned.

"Señor Whitehorse! *Gracias a Dios,*" she said, lifting her apron to dab at her eyes. "You will find our Teddy, sí?"

"Sí," he replied, his jaw tight. "I will find him."

He took a seat at the table, taking care to keep his gaze away from Abby. He couldn't bear the thought of looking at her, of seeing the pain in her eyes. Not yet.

He looked at Marita. "Tell me what happened."

The woman drew a shaky breath, her fingers twisting a corner of her apron. "I call everyone for supper. Susanna was playing on the ramada. Cesar came in from the garden. But Teddy—" she gulped back a fresh onslaught of tears—"not come."

Cesar reached across the table and placed his gnarled hand atop his wife's. "We searched for him," he said, his voice raw. "Marita checked the house and the yard. I looked in the barn and all over outside. I think maybe he did not come when Marita called because he is hurt. But when I could not find him, I begin to worry that maybe something—" he cleared his throat—"that something else happened to the *niño.* That is when I told Marita I must get you or Señora Abby."

"I rode in just as Cesar was ready to leave," Abby said. "I searched for Teddy again, checking all the places he liked to play. I thought . . . I hoped maybe Cesar didn't know all of them." She turned her hands palm up on the table. "My son is gone."

The pain-filled words, coupled with her helpless gesture, pierced Chino to the quick. He should have known something like this would happen. If he had taken time to think the situation through, he would have realized that leaving Abby's children with the elderly Zepedas would put them at risk. He shoved that thought aside. There would be plenty of time later to lecture himself on what he should have done.

Finally, he said, "When was the last time you saw the boy?"

"He was here at noon," Cesar replied. "After we ate, he went outside."

"I saw him after that," Marita said. "It was early afternoon. Nestor came in while I was washing dishes."

"Nestor?" Chino's eyes narrowed. "What did he want?"

"Something to eat. He say he was hungry, so I feed him."

"How long was he here?"

Marita shrugged. "Not long. While he eat, Teddy came into the house. Nestor ask him if he want to go check on Señor Whitehorse's stallion when he finish eating."

"Teddy agreed to go with him?"

"Not at first. But Nestor say you asked him to

check the horse when he came back to the ranch. That you are worried the horse did not have food or water. Then Teddy say yes."

Chino must have made some sort of sound, because he suddenly felt everyone staring at him. He glanced at Cesar, then Marita and finally Abby.

"Is something wrong?" Abby asked. When he didn't respond, she leaned forward. "Chino?"

"You know Egusi. He is proud. Stubborn. Still half wild. Why would I ask someone who does not know him to care for such a horse?"

"You didn't ask Nestor to check on him?"

Chino shook his head. "I have not seen Nestor since yesterday afternoon." He shifted his gaze back to Marita.

"What happened after Teddy agreed to go with Nestor?"

"I tell Nestor, Señora Abby does not want the children to be alone. That he must bring Teddy back to the house after he check on your horse. He tell me he will make sure Teddy is with Cesar before he leaves."

She twisted her apron again, more tears streaking her brown cheeks. "I think—" she sniffled—"Teddy is with Cesar until I call them for supper."

Chino turned to Cesar. "Nestor did not speak to you?"

The older man shook his graying head. "I did not see my nephew today. I had no idea he was here until

Marita asked me why Teddy was not with me when I come to supper."

Abby stared at Chino, watched his expression change, saw the slight narrowing of his eyes. "What are you thinking?"

When he didn't respond, she said, "You're not thinking Nestor had something to do with Teddy disappearing, are you?"

His mouth thinned. "He was the last one with the boy."

"Yes, but you know how persuasive Teddy can be, and he's trying so hard to act grown-up. Maybe he promised Nestor he would go to Cesar. But on his way, something probably caught his attention. A bird. A snake. Or one of a hundred other things could've captured his attention and made him forget his promise."

"Nestor left hours ago," Chino replied. "If Teddy did as you said, where has he been? Why did you not find him?"

"Maybe he wander off," Marita said, "and get lost. Or maybe he is hurt."

"I don't think so," Abby said, shaking her head. "He knows better than to take off on his own. I've warned him time and again to stay close to the house. Other than fetching the cows, he never goes far."

"And if he was hurt," Cesar said, "we would have found him."

"Yes, or heard him calling for help." She turned

her gaze on Chino. "So what could've happened to him?"

The hard set to his jaw, the tightness around his mouth made her blood run cold. "You don't think he's de—" The possibility was so horrendous, so mind-numbing, that she couldn't say the word.

"No, he is not dead," Chino replied, hoping that wouldn't change, for Abby's sake as well as his own. If anything had happened to her son while the safety of everyone on the ranch rested on his shoulders, he wasn't sure he could—He halted that line of thinking, forcing himself to concentrate on the present. "The boy could have left with someone."

Marita's brow wrinkled. "That cannot be. I was here with the *niños* and Cesar all day. The only person I see was Nestor."

Abby pressed a hand to her mouth. If Chino was right about Teddy leaving with someone, then that meant his other suspicions also could be correct. She forced back fresh tears. "It had to be someone else," she whispered.

Chino watched the emotions flicker across Abby's face, sharing her agony. He longed to go to her, offer the comfort of his embrace and his strength. But he didn't move. "Would Teddy leave with someone he did not know?"

She shook her head. "I don't think so. Susanna is the more open of my children. Though she still wouldn't go to anyone—" a weak smile hovered on the corners of her mouth—"like she did with you. But Teddy was wary of strangers." She shook her head again, more vehemently. "No, I'm sure he wouldn't go with someone he didn't know. Not willingly. Not without a lot of kicking and screaming."

Chino looked at Cesar. "Did you see signs the boy tried to get away from someone?"

"No," he replied. "Nothing like that."

Chino fell silent, leveling his gaze on Abby. She knew he was waiting for her to accept the conclusion he'd already drawn. Though she hated the idea, there simply was no other logical explanation for Teddy's disappearance.

She closed her eyes for a moment, took a deep breath, then met Chino's stare. "Where do you think Nestor took him?"

Marita gasped. "How can you say this? Why would Nestor take Teddy and not say something to me? Or to his *tío*?"

Abby turned toward Marita, took one of the woman's hands between hers. "Chino thinks—" she drew another deep breath, looked over at Cesar, then back at Marita—"and I'm afraid I have to agree, that Nestor is working for Neville Warner."

Marita's mouth opened, but no sound came out.

Cesar scowled. "Why would my nephew do such a thing?"

"Money," Chino said.

Cesar jerked as if he'd been struck. "Money means

nothing," he said with a wave of his hand. "Love. Family. Working with the soil to grow food. Those are what is important."

"To you. Maybe not to Nestor."

"No." Cesar slapped a hand on the tabletop. "I still do not believe it. My brother did not raise him to desire money above all else."

"I know this isn't easy," Abby said, releasing Marita's hand, "but think about it. Nestor working for Warner would answer a lot of questions. Like how Warner found out about Chino. How he knew when to send someone to shoot at the horses, and where to send men to steal half my cattle. And how someone could take one of Susanna's kittens from the barn and . . . um . . . do what he did, right under our noses."

Abby's heart went out to the couple. She knew her accusations against Nestor had hurt Marita and Cesar, but they had to know the truth.

After a few minutes, Cesar said, "All those times he was gone all night, when he said he was checking cattle or the horses, you think he lied? That he went to see Señor Warner?"

Abby looked over at Chino. At his nod, she said, "Yes. Nestor probably was supposed to check in with Warner. To let him know about our plans here, and to get his orders."

"How could he do this to us?" Marita said with a sob, burying her face in her apron.

Abby swallowed hard, then shifted her gaze to Cesar. His work-gnarled hands curled into fists and his face crumpled with anguish.

"How can a man so cruel be my flesh and blood?" he asked, staring at his hands. "He must be filled with much evil. Who else would do that to a helpless kitten?" He lifted his head, his tear-filled eyes pleading with Abby. "Forgive us, Señora Abby, for bringing him to your ranch. We had no idea he was such a vile—"

"No, Cesar," she said, reaching out to wrap her fingers around one of his clenched fists. "This isn't your fault. When Nestor showed up here, you said you hadn't seen him since he was a boy. There's no way you could've known what kind of man he'd become."

He relaxed his fists, then acknowledged her words with a weary nod. "If my brother had lived to see this, to know the things his son has done, he would be sick—" he touched his fingers to his chest— "here. Just as my heart is sick at what my *bastardo* nephew has done."

"Stop fretting," Abby said, giving his fingers a quick squeeze. As she withdrew her hand, she glanced at Marita. "Both of you. Everything will be okay." She looked again at Chino. "It will, won't it?"

He met her gaze, his eyes flashing with a fierceness she'd never seen. "Yes," he said, his voice equally fierce. "I will find your son. I give you my word."

He rose and started across the room.

Abby jumped up and followed him to the door. "Where are you going?"

"To look for their trail," he said.

"Now? It's almost dark."

"There will be a full moon."

"But, wouldn't it be better to wait until morning?"

"I will not leave until sunrise. My horse needs rest, so I will use the time to find a trail and prepare for the journey."

"You need rest, too."

"There will be time for sleep after I find Teddy." He started to leave, then turned back to her. "If Marita has extra tortillas I could take, I would be grateful."

"Yes, of course. You're welcome to whatever we have."

Before she could say anything more, he stepped outside and closed the door behind him.

Abby waited on the ramada for Chino to return. The time crawled by, minutes feeling more like hours while her mind conjured every kind of horrible scenario about what could happen to Teddy. The idea of her son suffering at the hands of a man who had tortured a kitten to death filled her with stark terror. Though the night air still carried a good portion of the day's heat, she shivered. Rubbing her arms, she paced the length of the ramada, her fears for Teddy's safety giving way to a moment of anger.

Damn you, Neville Warner. Damn you to hell for doing this to me and my family.

At one end of the ramada, she stopped her nervous pacing to stare into the deepening darkness. "Please, God," she whispered into the night, "please don't let Nestor hurt my son."

She had no idea how long she stood there, but a noise behind her pulled her attention from her tormenting thoughts. Turning, she saw Chino approaching her. Moonlight filtered through the ramada's beamed roof, wrapping them in a cocoon of pale silver.

"Did you find anything?" she asked, taking a step toward him.

He nodded.

"Well, good, then you'll know where to start in the morning. Marita packed you some food. It's on the table."

He nodded again, then said, "I spoke with Cesar. He checked Nestor's room. All his belongings are gone."

"Obviously, he doesn't plan to come back here. This must be Warner's final effort to get me to sell." She rubbed her arms again. "If only I knew for certain that Teddy's all right."

"Warner knows you will not agree to anything until you are sure your son has not been hurt."

"I hope you're right. But now that I know what

315

Nestor is capable of, what he did to that poor kitten, I worry—"

"No! You should not worry."

"I know," she replied, trying to summon a smile, "but that's easier said than done." Sobering, she said, "I wish I'd listened to you sooner. If I had taken your suspicions about Nestor more seriously, we could've confronted him. Then he wouldn't have taken my son to God only knows where."

"I should not have listened to Nestor yesterday. I did not trust him, yet I agreed to let you split up. When I saw him later, he told me he was going after some of the horses and would not be back last night. Again I did nothing to stop him."

"You had no way of knowing what he was planning. If we hadn't split up to search for the horses, he would've found some other way to carry out Warner's plans. I'm just beginning to realize I didn't know Nestor at all. I had no idea he could be so cunning or so resourceful. Not to mention a skilled liar."

"I have met men like him," Chino said, his voice a harsh whisper. "I should have known he did not speak the truth." He huffed out a deep breath. "It is my fault Teddy is gone."

"Chino, don't be ridiculous. This isn't your fault."

When he opened his mouth to respond, she held up a hand to stop him. "We both made mistakes where Nestor's concerned, so if you insist on placing blame, then we should share it equally."

She could tell by the way his lips thinned that he wasn't satisfied, but apparently he decided to let the topic drop.

Several seconds passed, then he said, "You should go to bed."

"There's no way I can sleep."

He reached toward her, then abruptly dropped his hand. "This will be over soon."

She released a deep sigh. "I pray you're right."

"I will also pray for Ussen to lead me to Teddy." He stared off in the distance for a moment, then said, "I will not return until I have found him."

She nodded, a lump forming in her throat. Though Teddy was her primary concern at the moment, she hadn't forgotten about trying to repair her relationship with Chino—provided he wanted to recapture what they'd shared. The possibility that she might lose both her son and the man she loved sent a sharp pain ripping through her chest.

When she could trust her voice, she said, "Once this is over, I think we should talk. I want to—"

"There is no need to talk. After I return with your son, I will leave."

Abby's pain intensified, threatening to double her over. When this man rode away from the Flying M for the final time, she never would be the same. She would go on living because she had to, because her children and the Zepedas relied on her, needed her.

But what about her own needs, who would see to them? The answer wasn't one she wanted to contemplate. Nor did she want to contemplate having to run the ranch alone. She'd done so before, but without Chino—the man who'd become an integral part of her life, the man she'd love until her dying breath—her heart would no longer be in making the Flying M a successful horse ranch. Yet based on what he'd just told her, she would be forced to face all of those things.

She swallowed hard, then said, "Have you decided where you'll go?"

He hesitated, then shook his head.

"Would you tell me, if you had?"

His eyebrows pulling together, he frowned, but again didn't speak.

"It's just as well. If someone from San Carlos were to show up here and ask about you, I can't very well tell them where you went, if I don't know."

"No one from San Carlos is looking for me."

"How can you be sure? I hear about troops looking for renegades all the time."

"Keja told John Clum he was the only one to survive when Warner and his men attacked us."

"You trust your brother-in-law, even though he works for Anglos?"

"Keja works for the White Eyes, but he is still Apache. He swore he would reveal the truth to no one. I believe him."

318

"That seems strange to me. I mean, after all the times you told me Apaches always speak the truth, I'm surprised Keja wasn't concerned about lying."

"Keja wanted revenge for the death of his sister and nephew, but he could not leave San Carlos. He knew I wanted revenge as much as he did. Knew I would not give up until I found the men who killed my family. For that reason, he did not tell John Clum, or anyone else, the truth."

Abby mulled that over for a few seconds, then said, "Well, whatever you decide to do, at least you'll have Egusi. He'll sire many valuable foals."

"Egusi will stay here."

"Yes, I know he'll stay here for now. I meant later, when you leave—" though the words nearly choked her, she managed to say them—"for good."

"No, I will never take him. I did not prevent your son from being taken, so I do not deserve such a fine horse."

Chapter Twenty

Long after Chino had left, Abby remained alone on the ramada, but eventually exhaustion, both physical and mental, caught up with her. Though certain she'd never be able to sleep, she decided to lie down.

After checking on Susanna, she went to her bedroom and stretched out on her bed. As her body began to relax, the tenseness in her fatigued muscles slowly seeped away, but her mind remained a disturbing jumble, filled with thoughts and images of what could happen to Teddy—each more abhorrent than the last.

Though she fought to hold back fresh tears, she couldn't stop the stinging in her nose, or the trickle of moisture from beneath her closed eyelids. What if Chino couldn't find Teddy? In spite of his promise to bring back her son, there were no guarantees he'd succeed. Not when men as evil as Neville Warner and Nestor Zepeda were involved. If Chino's efforts proved futile, how would she survive? Knowing Chino soon would be leaving her was painful enough—a loss from which she never would fully recover—but to also lose a child—She drew a shuddering breath. The pain was too great to contemplate.

Trying not to focus on the negative, she pulled up memories of happier times. Watching Teddy riding a horse for the first time, her heart in her throat while Alan gave the boy instructions and a smile of encouragement. Teddy and Susanna splashing in the creek on a hot summer afternoon, their squeals of laughter filling the air. Teddy's face scrunched in concentration, listening intently to one of Chino's lessons.

Chino. The other half of her soul. The man who'd brought so much joy into her life, who'd captured her heart as no other man ever had or ever would. And yet there would be no future for the two of them. What a sad and ironic twist of fate—finding the true love of her life, only to have him snatched away. When more tears threatened, this time she didn't fight to hold them back.

Eventually, her overactive brain calmed enough for her exhausted body to win the battle for some much-needed rest. Rolling onto her side, she slipped into a light doze.

Holly Harte

*   *   *

She awoke to sunlight pouring in through her bedroom window, her head pounding from too many tears and too little sleep. Bracing herself for a long day, she sat up and swung her legs to the floor.

By keeping herself busy, getting Susanna dressed and helping Marita with breakfast, she made the first hour pass quickly. After that, time dragged. Tasks she normally did by rote took much longer because of her sluggish concentration. Though she knew it was too soon for Chino to return with Teddy, she kept pausing, straining to listen, hoping to hear something signaling their arrival. Each time she heard nothing. With a sigh, she returned to her work, offering more prayers to protect both the man and the boy she loved.

When Marita called her to dinner, she wanted to refuse. She wasn't hungry, and she wasn't sure she could choke down any food. Even so, she had to try for Susanna's sake. And for her own. She couldn't afford to fall ill, not now when she needed to be strong.

Resigned to eating at least a few bites, she sighed and went into the kitchen. After settling her daughter at the table, she moved to her own chair. Before she could take a seat, the sound of pounding hooves chased away all thoughts of food.

She gave Cesar a signal to stay in the house, then ran for the front door and stepped outside.

A lone horse galloped toward the house, kicking up a thick cloud of pale dust. Abby took several steps into the yard, lifting a hand to shield her eyes from the sun's glare. Disappointment washed over her. The horse was a strawberry roan, not Chino's dark bay.

As the rider came closer, she tried to make out the man's identity. He wore his hat pulled low on his forehead, keeping all but his mouth and chin in shadow. Even though she couldn't see the rest of his face, she knew he had to be one of Warner's henchmen.

The horse and rider continued bearing down on Abby, yet she stood her ground. Certain this man's purpose for coming to the Flying M had to do with Teddy, she refused to show any cowardice, or any other weakness he could report to his boss. She wouldn't give him the satisfaction.

The rider waited until the very last instant, then yanked back on the reins and brought his horse to a skidding halt several feet in front of Abby. She never flinched, though her heart pounded a wild cadence against her ribs.

A choking haze of dust swirled around them, settling on Abby's clothes, and burning her eyes.

When the dust cleared, the man said, "You are Señora Madison?"

"Yes. What do you want?"

"I want nothing, señora," he replied, opening one

of his saddlebags and reaching inside. "I come here to give you something."

Abby tensed, but didn't reply, watching his every move.

He smiled, the white of his teeth stark against his swarthy skin. "I am not here to hurt you."

Though he hadn't added the words, "this time," she felt certain he meant for them to be implied. Forcing the stiffness from her shoulders, she kept her expression bland. "Give me whatever Warner sent you to deliver, then get the hell off my ranch."

He laughed. "Señor Warner say you are hot-blooded. I think he is right." He withdrew an object from the saddlebag, then tossed a small packet toward her.

As soon as she caught the packet, he said, "*Adiós,* Señora Madison." Flashing a grin, he swung his horse around and galloped away.

She waited until she was certain he hadn't changed his mind about leaving before looking at what she held. The packet was actually an envelope. Turning it over, she found her name written across the front in a bold scrawl.

She took a deep breath, then broke the envelope's seal and withdrew a single sheet of vellum. With unsteady fingers, she unfolded the stationery, then gasped. A lock of dark brown hair lay tucked in the crease.

"Oh God, Teddy," she whispered, touching the

silky hair with a fingertip. "If he's hurt you—" She bit her lip and squeezed her eyes closed, desperately trying to push down her panic. She couldn't afford to lose control—not when the life of her son remained at stake.

When she'd regained her composure, she blinked several times to focus on the message written in the same bold scrawl as appeared on the envelope.

The deed to the Flying M for your son. Noon, day after tomorrow. Diablito Mountain. Come alone.

The terse missive contained no signature, but then, none was needed. Only one person was low enough, relentless enough to resort to kidnapping and blackmail in order to get his hands on her ranch.

She released a long sigh. Though fear for Teddy's safety still clung to her like the spines of a prickly pear, knowing the rules of the game gave her some measure of relief.

She walked back to the house, her only hope still pinned—now more firmly than ever—on Chino. But along with that hope came a new worry. She knew about the deadline she'd been given, but Chino had no way of knowing. If he didn't return with Teddy within forty-eight hours, she would have no choice except to meet Warner's demand.

* * *

Chino left his horse beneath a stand of trees in a small canyon a mile from the headquarters of the Warner Land and Cattle Company, then set off at a lope. Staying in shadow as much as possible, he moved with easy strides, his footsteps silenced by his moccasins. In only a few minutes, he arrived at the cluster of buildings making up the ranch headquarters. Of the main house, barn, bunkhouse and several other outbuildings, light shown from the windows of only the house and bunkhouse.

As he'd done all day, after following Nestor's trail here, he hunkered down to monitor the goings-on of Warner and his men.

An occasional laugh drifted to him from the bunkhouse, the door opened and closed several times as men went outside, then returned a few minutes later. Finally, the windows went dark, first in the bunkhouse, and then the main house.

Chino remained in his hiding place, patiently waiting to make sure everyone had settled down for the night. When he decided sufficient time had passed, he rose and started toward the barn. Slipping inside the door, he stopped, listening for any sign that his presence had been detected. Hearing only the snuffle of horses and the clomp of a hoof, he eased farther into the building.

He stopped at each stall, checking the horse inside. By the time he checked the last stall, he was forced to admit the truth. Nestor's horse was not there. Which meant the man's visit to the Warner ranch had been brief. He'd probably left long before Chino reached the headquarters that morning. Too late, he realized he should have known Nestor never would have left such an easy trail to follow if his final destination had been Warner's ranch. But he'd been so determined to find Abby's son, to make sure Warner wouldn't cause the death of another child, that he'd let the obvious slide past him.

Though furious with himself for not foreseeing this possibility, Chino carefully and methodically began checking each building, silently entering and leaving without causing anyone to raise an alarm. Only after making certain Teddy was not being held in one of the ranch buildings did he head back to where he'd left his horse.

At first light the next morning, he resumed looking for Nestor. Since he had no idea what the man's next destination would be, finding the right trail could require a great deal of time and patience. He worked in a circle around the ranch headquarters, taking care to stay out of sight of Warner's men.

He immediately eliminated most of the trails he came across, because they were made by more than one horse. Though Chino acknowledged that Nestor might have put Teddy on a second horse, he didn't think the man would risk giving the boy his own mount.

Whenever he found a trail made by a single horse,

he dismounted and checked the ground carefully. The amount of moisture in the blades of grass crushed by the horse's hooves would tell him the age of the trail. In each case, the grass was too dry, making the trails too old, left at least a day before Nestor would have passed through those areas.

The sun beat down on him from high overhead before he found another trail with just one set of hoofprints. Again he dismounted and checked the grass. Sufficient moisture in the blades told him the trail was fresh enough to be Nestor's. As he straightened, he debated whether to follow this trail or keep looking.

Since he'd already spent half a day searching, he made a decision, then turned toward his horse. Swinging into his saddle, he prayed the Spirits would send him a sign that he'd made the right choice. His stomach rumbled, but he ignored his hunger. The need for food could wait. Finding Teddy was much more important.

Abby bit her lip to stop herself from vocalizing the scream inside her head. Though she'd tried to continue a normal routine in order to insulate Susanna from her fluctuating emotions, her efforts had met with little success. Her daughter had become a child she didn't recognize, trying her patience at every turn. Whining and clingy one minute, mouthy and demanding the next, and then abruptly turning belligerent and distant.

The girl's latest show of temper—sassing Marita, something she never did—had earned a slap on the bottom, resulting in an angry scowl directed at Abby. Refusing to shed the tears shining in her green eyes, the girl had lifted her quivering chin and flounced out of the room.

Abby sank into a chair with a sigh. "What am I going to do with that child? She's never behaved this badly for an entire day."

"We are all tense," Marita replied. "Worried about Teddy. Susanna feels this."

"I'm sure you're right. I've tried so hard to hide what I'm going through, to assure her that her brother will be home soon." She sighed again. "But not hard enough, I guess."

Marita moved closer to Abby's chair and gave her shoulder a squeeze of encouragement. "When Señor Whitehorse returns with Teddy, everything will be as before."

Although Abby nodded her agreement with Marita's statement, she knew the truth. Not everything would be as it was before.

Chino's progress in finding Nestor and Teddy was slow. When the man left the Warner ranch, he'd been more cautious, probably at his employer's insistence in case he was followed, making sure he didn't leave an easy trail to read. He'd taken care to hide his tracks whenever possible. He used streams as roads, keeping his horse in the water for a long distance upstream before coming back onto land. And he purposely chose to cross over solid rock whenever the opportunity arose.

Each time Nestor's trail stopped abruptly, Chino had no trouble finding where the trail resumed. Though the extra minutes spent searching put him farther behind his prey and added to his growing frustration, at least he knew he had made the right choice.

Several hours after deciding which trail to follow, he'd come to a clearing with a small spring on the opposite side. He dismounted and crossed the clearing carefully, checking the ground for tracks. Based on the marks in the dirt, someone had attempted to cover his presence at the spring, but not as thoroughly as he assumed. At the edge of the spring, Chino found several footprints which had not been entirely obscured. One was the footprint of a man, the other clearly that of a boy. After murmuring a quick prayer of thanks and allowing his horse to get a drink, Chino again resumed his search, relieved and invigorated to know he was following the right trail.

He rode until darkness forced him to stop for the night. Heavy clouds were building. They already filled the western sky and quickly pushed eastward.

Soon the moon would be covered. Since Nestor's trail was difficult to read even when the sun shone, especially since he was now heading into the mountains, continuing without any light would be unwise.

Resigned to another long, sleepless night, he selected a place to make camp. After hobbling his horse, he spread a blanket on the ground and lay down, hands folded behind his head.

He stared at the churning clouds, saw a streak of lightning in the distance, then another. He smiled. Though he'd been taught to fear lightning, surviving a near lightning strike at the age of fifteen had changed his beliefs. If not for getting caught in a sudden thunderstorm while hunting with Nacori and Tu Sika, his closest friends, and being tossed to the ground by a powerful bolt of lightning, he would not have received his first vision, or been given horse power. On that day, he had stopped fearing lightning, and began viewing the phenomenon as an old friend.

He closed his eyes, thinking of the friends who'd shared that life-changing experience. He hadn't seen Bearclaw, whose boyhood name was Nacori, since leaving San Carlos, though he had heard rumors his friend was one of the Apache who went with John Clum on a trip East to meet the Great Father of the White Eyes. Perhaps one day he would see Bearclaw again, so he could ask if the rumors were true.

He had seen Nighthawk, once called Tu Sika,

more recently. In Tucson a year earlier, he'd stopped to see his friend before traveling to Mexico to find the two men who'd killed his wife and son.

More memories surfaced. The sound of gunfire. The cry of pain. The stunned expression on his wife's face. The ground turning red with blood. Hers. Their son's. And then his own.

With the low rumble of thunder as a lullaby, he pushed the disturbing sounds and images from his mind and allowed sleep to embrace him.

From a hill above the herd, he pulled Egusi to a halt and watched the horses in the valley below. His chest swelled with pride at their number, many more than the first time he'd seen the beautiful animals. Searching the herd for the yellow mare and her new foal, he smiled as the black colt frolicked beside his dam, his long legs no longer wobbly.

"You made a fine son," he said to the stallion, remembering the day Egusi had covered the mare and started a new life growing in her belly.

The colt was black now, but according to Abby, his coat probably would lighten as he grew older. Whatever his final color turned out to be, he would make an excellent addition to the herd. But Abby talked of selling the colt, saying he would bring a hefty price when he was older. Though Chino agreed with her assessment, he wasn't sure he wanted to

*sell. Something told him the colt would be as good
as, maybe even better than, his sire.*

*He would have to convince Abby they should keep
the horse. His lips curving into another smile, he
knew just how he would change her mind.*

Chino awoke with a start. Disoriented and wondering what had awakened him, he lay still for several
seconds, listening to the sounds around him. Then
the events of the past several days rushed back. Warner's last visit to the Flying M. Men pretending to be
Apache scattering the herd. Nestor taking Teddy.

Anger and frustration bubbled up inside him.
Abby had been through enough; she shouldn't have
to endure losing a son as well. He would do everything possible, even give his life, to make sure she
didn't. She had family to take care of, a ranch to run,
a herd of horses to—Her horses. His dream came
flooding back, squeezing his heart in a tight grip.

He knew he had no control over what he saw in
his dreams. Knew he couldn't make himself stop
dreaming about anything or anyone—he'd already
tried and failed after the deaths of his wife and son.
Even so, he prayed his dreams would no longer center around Abby. The pain was too great.

He didn't try to sleep after that, for fear his prayers
wouldn't be answered.

Chapter Twenty-one

As soon as the cloak of darkness lifted, Chino rose and prepared to continue following Nestor. In spite of his lack of sleep, he was anxious to get started, anxious to have something to occupy his thoughts besides unwanted dreams about a future that couldn't be.

While saddling his horse, the flesh on the inside of his thigh began to shake. Pausing in his task, he allowed himself a moment to relish the relief rushing through him. He blew out a deep breath, then tightened the cinch and stepped into the stirrup. His mood much improved by the sign that told him he was close to the end of his search, he started down the trail.

He'd ridden a mile or more, his concentration entirely dedicated to reading the ground in front of his horse, when he heard something behind him. The sound didn't totally register. But the second time he heard the noise, his senses went on full alert. Pulling his rifle from the scabbard, he brought his right leg up and over the saddle horn and slid to the ground. He lifted the rifle to his shoulder, then took several steps back down the trail.

Twenty feet farther, a thicket of brush rustled. His gaze glued to that spot, he thumbed back the hammer, then curled his finger around the trigger. Holding his breath, he inched closer.

The thicket shook again, more violently, then suddenly the brush parted and Teddy burst through the opening.

"Chino, don't shoot," the boy shouted. "It's me."

Instantly, Chino uncocked and lowered the rifle. His heart pounding, he dropped to his knees.

Teddy raced toward him. Skidding to a stop, he placed one grubby hand on Chino's cheek. "Are you okay?"

Chino nodded, stifling the urge to laugh at the absurdity of the question. Teddy was the one who'd been kidnapped, yet his first words concerned someone else's welfare. Moving his gaze over the boy in a quick check for injuries, he noticed a few scratches on his face and arms, along with a smudge or two of dirt, but nothing serious. Releasing a deep breath, he said, "What about you? Are you hurt?"

Teddy shook his head, then wrapped his arms

around Chino's neck with a sob. "I'm so glad yer here," he said in a broken whisper, his chest quaking with another sob. "Nestor said nobody'd be able to follow our trail. Not even an Injun." He hiccuped. "I told him that wasn't so. That you could find us, but he . . ." His voice dropped even lower. "He laughed at me."

An enormous lump formed in Chino's throat as he hugged the boy tight, relishing the feel of the small body pressed against his chest.

"He did not do anything else to you?"

"He used his knife to whack off a hunk of my hair." He lifted a hand to touch the back of his head. "But that didn't really hurt."

Maybe Nestor hadn't harmed Teddy physically, but Chino still hoped he'd have the chance to make the man pay for everything he'd done to Abby's family.

He swallowed hard, quelling the sudden bloodlust humming through him. "How did you get away?"

Teddy sniffed, then pulled his arms from around Chino's neck. Taking a step back, he swiped at his damp cheeks with the heels of his hands. "Yesterday, when we stopped for the night, I waited 'til he spread out our bedrolls, then I told him I had to puke."

"You were really sick?"

Teddy shook his head. "I was just pretendin'."

"He believed you?"

"Yeah. He cursed at me, but then he said not ta do it anywhere near him. A little while later, I told him I had to puke again. He yelled, 'don't tell me about it, just go do it.' After that, I got up a couple more times and headed for the tall grass."

The boy flashed a quick smile, amusement dancing in his eyes. "The last time I got up, he was snoring, so—" he shrugged—"I took off."

Chino returned the boy's smile, then immediately sobered. "You were very brave, but you took a great chance by running away."

"I know," Teddy replied, scuffing the toe of his boot in the dirt. "Are you mad at me?"

"No. I am proud of you. Your plan was good, and it worked." He straightened, then frowned. "I am not sure your mother will agree."

"Yeah, probably not," the boy replied with a sigh. Then he tilted his head and looked up at him. "But she'll be really happy to see me, so I bet we can convince her I did the right thing. Don't ya think?"

Chino smothered the urge to laugh. Maintaining a stern expression, he said, "We will try."

As Chino turned and started toward his horse, Teddy said, "Ya got anything to eat?"

This time he couldn't halt a hoot of laughter. "Marita filled a bag of food for me."

"Great. I'm starved." The boy's stomach picked that instant to growl, making Chino laugh even harder.

A few minutes later, Chino turned his horse in the direction of the Flying M. Teddy rode behind him on the bay, one hand gripping his shirt for balance, the other holding a rapidly disappearing tortilla.

Abby stared at the clock, wishing she could make time stand still. If Chino didn't return with Teddy in the next few minutes, she would have no choice except to comply with Warner's demand. The more she thought about the gall of the man who'd brought about her current situation, the more she wanted to scream her outrage. She huffed out a breath. For all the good screaming would do.

She glanced around the *sala*, her heart aching at the idea of having to move from her home. Just the thought of living somewhere else intensified the ache. As much as she hated to consider the idea, maybe she should try striking a deal with Neville Warner, offer to sell part of the Flying M.

She gave her head a shake, instantly dismissing the idea. She doubted a man so bent on possessing the entire Santa Cruz River valley—by fair means or foul—would settle for anything less than every square inch of the Flying M. Releasing a deep sigh, she picked up the deed to the ranch, then moved toward the door.

A half hour after Cesar watched Abby ride away from the barn, he heard the pounding of hooves.

Grabbing his rifle, he rushed to the barn door and peered outside. What he saw made his blood run cold.

Three men rode into the yard, weapons drawn, heading for the house. Recognizing them as employees of Neville Warner, Cesar made a sound of disgust.

"*¡Todo lo que dice es mentira!*" he muttered under his breath.

"Who says only lies?"

Cesar whipped around, his heart leaping to his throat. "*Madre de Dios*. I did not hear you come in, señor."

Chino stepped from the shadows. "I saw the men riding toward the ranch and came in from a different direction."

"You found Teddy?"

Chino nodded. "I left him with my horse near the creek." He moved to look out the door. "Those are Warner's men. What new lie has he told?"

Cesar told Chino about Warner's note offering to exchange Teddy for the deed to the ranch. Then he nodded at the men riding toward the house. "His men coming here now proves he lied. He never planned to let any of us leave. Not alive."

Chino's jaw tightened. "We must work quickly, so I can go to Abby."

"Sí," Cesar replied, lifting his rifle. "I am ready."

Chino told the older man what he planned to do, then the two went outside.

Just as the riders dismounted in front of the house and started toward the door, Chino's call swung all three of them around. The men lifted their weapons, but not quickly enough.

A series of rifle shots rang out in rapid succession. Two of the men grunted, then fell where they stood. The third swore viciously, then staggered forward, only to be jerked off his feet by another bullet. He collapsed without making a sound.

Chino racked another shell into his rifle's chamber, then approached the men lying on the ground. He jabbed his toes into the ribs of each one. None of them moved or made a sound. Satisfied the three posed no further threat, he looked up at Cesar. "Go get Teddy and my horse, *por favor*. Both are tired and hungry."

Cesar bobbed his head. "I will see to them."

"I need to borrow one of the other horses," Chino said, turning and starting toward the barn.

"Sí, señor, take whichever one you want."

"*Gracias,*" Chino called over his shoulder. "I will be back soon."

Cesar watched him walk away, then murmured, "*Vaya con Dios, mi amigo*—go with God, my friend."

* * *

Abby pulled her gelding to a halt on the edge of a rocky ridge near the top of Diablito Mountain. As she dismounted, Neville Warner stepped from behind a pile of boulders on the opposite end of the ridge.

"Right on time, my dear," he said, moving closer.

Abby longed to tell him she wasn't his dear—plus a few other choice words—but she held them in. She wouldn't risk Teddy's life by saying something stupid.

"Where's my son?" she asked, trying to maintain a level tone.

"He'll be here soon. Then we can conclude this little—" he smiled—"transaction. I assume you followed my instructions and brought the deed with you."

"Yes," she replied, imagining herself slapping the smug look off his face.

"Good. Then we'll just wait for my associate and your son to arrive."

The minutes dragged by. Though Abby found waiting nerve-racking, Warner took the delay with even less grace. He began pacing, muttering under his breath and periodically checking his pocket watch. His agitation growing each time he looked at the watch, he clicked the cover shut with more and more force.

Another few minutes passed, then the sound of an

approaching horse had Warner rushing to meet the rider.

Abby's heart thumped wildly as she watched Nestor dismount. Disbelief and panic clutched at her insides when she saw that Nestor was alone. Unable to move, she could only watch in stunned silence while the two men talked. They were too far away for her to hear more than a word or two, but she could tell the conversation was quickly becoming more heated.

Warner grabbed Nestor's arm, his face twisted with rage. Nestor jerked free, stumbled backward, then caught his balance and leveled a fierce glare at Warner. He shouted something, his words whipped away by a gust of wind, then turned toward his horse.

Before Abby realized Warner's intentions, he drew his pistol and shot Nestor twice in the back. Her mouth dropping open in shock, she watched Warner calmly turn and walk toward her as if he hadn't just killed a man.

"There's been a change in plans," he said, moving closer, the pistol still in his hand.

"Where's my son?"

"Seems the brat slipped away while that useless Mex—" he nodded toward where Nestor had fallen— "was sleeping."

Fury replaced Abby's shock. "For God's sake, why

did you kill him? He's the only one who knew where to look for Teddy."

"I don't tolerate irresponsibility in my employees," he replied. "Besides, what's the difference if the kid dies in the desert or here with his mama. Either way he's dead."

Abby's blood chilled at his words. "What are you saying?"

"You're a smart woman. You ought to be able to figure it out."

In spite of her fear for her son, her temper flared to life. "Spit it out, dammit."

Warner's eyebrows shot up, and he smiled. "Ah, still the spitfire. You'll probably fight me to the end." He stared at her thoughtfully for a moment, then said, "On second thought, maybe you'll lose that smart mouth when you find out there's nothing left for you on your ranch."

As the implication of his last statement sank in, Abby swayed on her feet. "No, this can't be happening." She didn't realize she'd spoken the words aloud, until he spoke.

He laughed, a demonic sound sending shivers up her back. The man was out of his mind.

"Oh, but it is, my dear. At this very moment, my men are at the Flying M. When they leave, there won't be a person living or a building standing. Like I said, nothing left for you to go back to."

For a moment Abby thought she was going to be

sick, her stomach roiling at the picture his words had painted. She swallowed the bile in her throat, then sucked in a deep breath. If she ended up dying by this man's hand, there was something she needed to ask first. "Did you have Alan killed?"

His glare turned icy. "That fool laughed in my face. Said he'd never sell me the Flying M." His lips curled into an evil grin. "I got him out of the way, though, didn't I?"

"Except that I wouldn't sell either."

"No, you were so damned determined to keep the land I needed. If only you hadn't ignored my warnings, then you could've moved your family to—" He laughed. "Well, it's too late for that. Now yer going to hand over the deed." He nodded toward her horse. "Get it. Now."

Abby backed toward her gelding, unwilling to turn her back and get shot the way Nestor had. She moved slowly, trying to give herself time to think. Her rifle was in its saddle scabbard, but the weapon was useless unless she could pull it free without alerting Warner.

"Hurry up," he called. "I don't have all damn day."

She reached her horse, then flipped open one of the saddlebags. Hoping her movements looked like she was digging around inside the saddlebag for the deed, she made a quick grab for her rifle. She managed to free the gun from the scabbard, but before she could pull back the hammer, several sounds assailed her in the same instant. The loud bark of Warner's pistol. An ear-splitting scream. And a sharp gasp of pain.

As she slid to the ground, her arm on fire from the bullet wound she'd suffered, she realized the gasp had come from her, but who had made the almost inhuman scream? More gunfire erupted; several rapid shots from Warner's pistol were returned by the single crack of a rifle. Another scream rent the air, grew fainter, then finally faded into silence.

Before Abby could get to her feet, a shadow fell across her. Uncertain who stood over her, she drew a deep breath, then lifted her gaze.

Her breath left her lungs in a whoosh. "Chino!"

He crouched next to her. "Where are you hurt?" he asked, his gaze moving over her.

"My arm."

He quickly checked the wound, relieved to find only a shallow crease in the flesh of her upper arm. It bled freely, but wasn't serious. He closed his eyes for a second. "I did not plan to let Warner know of my presence. But when I saw him fire his gun at you, I could not hold back my scream of rage."

She lifted her uninjured arm and touched his face. "So that was you. I wondered who made such a bloodcurdling—" She blinked up at him. "Teddy! Warner said Teddy ran away from Nestor. We have to find him."

"I found him. I left him at the ranch."

"He's okay?"

When he nodded, tears sprang to her eyes. "Thank you. I can't wait to see him." Remembering what else Warner had told her, she grabbed Chino's arm. "Warner also said his men were at the ranch, that they were going to—"

He pressed a finger to her lips. "Everyone is safe. Cesar and I stopped his men."

She released his arm, and let out a long sigh. "I don't know how I'll ever repay you for everything you've done."

"There is nothing to repay," he replied. "My revenge is complete. That is enough." He rose. "I need to make sure he cannot hurt anyone else."

Abby tested her injured arm. The wound stung like the dickens but otherwise didn't bother her. She got to her feet and was sliding her rifle into its scabbard when Chino returned.

"Well?" she said.

"Dead. I cannot tell if he died from a bullet or when he fell off the ridge."

"Doesn't matter at this point, does it?"

Chino shook his head. "Can you ride?"

"Yes, I'm fine. I want to go home."

Home. Chino wished the Flying M could be his home, but he knew he didn't deserve to live on such a wonderful place. Shoving those thoughts aside, he said, "What about the bodies?"

"We'll stop in Arivaca and send word to Warner's

ranch. Whoever's there can fetch the bodies and see to the burials. I don't think Cesar will mind."

He nodded, then said, "I will get my horse."

As he started to walk away, Abby said, "Chino, I still think we should talk."

He turned. "If you want to explain why you thought Apache scattered your horses, it is not necessary. I understand."

"That's part of what I want to say, but—"

"No," he said, his voice sharp. Something flickered across his face—pain or regret, she couldn't tell which—then he released a deep breath. "You know I am leaving. There is nothing else to say."

"Yes, there is. I want you to stay. You must know I love you. My children love you. We could have a good life together."

He crossed his arms over his chest. "I am Apache. Have you forgotten you hate my people? Someday, this love you say you have for me would also turn to hate."

"That's not true. I could never hate you. I admit, I blamed the Apache for killing Alan, and I hated them for it. But even before I found out Warner was behind Alan's death, getting to know you made me realize I was wrong to blame all Apache for what I thought a few of them had done. As Cesar pointed out, there is good and bad in all people." She moved closer, placed a hand on his arm. "You are definitely one of the good, and I love you."

A muscle worked in his jaw, but he didn't respond.

"You love horses," she said, hoping she was getting through to him. "You could continue working with Egusi." She withdrew her hand and dropped her gaze. "If you don't love me, that's okay. Maybe . . ." She drew a shuddering breath. "Maybe someday you'll come to love me a little. I'd be content with that."

Chino blinked with surprise, shocked she didn't realize how he felt about her. "A little love is not good enough for you, Abigail Madison. You deserve all of a man's heart."

She lifted her head, her lips trembling with a weak smile. "Any of your love would be enough. Please, just promise me you'll think about what I said."

Though he didn't want to agree, didn't want to give her hope, he nodded.

The long ride back to the Flying M was accomplished as quickly as possible and in total silence. Then once Chino and Abby arrived at the ranch, the excitement of having her entire family reunited didn't allow the two of them any time alone. For that Chino was grateful.

He had thought about what she'd told him, over and over. But as much as he wanted to stay, as much as he loved her, he couldn't convince himself that he deserved the life she'd offered him.

While Marita saw to Abby's arm, he slipped away.

His lack of sleep finally catching up with him, he headed for the bunkhouse. Stretching out on his bunk, he hoped his exhaustion would allow sleep to come immediately. He closed his eyes, but his mind refused to cooperate, keeping him awake by repeating Abby's words and filling his head with an assortment of images. Teddy and Susanna. Egusi and the other horses on the Flying M. But mostly, the images were of Abby.

He saw her helping her children with their lessons, leaning over her gelding's neck to urge more speed, and lying on the rumpled sheets of her bed. He saw the wild tangle of her hair, the flush staining her cheeks and the green flecks sparkling in her eyes. As he watched himself bend down to press another kiss on her swollen lips, he heard a voice in his head—a voice he recognized instantly—say, *"Daaka."*

Hearing his wife speak to him came as a shock. Not once, since her death, had she spoken to him, so why now? He mulled over that puzzle for a long time. When the answer came to him, he smiled, then the darkness of sleep claimed him.

Some time later, Chino awoke to the sound of someone saying his name. He opened his eyes to find Abby standing inside the bunkhouse.

"Sorry to wake you," she said. "But you've been sleeping so long, I was starting to get worried."

Chino sat up, then swung his feet to the floor. "How long have I been asleep?"

Abby moved closer. "Almost twenty-four hours."

His eyebrows rising at her response, he said, "No, not that many hours. When I first came in here, I did not sleep right away. I was awake for a long time."

"I know what you mean," she said with a smile. "Sometimes when I'm completely exhausted, I just can't fall asleep. Anyway, Marita will have supper ready soon, so if you're hungry—"

"I must speak to you first." He held out a hand to her. "Come. Sit beside me."

Her smile faded, defeat replacing the happiness in her eyes. "You want to tell me you're still leaving," she said, dropping onto the bunk next to him.

He lifted a hand and touched the indentation in her chin. "I have wanted to stay, probably from the moment I came here. At first I thought the Spirits must have other plans for me, that you could never want a hated Apache in your life. But then I had dreams of making my home here. I saw myself working with Egusi and other horses from the herd. I saw myself becoming a father to your children and you greeting me when I came into the house. I saw you carrying my child."

Ignoring Abby's soft gasp, he continued. "But then I could not stop Teddy from being taken from you, and I thought I did not deserve to have the happiness I saw in my dreams."

"Chino, we've been over this before. You're not to blame for Teddy being kidnapped. Besides, you got him back, didn't you? So, don't tell me that's the reason you won't stay."

"That was a reason, but no longer."

"I don't understand."

"I spent much time thinking about what you said yesterday, thinking about my future. But something inside me would not let me believe what I wanted was the right choice. Now I know it is. I want to stay."

Though his statement sent a thrill through Abby, she tamped down her growing excitement. "You want to stay, even though you don't love me the way you said I deserve?"

He chuckled. "Yes, I want to stay. But you made a mistake. You think I do not love you, because I never told you how I feel."

Her eyes went wide, her heart pounding even harder. She swallowed the lump in her throat, then managed a whispered, "Go on."

"You said any of my love would be enough. But you will have much more. You have all of my love, all of my heart, forever."

Her throat tightened painfully. "Are you sure? I mean—" her voice cracked from the hope surging through her—"you always speak the truth, but do you truly love me that much?"

Holly Harte

"Yes, *lika*." He lifted her chin with his knuckles, then lowered his head toward hers.

"Oh, Chino," she whispered, accepting his mouth for a quick, fierce kiss. When he lifted his head, she said, "You called me *lika* again. What does it mean?"

"Sweet," he murmured, running a fingertip over her lips. "You taste so sweet."

She smiled, then released a deep sigh. "I don't know what changed your mind about staying, but I'm glad you did."

He lifted a strand of her hair and pushed it over her shoulder. "My wife spoke to me."

"I beg your pardon?"

"I was also surprised," he replied with a smile. "I had decided I wanted to stay, even though I was not sure this was what the Spirits planned for me. Then I was thinking about you, of kissing you. That is when I heard my wife's voice."

"What did she say to you?"

"*Daaka.* Apache for it is right. She told me I had made the right decision."

Tears stinging the backs of her eyes, she gulped down a sob. "Remember when I told you I thought your coming to my ranch was supposed to happen?"

He nodded. "That was after you showed me Egusi."

"Yes, and I also said our meeting was destiny." Looping her arms around his neck, she pulled him closer. "Now I know that is true. We were meant to

352

be together." She gave him a quick kiss. "Forever."

"I agree," he murmured against her mouth.

"Good, then how about showing me how much you love me?"

He laughed. "I thought supper will be ready soon."

She raked her teeth over his lower lip. "Supper can wait. There's another hunger we need to take care of first."

Laughing even harder, Chino didn't resist when she pushed him onto his back.

Epilogue

Two years later

Abby stood in the doorway of the *sala,* watching a scene she never tired of—Chino and the children. Gathered around the low table in the center of the room, they were waiting for her arrival so they could begin their lessons.

Soon after she and Chino had become man and wife, he'd asked her to teach him to read. Though she immediately agreed, curiosity made her ask him why he'd changed his mind. His answer not only surprised her, but also touched her deeply.

After he'd learned about Warner's note, Chino confessed that he'd made a chilling realization. If she had been kidnapped instead of Teddy, and Warner had sent the note to Chino, he wouldn't have been able to read the man's demands. Even when she pointed out that Warner was no longer a threat and the likelihood of a repeat situation was practically nil, Chino remained adamant. He refused to allow himself to be in a circumstance where his inability to read might bring harm to those he loved.

Chino Whitehorse was such a special man. He had taken her children into his heart and loved them as if they carried his blood. He had helped create a successful and prestigious horse ranch out of the Flying M, which they had renamed Destiny Ranch. He had given her a beautiful daughter—conceived, she was certain, on the day he told her of his decision to stay—with his dark eyes and hair the color of polished mahogany. Her gaze moved to the fifteen-month-old girl sitting in Chino's lap. Elizabeth, whom they called Libby, already had her adoring papa wrapped around her little finger.

Her heart near to bursting with love, she stepped into the *sala*.

"I see you're all waiting for me."

All four gazes lifted to look at her. Teddy wore his usual less-than-enthusiastic expression at the prospect of more book learnin'. Susanna beamed a mischievous smile, eager to begin so her latest prank on her brother would be discovered. Libby chortled, waved a fat fist and flashed an impish grin.

Chino also had a smile for his wife. "I am ready for my lesson, *lika*."

Though his words seemed innocent enough, the gleam in his eyes told her he was referring to the lessons conducted in the privacy of their bedroom. Trying to ignore the blush climbing up her throat and cheeks, she strove for a no-nonsense tone when she said, "Good, then let's get started."

As she took a seat on the sofa beside Chino, Susanna said, "Papa told us you got another brother or sister in your tummy."

Abby blinked, shifting her gaze from her older daughter to her husband.

He shrugged, his expression clearly revealing his obvious pleasure at the news she'd given him just the night before. Pleasure he apparently couldn't help sharing.

When she'd realized she was pregnant again, she hadn't been sure how Chino would react. She still remembered his reaction to her advances when Libby was almost two months old. At first, she thought he was afraid it was too soon for her. But when she tried to assure him she was fine and more than ready to make love again, he'd given her the true reason for his resistance.

The Apache life-way, he'd informed her, taught a man not to get his wife with child again until the first child could walk. And the only sure way to prevent

Apache Destiny

another pregnancy was not resuming an intimate relationship.

Abby had been speechless with shock. Though she
never tried to belittle or dismiss his beliefs, that time
she wasn't going to give in. By exercising a great deal
of patience, along with some carefully chosen words,
she finally convinced him the Apache life-way—at
least in that instance—need not be followed to the
letter.

But she'd worried needlessly about telling him of
the new life they'd created. He was delighted. Susanna's voice pulled her from her musings.

"Momma, are you okay?"

Abby smiled. "I'm fine, sweetheart. And your
papa's right. Next spring you'll have a new brother
or sister."

"This one better be a boy," Teddy muttered under
his breath, apparently not relishing the idea of
having another sister to pester him.

Chino chuckled. "Your mother and I tried very
hard to make a boy," he said, watching Abby's blush
deepen. "But we cannot promise to give you a
brother. If not, we will try again."

Abby's eyebrows shot up. "Try again?"

He lifted a hand and stroked her flushed cheek.
"Only if you want another child."

She drew an unsteady breath, nearly overwhelmed
by the perfection of her life. She had no idea why

357

she'd been allowed a second chance at love. But every day, she offered prayers of thanks to both her God and Chino's Ussen for bringing this man, her Apache destiny, into her life.

White Dove

Susan Edwards

White Dove was raised to know that she must marry a powerful warrior. The daughter of the great Golden Eagle is required to wed one of her own kind, a man who will bring honor to her people and strength to her tribe. But the young Irishman who returns to seek her hand makes her question herself, and makes her question what makes a man.

Jeremy Jones returns to be trained as a warrior, to take the tests of manhood and prove himself in battle. Watching him, White Dove sees a bravery she's never known, and suddenly she realizes her young suitor is not just a man, he is the only one she'll ever love.

___4890-6 $5.99 US/$6.99 CAN

Dorchester Publishing Co., Inc.
P.O. Box 6640
Wayne, PA 19087-8640

Please add $2.50 for shipping and handling for the first book and $.75 for each book thereafter. NY, NYC, and PA residents, please add appropriate sales tax. No cash, stamps, or C.O.D.s. All orders shipped within 6 weeks via postal service book rate. Canadian orders require $2.50 extra postage and must be paid in U.S. dollars through a U.S. banking facility.

Name_____
Address_____
City_____ State_____ Zip_____
I have enclosed $ _____ in payment for the checked book(s).
Payment <u>must</u> accompany all orders.☐ Please send a free catalog.
CHECK OUT OUR WEBSITE! www.dorchesterpub.com

White Nights — Susan Edwards

Eirica Macauley sees the road to better days: the remainder of the Oregon Trail. The trail is hard, even for experienced cattle hands like James Jones, but the man's will and determination lend Eirica strength. Yet, Eirica knows she can never accept the cowboy's love; the shadows that darken her past will hardly disappear in the light of day. But as each night passes and their wagon train draws nearer its destination, James's intentions grow clearer—and Eirica aches for his warm embrace. And when darkness falls and James stays beside her, the beautiful widow knows that when dawn comes, she'll no longer be alone.

Lair of the Wolf

Also includes the fifth installment of *Lair of the Wolf*, a serialized romance set in medieval Wales. Be sure to look for future chapters of this exciting story featured in Leisure books and written by the industry's top authors.

___4703-9 $5.50 US/$6.50 CAN

White Flame — Susan Edwards

Searching for her missing father, the determined Emma O'Brien sets out for Fort Pierre on the Missouri River, but when the steamboat upon which she is traveling runs aground, she is forced to travel on foot. Braving the wilderness, the feisty beauty is soon seized by Indians. Surrounded by enemies, Emma learns that only Striking Thunder can grant her release. The handsome Sioux chieftain offers her freedom but enslaves her with a kiss. He takes her to his village, and there, underneath the prairie's starry skies, Emma learns the truth. The danger Striking Thunder represents is greater than the pre-war bonfires of the entire Sioux nation—and the passion he offers burns a whole lot hotter.

___4613-X $4.99 US/$5.99 CAN

WHITE WOLF

SUSAN EDWARDS

Jessica Jones knows that the trip to Oregon will be hard, but she will not let her brothers leave her behind. Dressed as a boy to carry on a ruse that fools no one, Jessie cannot disguise her attraction to the handsome half-breed wagon master. For when she looks into Wolf's eyes and entwines her fingers in his hair, Jessie glimpses the very depths of passion.

___4471-4 $5.50 US/$6.50 CAN

Velda Sherrod

Lord of the Plains

To save her sister, saloon singer Kate Hartland plays the hundred-dollar whore. Trembling in her innocence, she seduces a handsome outsider who appears safe, kind, and Irish. But the virile stranger turns out to be anything but safe. He awakens a dangerous passion, incites torturous longings, and worst of all possesses hated Comanche blood.

As Sean O'Brien he takes her virginity, claiming her in the most primitive sense. As Grayhawk he saves her life, making her his wife in the eyes of the Comanche. As he risks death to unite the white settlers and the Indians in peace, he also risks his spirit to unite body and soul with the lass who has captured his heart.

___4901-5 $4.99 US/$5.99 CAN

Dorchester Publishing Co., Inc.
P.O. Box 6640
Wayne, PA 19087-8640

Please add $2.50 for shipping and handling for the first book and $.75 for each book thereafter. NY, NYC, and PA residents, please add appropriate sales tax. No cash, stamps, or C.O.D.s. All orders shipped within 6 weeks via postal service book rate. Canadian orders require $2.00 extra postage and must be paid in U.S. dollars through a U.S. banking facility.

Name_____
Address_____
City_____ State_____ Zip_____
I have enclosed $_____ in payment for the checked book(s).
Payment <u>must</u> accompany all orders.☐Please send a free catalog.
CHECK OUT OUR WEBSITE! www.dorchesterpub.com

DESERT RAIN

SPIRIT WALKER

Once Desert Rain blended her voice with Arm Bow's in nightly ecstasy. But then her young husband is killed, taking her reason for living with him. Shattered by grief, Desert Rain steals away from her village, eager to join her beloved Arm Bow in the After World. A frantic search party sets out after her, fearful she will soon achieve her goal—they know the legends of the mysterious warrior who is said to be able to travel between this world and the next—the shadowy Spirit Who Walks Like a Man. But how could they know that Desert Rain has already encountered the spirit warrior? In his arms her desire for life is reawakened. With his deep voice he calls her to join him, their bodies harmonizing in a song just by them.

___4919-8 $5.50 US/$6.50 CAN

Dorchester Publishing Co., Inc.
P.O. Box 6640
Wayne, PA 19087-8640

Please add $2.50 for shipping and handling for the first book and $.75 for each book thereafter. NY, NYC, and PA residents, please add appropriate sales tax. No cash, stamps, or C.O.D.s. All orders shipped within 6 weeks via postal service book rate. Canadian orders require $2.00 extra postage and must be paid in U.S. dollars through a U.S. banking facility.

Name_____
Address_____
City_____ State_____ Zip_____
I have enclosed $_____ in payment for the checked book(s).
Payment <u>must</u> accompany all orders.☐Please send a free catalog.
CHECK OUT OUR WEBSITE! www.dorchesterpub.com

MADELINE BAKER
Chase the Lightning

Amanda can't believe her eyes when the beautiful white stallion appears in her yard with a wounded man on its back. Dark and ruggedly handsome, the stranger fascinates her. He has about him an aura of danger and desire that excites her in a way her law-abiding fiancé never had. But something doesn't add up: Trey seems bewildered by the amenities of modern life; he wants nothing to do with the police; and he has a stack of 1863 bank notes in his saddlebags. Then one soul-stirring kiss makes it all clear—Trey may have held up a bank and stolen through time, but when he takes her love it will be no robbery, but a gift of the heart.

___4917-1 $5.99 US/$6.99 CAN

Chase the Wind
Madeline Baker

Elizabeth Johnson is a woman who knows her own mind. And an arranged marriage with a fancy lawyer from the East is definitely not for her. Defying her parents, she sets her sights on the handsome young sheriff of Twin Rivers. But when Dusty's virile half-brother rides into town, Beth takes one look into the stormy black eyes of the Apache warrior and understands that this time she must follow her heart and not her head. Before she knows quite how it's happened, Beth is fleeing into the desert with Chase the Wind, fighting off a lynch mob—and finding ecstasy beneath starry skies. By the time she returns home, Beth has pledged herself heart and soul to Chase. But with her father forbidding him to call, and her erstwhile fiancée due to arrive from the East, she wonders just how long it will take before they can all live happily ever after. . . .

___52401-5 $5.99 US/$6.99 CAN